WHAT SHE FEARS

Also by Jane Gorman

The Adam Kaminski Mystery Series
A Blind Eye
A Thin Veil
All That Glitters
What She Fears

WHAT SHE FEARS

*Book 4 in the Adam Kaminski
Mystery Series*

Jane Gorman

Blue Eagle Press

In memory of Gerald Horgan, the Dingle
Photographer.

CHAPTER ONE

THE HOT PINK in the scarf finally caught his attention. He should have noticed it sooner. He *would* have noticed it sooner if he hadn't been preoccupied with his own concerns. Concerns that paled in comparison to those of the woman half covered by the low bushes that separated the footpath from the River Corrib.

Detective Adam Kaminski stepped off the path toward the body. She lay face up, her right arm flung over her head as if, had she been standing, she were hailing a taxi or waving a flag. Perhaps she had been trying to attract attention, flailing for any possible help during her last, horrible moments.

She looked surprised, her eyebrows frozen in an expression of amazement, her eyes wide open though forever unseeing. Adam bent closer, examining the corpse without touching anything. He knew better than that.

Her pale face lay buried beneath a wave of dark curls, but he could see that she wore makeup, her eyes lined with some kind of charcoal, her lips still ruby red, even in death. She was dressed for a night out, one high-heeled pump still on her left foot, the other not visible from where Adam crouched. A long earring lay on the ground near her head, like a colorful cut-stone flower tossed aside. Her clothes were bright. Flamboyant. He really should have noticed her sooner.

Her body lay off the main pedestrian path that crossed Nun's Island from the cathedral, along the banks of the River Corrib toward the bridge that led to National University of Ireland, Galway. A back entrance used mostly by students. He'd only come this way because of the time he'd spent reading about the area. It seemed a pleasant walk.

In the summer months, the path would be lined with tiny pink wildflowers, lilac and flowering japonica, but at this time of year the trees were bare, the honeysuckle branches dark, the low bushes only sparsely colored skeletons of their summer selves. The ground still held a trace of dampness from the morning's rain and it released an earthy, loamy scent with each step.

Adam was just at the point where the path turned toward the cable-stayed bridge that crossed the narrow branch of the Lower Corrib, past the old lime kiln and the exposed expanse of grass and gravel that opened up to the university campus.

As it was, he'd actually passed by before the hot-pink scarf caught his eye and he'd turned his head to look back. His eyes had been open, but he'd been looking inward, excited about his upcoming meeting. And, he could admit it, apprehensive.

His last conversation with Sylvia in Philly had been an argument. No surprise there. They'd made up since on the phone, but he wanted this visit to be special. To show her how much he loved her and how much she meant to him. Sylvia Stanko, soon to be Mrs. Adam Kaminski, had no idea Adam was joining her in Galway.

He'd booked his ticket from Philadelphia without telling her and read everything he could get his hands on about Galway, from tales of mythical Irish warrior queens to tourist guides to the city's pubs and parks. With Sylvia's work schedule finagled from her — without, he hoped, raising her suspicions — he'd set out that afternoon to see the town. Walking through the streets gave him a feeling for the city that no book could. He'd timed his walk to end at the university at ten minutes before seven, just before she was due to be done with her meetings for the day.

Executing his plan had been remarkably simple, really. Until he stumbled onto a murder.

CHAPTER TWO

"DETECTIVE SUPERINTENDENT Sayers will be talkin' with you in just a moment, sir. Please wait here."

The round, boyish face with barely a hint of whiskers looked incongruous balanced on top of the uniform of the An Garda Síochána, but Adam took the warning seriously. His age notwithstanding, the young man's instruction was a lawful order and Adam would comply.

The sun had risen less than an hour before, if the slightly lighter color tinting the clouds heavy in the sky above them could be called sunrise. Throughout the night, as Adam kept watch over the growing crew of law enforcement and medical personnel who claimed the crime scene as their own, a briny mist had spread over the low ground near the river. As the sun's light grew, the mist slid away, slinking back to the safety of the running water.

The crime scene crew had taken over efficiently and effectively. Yellow caution tape created a taut fence around a broad swath of ground, reaching from the river bank, across the path and narrow strip of grass, and ending on the far side of the bushes that lined the corridor. Any pedestrians getting an early start that morning and hoping to use this path as a shortcut to or from the university were being waylaid and redirected by an eager team of young officers.

Halogen lamps on thin metal brackets marked the

borders of the technicians' territory, shining a bright, unforgiving light deep into the recesses of the bushes, creating a shimmer along the surface of the cropped grass and gravel path. Every piece of cloth, metal, plastic, or flesh jumped out in the brightness, exposed to identification, analysis, and speculation.

Though the techs were clearing away the bulk of their equipment now, having spent the past six hours poring over the grounds in great detail, their work was only just beginning. All of the evidence — and the suspicious items that would later prove to be nothing more than a waste of time — would be taken back to their labs for deeper analysis.

Adam took a breath, calling on his last reserve of patience as the young garda returned to his assigned task of monitoring the boundaries of the scene. He'd been told to wait. Repeatedly. After he'd used his cell phone to call in his gruesome discovery, ignoring the painfully high fees that he knew would be tacked on to the international call; after he'd shown the garda who first appeared on the scene what he'd found; after they'd called it in to their superiors, calling out the big dogs and the crime scene techs; throughout it all, Adam had been told to wait.

The mindfulness training he'd been subjecting himself to in an effort to control his anger was certainly coming in useful. He focused on his breath. He focused on one object in front of him. He listened to the sounds of Galway slowly waking up around him. The heavy hydraulics of the early morning delivery vans, the clinking of bicycle chains, the joyful ringing of the bells high above in the double bell towers of the cathedral. Bit by bit, the rest of the city woke up, came to life, moved into action.

Adam, pushed to the side to watch as others examined the crime scene, simply waited.

The order to stay put had prevented him from finding Sylvia. He was pretty sure, based on the detailed information about himself he'd had to provide to the gardaí, that she knew by now he was in Galway. He'd needed to give them her name and contact information to justify his presence in that part of town at that time of night. He'd needed to prove to them that he was exactly who he claimed to be: a cop from Philadelphia on vacation in Galway to surprise his fiancée as she coordinated a joint fundraising event at the university.

He glanced at his watch. By now, she knew exactly where he was and why. It certainly would have come as a surprise to her, which had been his goal, after all. Just not the way he'd wanted her to find out.

He shoved his hands deeper in his pockets, shifting his weight from side to side. The bustling activity of the crime scene moved about in front of him, as if on a stage, the actors performing for an audience of one. Only for him. Despite his efforts to be calm and wait patiently, he couldn't help but keep a close eye on their activities.

He noted the easy identification of the victim by the earliest gardaí on the scene, the victim a well-known member of the university faculty. He watched and listened as the doctor examined the body, confirming his early speculation about time of death, narrowing it even more to between 6:00 and 6:30 that evening. He noticed the photographer focusing on a few light footprints in the grass and observing the marks left by what was likely a small sports shoe, perhaps prints left by a boy running to a football match, perhaps not linked to this investigation at all.

Reminded yet again, unnecessarily, by the young garda of his requirement to wait, Adam turned to the small gathering of techs around a long table, on which lay a collection of plastic and paper bags, plastic gloves, tubed cotton swabs, and similar items of detection. His focus on their activity around the table prevented him from noticing his assailant in time. He let his mindfulness slip.

Two strong hands grabbed his shoulders from

behind, swinging him around and grabbing for his collar. The pull knocked Adam off balance. He caught himself with his hand on the ground and looked up into a gaunt, sallow face.

"You. What did you do to Moira?" The man's voice stayed low, his words, in a clear American accent, issuing through narrow lips.

Adam tensed, ready to defend himself if necessary, but the man seemed to have used up all his energy on his first attack. His entire body slumped, but he kept his narrowed eyes trained on Adam. He'd been crying, his clothes were wrinkled, and he smelled like yesterday's beer. A sheen of stubble covered his chin, though Adam suspected it was artful rather than accidental.

"Why did you kill her?"

Adam ignored the accusation. It took only a second and a few quick movements to twist one of the man's arms behind his back, restraining him without hurting him.

"Professor Rourke, stop it. You, let him go." Two gardaí jogged over.

Before Adam had a chance to defend his actions, Professor Rourke repeated his accusation. "He killed her."

Adam loosened his grip and lowered his gaze, trying not to further antagonize the man. "Professor Rourke, is it? I'm very sorry for your loss, sir, but I did not kill her. I just found her body and called it in."

"Her body…" Rourke looked over at the heavy black plastic that now encased the corpse, then turned back to the guards who'd escorted him in. "I can't think of Moira that way. I just can't."

"Professor Rourke." The call came from a tall woman wrapped in a black raincoat striding across the grass toward them. "Control yourself, Sean. You shouldn't even be here." She cast a meaningful glance at the guards.

"He said he could identify the body, Detective

Superintendent Sayers. He said he knew where she'd been last night," one of the young men said defensively.

"Then I'll talk to him down at the station." She threw a glance at Adam. "And you, too. Come on with me."

She turned on her heel, a heel that was safe and dry in a dark gray rubber boot, and didn't wait to see that Adam and Sean Rourke followed her. A woman used to having her orders immediately obeyed.

CHAPTER THREE

SEAN ROURKE PACED back and forth across the office, no more than three steps carrying him fully across the narrow room, then three more back again. Each time, he stopped in front of the window that looked out over the shallow stream that, once upon a time, had given Mill Street its mill and hence its name.

"Sit down, Professor Rourke. Please." Isabel Sayers' voice was calm. Professional. Strong.

Sean glanced at her and retook the seat next to Adam. Isabel leaned over her desk, her long fingers clasped together in front of her, decorated only with a simple gold band on her right hand.

"I understand that you're upset, Professor Rourke, and I am truly sorry for your loss. But I need to know, why did you attack Detective Kaminski back there? What did you know, or think you know?"

"Detective?" Sean flinched. "I had no idea you were a detective. I was told you were from Philadelphia."

Adam clamped his lips shut tight at the description, working to hide the smile that threatened to escape. "Yes, I am from Philadelphia. And I'm a detective. They're not mutually exclusive."

"No, no, of course not. It's just when they said who you were, no one said anything about being with the police."

"Would that have made a difference to the way you

reacted?" Isabel asked.

Sean shrugged. "Maybe. I don't know, maybe not."

"Tell me what you told the officers, Sean." Isabel spoke calmly, soothingly. "What do you know about Moira Walsh that will help our investigation into who killed her?"

"Nothing. Really, nothing. I just... I just wanted to see her. I couldn't believe it. I know, they told me, but not really. It couldn't be real, you know?"

Adam knew. He'd seen that reaction enough times from the loved ones of murder victims. He'd felt that reaction himself when he'd first learned about his students, gunned down in a drive-by shooting in Philadelphia. Violence was always hard to accept. Hard to believe.

"You were involved with Moira?" Adam asked.

Sean put his head to the side. "Well... I wouldn't say involved. We'd been... well, we'd been together a couple of times over the past few months. It wasn't serious. At least, not yet. What could have been? Who knows." He stood and walked to the window to stare once more at the old, worn, broken mill wheel that blocked the stream outside Isabel's window.

"Really, I guess, to be honest, we were just colleagues. Friends. Perhaps we could have been something more. I needed her."

"You needed her?"

He shrugged, looked down at his feet. "You know how it is. You get ideas. You think you have plans."

"I do." Isabel's tone was firm, offering complete understanding. "When was the last time you saw her?"

Sean pursed his lips, blinked a couple of times, then turned his face back to the window.

"Did you see her last night?" Isabel persisted.

"I... no, no, I didn't. I mean — I saw her yesterday, of course, in the afternoon. But not last night, not..." He laughed and glanced back and forth between the two detectives. "Sorry, I mean no, I didn't see her last night."

Isabel looked at the papers on her desk, her fingers moving so that her ring tapped against the hard surface, then looked back up at Sean. "Do you know where she was going, then? Along that path?"

"Me? Why would I know where she was going?" His face turned a slight shade of pink.

"I'm just asking a few questions, Sean, that's all. Anything you know may prove to be helpful in tracking down the person who did this to her."

"What do *you* know? What can you tell *me*? Who killed her?"

"Not much at this point, I'm afraid. She was strangled. With her own scarf. Not much of a struggle. Either she knew her assailant or was completely taken by surprise."

Adam remembered the look of surprise frozen on her face. "Strangling — that requires some strength, doesn't it?"

Isabel nodded. "Most likely a male assailant. Statistically speaking. But we're keeping our options open at this point."

"What can I do to help?" Adam tried to bite back the words as soon as he'd said them, but the offer to help had come so naturally to him he hadn't thought through the consequences.

"You? Nothing, for now, Detective Kaminski. You do understand you're still a suspect?" Isabel gave him a stern look.

"Of course, I found the body. But I didn't know her. I have no connection to her."

"Perhaps not. But your fiancée does. Ms. Sylvia Stanko?" Isabel glanced down at her notes to check the name as she said it.

"Does she? I didn't know."

"They were working together on an event later this week, a fundraiser."

Adam nodded. He knew that was why Sylvia was in Galway, just hadn't known the victim was also involved in the event. "So what are you telling me? Don't leave town?" He smiled his most charming smile, exposing his dimples, and Isabel seemed to bend, just a little.

"Something like that, yes." She smiled too. "But that's about it. Unless there's more you can tell me."

"Look, if I'm stuck here until you solve this, I might as well help. If Sylvia knew her, worked with her, perhaps I could learn something useful."

Sean let out a low moan and turned back to the window. Isabel and Adam both flinched, but let him be.

"I can't let you get involved, Detective, though I appreciate the offer. You will stay out of this, yeah?"

Adam shrugged, an exaggerated movement designed to convey acquiescence.

Isabel nodded at him, then looked back at Sean.

"I need her," he mumbled again.

"I have a few ideas about where to start. People who knew Moira, who worked with her." She glanced at the clock on the wall. "I'll need to leave now to catch one of them. A man who knows a little bit about everything that goes on in this town." She grinned. "Particularly if it's not quite legitimate."

CHAPTER FOUR

"THE COUNCIL MEETING should just be ending." Isabel checked her watch again as she spoke, walking toward the car park. "I can catch Conn O'Flaherty there, I'm sure. You should—"

"Adam!"

Isabel and Adam both turned at the call. Isabel scowled at the interruption, but Adam felt his mood lighten as a smile spread across his face, his heart beat a little faster. "Sylvia."

She ran toward them across the parking lot and grabbed him, throwing her arms around him. "What is going on? What happened? What are you doing here? Why are you in Galway? In Ireland?" As she spoke she attacked his face with kisses, covering every inch of exposed skin with tiny pecks.

"Sylvia, God am I glad to see you." He held her tight, holding her against himself, forgetting his apprehension about seeing her, forgetting their fights, forgetting everything except how good she looked. How good she smelled. How right she felt in his arms. "I'm sorry, I'm so sorry."

"You should be sorry," Sylvia responded, stepping back out of his clasp and slapping him lightly on the arm. "What the hell were you thinking? And what are you involved in?"

He laughed out loud at the dramatic shift in her mood

and her questions. Typical Sylvia. "Sylvia." He gestured toward Isabel. "This is Detective Superintendent Isabel Sayers. Isabel, my fiancée, Sylvia Stanko."

The two women shook hands, but Isabel's expression reminded Adam of her earlier comment identifying Sylvia as a potential suspect.

"Is it true then? Is Moira dead?" Sylvia's eyes moved from one of them to the other. "What happened?"

"That's what we're going to figure out. Detective Kaminski—" Isabel jerked her head to the side and Adam stepped toward her, away from Sylvia. "I'll need to talk with you again." She looked pointedly at Sylvia. "Both of you." With that, she headed toward her car.

Sylvia waited until Isabel was out of earshot before she spoke again. "Adam, I still don't understand. Why are you here and why are you involved in this?"

"I'm so sorry, I really am." He put his arms around her as he spoke, holding her tight again, trying to dispel the anger he knew she felt. "I wanted to surprise you. Honestly, that's it. And trust me, this is not the surprise I had in mind."

"Surprise me with what?" She pulled away to look up at him.

"Just being here. To see you. I thought we could spend a few days together in Galway, a little vacation or something." He shrugged. "You know I wanted to come here, to look up that artist. It seemed the perfect opportunity."

Sylvia nodded and Adam could almost see the calculations going on behind her eyes. "That was very sweet of you, darling. But you could have just called me and told me you were coming."

"I know. It was meant to be a surprise. I thought…"

She held up a hand. "I understand. A surprise, a romantic gesture. That is so like you, Adam, always looking for the romantic opportunities." She placed her hand gently on his face. "That is why I love you. But a murder? That is not romantic." She smiled as she spoke

14

and Adam ignored the questions and doubts her reaction had raised in him.

"Believe me, this was not my idea. I found her body. Last night, when I was coming to find you." He took her arm and walked back down Mill Street toward Bridge Street and the River Corrib. "I'm not involved in this. Isabel is handling the investigation. You and I can spend some time together."

"No." Sylvia's response came quickly. Adam felt his doubt rising again but pushed it down. She continued, "No, I mean, I'm glad you are here, of course. But I still have my event to plan. It is in just a few days. I will be very busy on this, Adam." She shook her head. "You should have called me, darling. I would have told you to wait a few more days before coming. Then I could spend all my time with you."

He took a deep breath, trying to dispel his disappointment, then let it out in a light laugh. "How could I be away from you for this long? You're my future, honey, you know that, right?" He stopped to look into her eyes. "Without you, I'd always be living in the past."

She smiled. This was a familiar conversation, one they'd had before, whenever either of them had doubts about their marriage.

"Always reading history, or studying your family's past." Her smile faltered and worry crept into her eyes. "Or figuring out who committed a terrible crime. This is so terrible about Moira."

They continued toward the river, walking hand in hand. He thought about what Isabel had said, about Moira working on the fundraising event. "Did you know her well?"

She pouted. "Not well, not really. She was always running off one way or another. She was excited about something when I saw her yesterday."

"What time did you see her?"

Sylvia looked at her watch as the bells of Galway

chimed the hour. "Darling, I have to get to the university. I'm sure they're waiting for me already, it is getting late."

"I was hoping we might grab breakfast?"

Sylvia stood on her toes to kiss his forehead. "It is too late for that, dear. I must get to work. There will be even more to do now… well, now we need to find a new faculty speaker for the event, and at such short notice…" Her eyes reflected her worries, her mind clearly far from Adam and the bustling street. "If only Moira had agreed to come to the museum with us."

"What are you talking about?"

Sylvia shrugged. "It is nothing. A few of us were planning to watch a new exhibit being installed in the museum yesterday evening, an archaeological display. Moira was supposed to come with us — she had some connection to the professor who created it — but then at the last minute she didn't come." She waved her hand away. "It didn't matter, he didn't come either, the whole process was postponed."

Adam kissed her lightly and watched as she got into a taxi to take her back to the school. The sudden change in Moira's plans last evening could be important. It wasn't much, but at this point in a murder investigation, every little bit helped.

Isabel had said she was going to a meeting of the city council. This was something she should know about, whether she wanted to see him or not.

CHAPTER FIVE

ISABEL HEARD THE scrape of chair legs being dragged across a wooden floor and picked up her pace toward the council room. Muffled voices carried into the hall, then the doors opened and two people burst into the hallway, rushing to their next meetings.

The room was filled with light, surrounded by windows, floor to ceiling — to indicate the transparency of government, she'd been told once. Hah, that was a joke.

A group of about ten stood around the long table in the front of the room. Chairs had been set up, theater seating style, on the other side of the room, presumably where the public could sit to watch the council meetings. There hadn't been many members of the public there that morning.

"Mr. O'Flaherty. Conn." Isabel flagged down a large, bald man who stood at one end of the table. He smiled when he saw her, a jagged gash through a granite face. His hands already gripped the cigar he'd be smoking once he got outside.

She slid between two askew chairs to get close enough to put a hand on his arm. "I have to talk with you."

"Detective Superintendent. A pleasure, as always." He grinned widely, then turned back to the other men. "Gentlemen, excuse me, please. I'll let you know what I decide."

"Working on the new bridge?" Isabel asked, knowing the council had a tough decision ahead of it.

"I'm making up my mind on that, yeah." Conn nodded without looking at her and stuck the cigar in his mouth.

"Others will have opinions on it, too, you know."

Conn shrugged. "I'll make up my mind. The lads will follow my lead." He spoke around the cigar and exhaled its sickly sweet smell with every word. "They always do."

Isabel kept her opinion to herself. It might be true, the members of council probably did go along with whatever Conn wanted. But she wasn't so sure it was completely voluntary. Which was why she needed to talk with Conn now.

"It's about Moira Walsh."

The rest of her thought was cut off as Peig Browne shoved two chairs out of her way, loudly and ungracefully, lunging toward the spot where Isabel and Conn stood.

"Peig, darling," Conn draped a heavy arm over Peig's shoulder as she reached them. She seemed to lose a few inches of her already diminutive five feet with the weight of his arm, flinching in response to his grin. "What can I do for you?"

"I just wanted to see if you'd worked anything out. With the council. About the bridge?"

She turned her eyes up to his, only briefly, then looked back down at the floor, her lips puckering into a pout. Isabel looked down to hide her grin. She recognized a snow job when she saw one; she'd never seen Peig act so deferential. Conn seemed oblivious.

"I haven't yet. But I imagine you have a position on it?"

"We need that bridge repaired, Conn. It's the only way we can increase our capacity. And you know we need to grow our tourism base."

Conn gnawed on his cigar and eyed the two women in front of him. "True."

"City revenue depends on it."

He nodded and pulled the cigar out of his mouth. "I get it, darlin'. I hear you."

The sound of voices drew Isabel's attention to the door, where Adam Kaminski entered the room. He stepped carefully around the mess of chairs, trying to catch her eye. She shook her head and turned back to Conn and Peig.

"I'm here on official business and I do need to ask you some questions. It's important."

"Of course." Conn spoke to Isabel but the direction of his gaze shifted as Adam approached their group.

"Detective Kaminski," Isabel fought to keep the annoyance out of her voice. "I'll find you when I need to talk to you. You can't be here right now."

"Detective? Don't think I've had the pleasure." Conn put out a beefy hand and Adam shook it. Peig took a step back, as if hiding behind Conn's bulk.

"Adam Kaminski," Adam introduced himself. "From Philadelphia."

"What's a Philadelphia detective doing in Galway then?" Conn asked with surprise.

"I need to talk with you about Moira Walsh, Conn," Isabel continued. "Adam, if you want to talk with me, you'll need to wait over there." She indicated the now empty chairs.

"Moira?" Peig's voice was small. "What happened to Moira?"

Isabel waited until Adam took a step back, then faced Peig and Conn. "I'm sorry to have to tell you both, but Moira Walsh is dead. Her body was found late last night outside the university grounds."

Peig sank into a chair, her face noticeably paler. Conn stayed standing, but put the cigar back in his mouth.

"What happened." He didn't ask it as a question. It was a statement.

"It seems she was strangled." Isabel kept her focus on the two people in front of her, gauging their reaction to the news, but the movement of Adam Kaminski pacing a few feet away was distracting.

"And why are you here now?" Conn asked.

"You worked closely with Moira. I thought you could give me some insight into what she was doing these days. I need to start somewhere, and you're often the man with information." Isabel wasn't above a little flattery to get what she needed, any more than Peig was.

Peig stood. "Look, I have to go. I'm so sorry to hear about Moira." She glanced at Conn as she spoke, as if asking permission to leave. When he nodded, she turned to Isabel. "I'll see you later, right?"

Isabel noticed that Adam's eyes followed Peig as she wove her way out of the room, swaying between the chairs in disarray. She turned her attention back to Conn.

"Damn, I'll miss her, sweet thing."

Isabel laughed at Conn's description of Moira. "No one but you would describe Moira Walsh as a sweet thing, Conn O'Flaherty."

He laughed with her, his wide mouth opening to expose perfect, straight white teeth. That didn't come cheap, with all those cigars he sucked on.

"He part of this investigation?" Conn asked, indicating Adam, who was clearly listening to their conversation.

"In a way. He found her body."

Conn shut his eyes and frowned. "Tell me, friend—" He raised his voice so Adam could hear. "What happened to our Moira?"

Adam must have been waiting for a reason to join, given the speed with which he moved closer to them. Isabel sighed and sank into a chair, followed by Conn and Adam.

"I wish I knew. I simply found her. After..." He paused. "How did you know Moira, Mr. O'Flaherty? Did you work together?"

Isabel opened her mouth to shut Adam up, to tell him

to leave, but Conn spoke first. He shifted in his seat, the thin plastic creaking under his weight, to look directly at Adam. "Something like that." He stared a moment longer, then turned his face back to Isabel.

She held his gaze, waiting him out. She knew he had more to add.

The room had completely emptied by now, leaving only the three of them seated around one end of the table. Shafts of light occasionally showed through the windows as the clouds passed quickly across the sky outside, creating an almost rhythmic motion of light and shade.

"Look, we were colleagues, right? You know that." He tossed a hand in Isabel's direction.

"I do, Conn, I just need to get your sense of her. What was she working on these days?"

"What makes you think her death has anything to do with her work?"

"I don't, necessarily." Isabel shrugged. "It's just one place I need to look, to poke around in. I'll also be talking to her family, her friends…"

"Ha!" Conn spat out a laugh. "If you're looking for accurate information about Moira, her parents are the last people you should ask, I can tell you that. And I'm not sure she understood what it meant to have a friend."

"Why do you say that?"

Conn shrugged, looked around the room, anywhere but at Isabel or Adam. "She was a little rough around the edges sometimes. You know that."

"You just described her as sweet."

Conn's grin came back, spreading across his face like a serpent, but he bit it back as quickly as it appeared. "She had a sweetness about her. In certain ways, if you know what I mean."

Adam's face darkened, but Isabel nodded. "I think I do."

It was the same old story. A strong woman who made difficult choices to support her career got labeled as mean, angry, or worse. And a strong woman who then sought out comfort, sought out relationships, got labeled as easy. Isabel could relate to facing difficult choices. Choices that could come back to haunt you. She realized she was playing with her ring and pulled her hands apart.

Out loud, she said, "Clearly, Moira wasn't perfect. I've heard rumors... about her integrity."

"I wouldn't know about that," Conn answered. "Look, like I said, we were colleagues. That's all. We spent some time together. When we were working on something, it was a lot of time." He raised a hand in the air and snapped his fingers. "Comrades in arms, that's what we were, comrades in arms."

"Why would you say that, Mr. O'Flaherty?" Adam asked.

Conn glanced sideways at Adam. "Look mate, if you'll be working on this investigation around this town, you might as well call me Conn. Everyone else does. Though I appreciate the respect, I truly do."

Adam nodded his understanding but didn't repeat the question. Conn shifted in his seat once more, directing his answer clearly to Adam.

"I've made a good living in this town, you see. I practically run the council these days."

"Are you a member of the city council?"

"Nah, nothing like that." Conn waved away the suggestion. "I don't need the title when I already have the power. You've been using my full name. D'you recognize it?"

Isabel was surprised to see Adam shake his head no. He said he'd read up on Galway. Surely the history of the original families would have been part of that reading.

Conn was still talking, and Isabel shifted her attention back to him as he filled Adam in on the significance of the fourteen tribes of Galway, the wealthy merchant families who, together, built Galway up from a small trading post into a rich, international city in the seventeenth century. Before Cromwell took it all away again.

"But your name's O'Flaherty," Adam said, interrupting Conn's story. Isabel smiled. So he had read about the families.

Conn stopped abruptly, the hand holding his cigar still held above his head in the gesture he had been using to describe Lynch's Castle.

"That's right. I'm of the O'Flaherty tribe. So you know, then? Never trust an O'Flaherty, they used to say. Lord protect us from the vicious O'Flahertys." His eyes flashed black for a moment, perhaps realizing he'd been goaded into talking by Adam. Then that wide grin cracked his face open and he laughed. "But not anymore, my friend. The O'Flaherty name is a name to be trusted now. Believe you me. And I'm proud of my ancestry. The O'Flahertys were a strong and powerful family back then just as they are today."

"But they were outsiders, literally kept outside the gates."

"Friends, enemies, what's the difference? This town traces its roots to those original families, and O'Flaherty is one of those families. I'm well established now, for sure. I support how many charities, donations to all kinds of deserving organizations. I've made this town my own."

"What does that mean?"

Conn's anger was beginning to show through. Isabel wasn't sure about Adam's technique, but he was certainly getting Conn to talk.

"I own the city council, man. I own the tourism board, and tourism is one of the biggest businesses in Galway these days." Conn turned his anger toward Isabel. "Look, you don't need to be asking these questions about me and what I do. You need to look to that university. That's where Moira's life was. No family or friends. Just her work. That's all."

"What was she working on?" Isabel asked.

"I'll tell you what." Conn plucked the cigar from his mouth as he spoke. "Nothing to do with me, but she talked a lot the past few days about that dig."

"Dig?" Isabel looked surprised.

"You know, up around Connemara. The American archeologist and his fancy necklace."

"Necklace?" Adam asked.

Adam's confusion was clear and Isabel felt guilty for feeling, just for a moment, superior. "It was an archaeological find from last summer. An artifact — a piece of jewelry remarkably intact — from the Roman period. Very pretty. And quite a significant find, from what I can remember."

Conn grinned at them. "Yeah, that's what had Moira's goat up lately. I don't know why." He held up a hand to forestall the question Isabel started to ask. "I just know she mentioned it a few times and was riled up about it. Something was off. But I don't know what."

He glanced back and forth between Adam and Isabel, clearly feeling back in control now he'd found a direction to send them in. "Sean Rourke. That's his name. You need to talk to him."

CHAPTER SIX

ADAM COULD SEE the office he'd been directed to, Sean's office, its door propped open, light escaping into the dark hallway. He approached the doorway and looked in. Isabel had shooed him away after their talk with Conn O'Flaherty. She was appreciative of his information about the sudden change in Moira's schedule, but not interested in including Adam in whatever meeting she had planned next. He didn't mind heading back to the university. Being on campus, enjoying the hopeful atmosphere, the deep, heavy aroma of the thick ivy stems that covered the limestone buildings... it all brought back bittersweet memories.

He'd taken it upon himself to find Sean Rourke again, and unless Sean had grown long blond hair that morning, the woman searching the bookcase was not him. Adam watched her, waiting for her to notice his presence. She was tall, big, athletic. And decidedly feminine. Her broad shoulders and strong hands reminded him of the powerful athletes who drew so much attention to the sport of beach volleyball, an impression she may have been trying to belie with her short skirt and bright jewelry. As she stood on her toes to reach a high shelf, Adam couldn't help but notice the shape of her legs, the curve of her back.

She grabbed the book she'd been aiming for, turning as she brought it down. She noticed Adam, gasped, and dropped the book. It hit the floor with a bang.

Adam stepped forward. "I didn't mean to scare you."

"You're American," was her only response.

"And from your accent, you're Irish."

She laughed and put out a hand to shake and he caught a whiff of a light, flowery perfume. "We don't all look like pixies. Jennifer Hughes. Pleasure to meet you. Are you a new student here? Or faculty?"

Adam shook his head. "I'm not. I am looking for Sean Rourke, though. Do you know where I can find him?"

Jennifer picked the errant book off the floor and carried it back behind the single desk in the room. She took the chair behind the desk, tucking a backpack under the chair as she sat. That left Adam the choice of standing or taking one of the three chairs that faced the desk. He sat.

"I'm not sure where Sean is right now. He should be around somewhere. I was hoping to see him myself."

"And what's your relationship with Sean?" Adam kept his voice friendly, but Jennifer frowned. His choice of words could've been better.

"My relationship with Sean? Who the hell are you?"

"Adam Kaminski. I'm a detective. From Philadelphia."

Jennifer's frown reset into an expression of delight. "A detective from Philadelphia. How exciting. What's this all about, then? Why do you need to find Sean?"

"It's about Moira Walsh. I don't know if you heard."

Jennifer looked down at the book she still held in her hand, her answer muffled as she kept her face turned down. "Yes, I heard. It's all over campus. It's terrible." She looked up. "But why are you looking for Sean?"

"He seems to have known Moira pretty well. And we heard she may have been working with him on something."

Jennifer grimaced. "Working with Sean? I hardly think so. Moira Walsh was... well, let's just say she didn't always adhere to the highest scientific standards. Not like Sean."

"So how do you know Sean?"

"Oh, right, sorry, I'm his student. In archaeology."

"You must be a graduate student."

"That's right. Finishing up my doctorate here. I came to work with—" she bit her lip, then started again, "I was invited after I met Sean at a conference a few years ago. To be part of his team, yeah?"

"Maybe Moira was able to help him with something? Be part of the team, too?"

"Ha. Moira was not a team player, I can tell you that. Besides, what did she know about archaeology? She was a statistician."

"A statistician? People just said she was a professor."

"Sure, she was on the Economics and Statistics faculty."

Adam settled lower into his chair. He hadn't come here intending to interview Sean's students, but he was perfectly willing to grab an opportunity when it presented itself. "So how have you liked working with Sean — being on his team? Were you part of his big discovery last summer?"

Jennifer shifted in her seat, recrossing her legs, sending out another wave of perfume. "Yeah, sure. I was there that day. It was just me and Sean, in fact. That was pretty exciting. But it only matters if we continue the work. If we find the encampment he expects to find."

"There's more?"

"We hope so. All we really found last time was a few trinkets. Valuable, sure, don't get me wrong. But the historical value — the scientific value — that depends on what we find next."

"I don't understand."

"Sean is convinced that what we found is just the tip of the iceberg. That there's an entire Roman encampment there, we just need to uncover it."

"And that's important?"

Her eyes grew large; she paused a moment, as if holding her breath, then burst out laughing. "You need to learn a little bit about Irish history, don't you? Yeah, that would be important. Seeing as how everyone right now believes there never were any major Roman encampments in Ireland. So, yeah, kind of a big deal. Changing history."

"Will you keep working with him on it?"

She looked uncomfortable again. "I guess so. I'll stick with him." She shrugged. "I need to finish my degree, anyway, don't I?" She glanced at the doorway, which remained empty, then back at Adam.

Adam stood. "If you see him, will you let him know I'm looking for him? Just to ask him a few questions."

"Sure. If I see him."

SEAN ROURKE STEPPED back from the doorway, avoiding Jennifer's gaze. Why was that detective from Philadelphia asking Jennifer questions? When Adam got up to leave, Sean stepped back behind a shelf in the hallway, easily hidden in the dark hall.

Sean watched him walk away, waited until he heard the door to the stairs close, then entered the office. Jennifer still sat behind his desk.

"Sean." She stood, walked over to him, and put her hand on his face. "Sean, what's going on? What happened?"

He brushed her hand away and pushed past her, claiming his own chair. "What did he want?"

"He was a detective. He's from Philadelphia but he's working with the Garda. Investigating Moira's murder. Why would he want to talk to you?"

"How would I know?" He didn't try to hide his irritation. She wouldn't care. "And he's not working with the police, if that's what he told you. I spoke to Detective Superintendent Sayers this morning. That man, Adam Kaminski, found Moira's body. He's a suspect, not a detective."

She leaned across the desk, putting herself physically closer to him, her breasts nestled together between her arms. Damn, she always got him that way. He turned his chair, turning his back toward her. She stood up straight.

"Well, I didn't tell him anything."

He spun back around toward her. "Tell him anything? What could you possibly tell him? What would you know about Moira's murder?"

She stepped back, her expression one of horror. "Of the murder? Nothing. How could I? I just meant…" She glanced around the room as if seeking her next words in the books that lined the walls or the straggly plants that struggled for survival on the windowsill.

"You meant what, Jennifer?" Sean had no intention of letting her off the hook. Whatever she was thinking about, he needed to know. He really needed to know. "What are you doing here, anyway?"

"I was looking for you." She tried on a smile but it didn't keep. "Clearing up some paperwork, but the bleedin' shredder's still busted." She waited, but Sean didn't respond. "Look, forget it. Okay?" She walked across the room determinedly, grabbed a book off the shelf as if that's what she'd been looking for all along. "I'll see you round, right? D'you need me for anything this afternoon?"

Sean shook his head. She left the room. It felt drastically emptier without her, a far greater change than the movement of only one person should have warranted. Turning in his chair, his foot touched the bag she'd forgotten about. He left his foot on it, drawing some comfort from knowing she'd be back for it.

He wondered about the Galway police and what their investigation would uncover. He couldn't worry about that. He had enough to worry about as it was.

CHAPTER SEVEN

ISABEL STARED at the upright panel map in front of her. It stood about eight feet tall, far taller than she, and she moved her head up and down as her eyes followed the colored lines and shapes marking buildings and paths through the campus.

Very pretty. If only they had a pretty colored diagram to help her find her way out of this mess at the station. She laughed out loud, then glanced around to see if anyone had noticed. She didn't want to be thought of as crazy. She had enough problems.

She let her fingers run over the smooth gold of her ring as she toyed with it, drawing comfort from the cold metal, from the certainty of its circle, from the warm memories it evoked. She blocked out the sounds of students calling to each other as they passed her, the smell of fresh-turned earth from the informal football matches on the green.

Her job would certainly be easier if the powers that be would let her get to work instead of pulling her in all directions at once.

Chief Superintendent McManus, head of the Garda's Galway Division, never failed to remind her that as long as Isabel was stationed at Mill Street she reported to him and would follow his protocols. After all, the responsibility for all investigations rested with the local Garda superintendent. The National Bureau of Criminal

Investigation, her former bureau, was only there to provide expertise and skill in assistance if needed.

She laughed again, without caring this time. Her old boss in Dublin would have a field day with that. His constant, if unsolicited, advice was that she stay aloof from local entanglements and local politics, as they could only hinder an investigation.

Isabel loved the idea of staying out of politics. If only she could. God knew she had enough worries of her own. Enough she had to forget already. She pushed down the thoughts of this latest staff meeting, let go of her ring, and focused again on the map in front of her. Even if she couldn't figure out where she belonged in the Garda, at least she could figure out where Moira was going.

She placed a finger on the spot where Adam had discovered Moira's body. From there, she moved her arm to trace the line of the various paths Moira may have been taking.

The murder had occurred on Nun's Island, the island that broke into the River Corrib in the heart of Galway. An interesting location. Known mostly as the site of the Galway Cathedral and the former site of the infamous Galway jail, it also offered a way to cut through to the university from downtown. In some ways, McManus was right. Familiarity with the town and its people helped.

She considered what she knew of the area. The main paths to the murder scene led either from the Cathedral or from the campus. It was a commonly used cut through to and from the city center and exposed to view from any number of people. A truly bold choice for a murder. Or a desperate one.

Isabel glanced to her right at the science building. Anyone walking to the murder scene to or from campus would pass before its ground floor windows. While it had been after regular hours, there still might have been people using the building. She made a mental note to check to see who was there at that time, to ask them who they'd seen passing that way.

A third option, much less traveled, would have the killer coming along the banks of the canal, on the island side. Isabel traced that line with her finger, following the path leading north from the murder scene, then banking south along the side of the canal past the cable-stayed bridge that led to the campus.

If the killer had come up along the side of the canal, there was less chance of being seen. But more chance of being remembered if he had been seen. It was a narrow, weedy path, very rarely used. Anyone seen making their way along that would be worth remarking on. But who to ask?

She went back in her mind to the question of whether the meeting was planned or chance. She could talk again with the last people to see Moira alive, the group planning the cocktail party. Sylvia Stanko, for example. She'd mentioned talking with Moira. According to Adam, she knew Moira had changed her plans at the last minute. She hadn't said anything about Moira having a meeting scheduled, but she might have heard something without realizing the significance. That happened far too often.

Isabel smiled and played with her ring. Maybe the detective from Philadelphia could make himself useful after all.

SHE HEARD ADAM and Sylvia before she saw them, standing off the main path, partially concealed by a high bush.

Sylvia's voice was a rough whisper that carried on the wind. Isabel couldn't make out her words, but the tone was clear. Adam did a better job of keeping his voice low, but Isabel could read his body language easily enough as soon as they came into view.

She stopped a few yards away, not wanting to

interrupt but also not wanting to eavesdrop. She took a heavy step. Coughed. Finally, she spoke.

"Detective Kaminski." She paused politely. "I've been looking for you."

Adam and Sylvia turned toward her as one. As she turned, Sylvia stepped close to Adam, and Isabel saw the transformation of her face from a scowl to a smile. A practiced smile. She was the type of slim, graceful woman men always seemed to find attractive. Isabel felt her shoulders curving in, as if trying to appear smaller, and she consciously pushed them back and stood taller.

"Detective Superintendent Sayers, how nice to see you again. Adam and I were just discussing…" Sylvia turned to Adam with a question on her face.

"How to handle this situation." Adam was curt. He didn't elaborate.

"Yeah, right. Tough situation, I get it. I'll tell you the same thing I told Adam this morning, Ms. Stanko. I will do my best to find out who did this. To bring justice, to give peace to Moira's loved ones. Then you can both go back to your normal lives."

She looked from one to the other, but neither seemed to find her words comforting. She tried a different tack.

"Sylvia, what do you know of Moira's schedule last evening? You saw her not long before she died. Did she mention that she planned to meet anyone, after she said she wouldn't be joining you at the museum?"

Adam stepped forward, moving slightly to his right so he stood in part between Sylvia and Isabel. An unconscious movement?

"I'm sure Sylvia would've told you already if she knew anything like that, wouldn't you?" He turned to face Sylvia with the question.

She shrugged, an elegant gesture. "She may have mentioned her plans, I do not know." Isabel was struck by the melodiousness of Sylvia's Polish accent. If only her own deep voice could sound so feminine.

She bit her lip and simply nodded her encouragement

for Sylvia to continue.

"I believe she had a number of meetings planned, yesterday and today. She was very engaged in planning our event, as you know." Sylvia glanced at Adam, then kept her eye trained on Isabel. "Of course she still had her own courses to teach, and I heard that she was involved in some private business ventures as well. With someone who worked with the city council."

Isabel nodded. "Conn O'Flaherty."

"She didn't mention meeting anyone in particular yesterday?" Adam asked.

Sylvia shrugged again. "I am sorry, I am. If she did, I do not remember it."

"What time did she leave the meeting last night?" Adam asked.

"I... I'm not sure. How could I be?" Sylvia's voice grew stronger as she raised her tone in a question.

"I'm sorry, I just... Well, what time did the meeting break up?"

Sylvia mumbled something Isabel couldn't make out. Adam frowned.

"I thought you weren't done until seven?"

"I stayed for... for more work that needed doing. Moira left at six, with many of the others."

Isabel didn't like the look Adam was giving Sylvia. There was something wrong with Sylvia's timeline, clearly. But Isabel liked even less the idea of getting involved in their personal spat. They had to work out their own issues. As long as Adam was professional enough to separate out any significant information and share it with her.

"Tell you what, I'll go find Sean. You two work out whatever it is you have to work out. Find me later."

CHAPTER EIGHT

THE DARK HALLWAY was an anachronism. Something that belonged more to the artifacts and remains dug up by the students and faculty of the archaeology department than to the modern science building.

Isabel stopped walking and heard the silence take over as the echoes of her footsteps faded away. The promising aroma of brewing coffee competed with the less appealing musty odor caused, no doubt, by the shelves, high, low, and in-between, that lined either side of the hall, creating the gloom and shadows she found herself walking into.

She paused, getting a feel for the place, trying to shake the uncomfortable feeling of sorrow the hallway produced in her. Other people might enjoy the dark and solitude, perhaps, but not her. She found no joy in digging through ancient vaults, unearthing old tomes in hidden recesses of the town library, or digging up details on suspects that predated the computerization of the Garda records.

The past didn't interest her.

She let her eyes accustom to the gloom, then walked forward. An open doorway to her right allowed a shaft of light to cross her path, and she turned as she walked by. A young woman, large, blond, sat stuffed into a narrow chair, a book held blatantly in front of her face, as if defying anyone to interrupt her reading.

Isabel kept going to the end of the hall, where she knew Sean Rourke's office lay. She knocked on the doorframe without hesitation, and the man inside almost jumped with surprise. She thought he'd've heard her footsteps as she approached. Perhaps she walked more quietly than she realized. Or perhaps he truly was absorbed in his writing.

Sean dropped his pen across his notebook, then closed it, leaving an awkward gap between the pages. He shoved the notebook into a desk drawer.

"Yes? Oh, it's you."

"Hiya, Sean. You feeling any better this afternoon? I hope you had a chance to get home for a rest?"

He shrugged, looked away, mumbled something incoherent.

"I'm here to talk to you about Moira. May I?" She gestured to one of the worn chairs facing his desk, and he nodded.

"How can I help you with that?" he asked. "I don't know what happened to her last night. Hell, I didn't really know her, did I?"

"That's not the impression you gave this morning, Sean. Accusing Adam Kaminski of killing her? Saying that you needed her?"

"Sure, yeah… we were becoming friends. That's all. But we didn't work together much. Different fields, you know?"

Isabel nodded, took a deep breath. The mustiness of the hall crept into the room, helped in no small part by the piles of books, the dying plants on the narrow sill, the collection of old objects that lined the shelves. It was a small space made even smaller by the collection of stuff that somehow brought Sean knowledge. Or comfort.

Sean grew even more uncomfortable as the seconds passed. "So, is there anything in particular you need to ask me?"

"I'd like to get your sense of Moira. What she was like as a friend — or as a colleague. Helpful? Friendly? Tiresome?" Isabel grinned as if making a joke.

"She was all right, I guess. She was helpful. Yes, definitely helpful."

"And what did she help you with?"

"Look, what is this about? Are you asking these questions of all the faculty at the university? Because that's an awfully slow way to go about your investigation if you are." Sean shoved his chair back and stood as he spoke, tripping over a backpack that lay on the floor. He picked the bag up and tossed it onto an empty chair, then turned back to Isabel.

"She didn't help me with anything in particular, she was just the helpful type, that's all. I'm sure others will agree."

"I've heard that she was particularly interested in your dig. The one you did last summer."

Sean made a pained expression and held up a hand. "Yes, I'm familiar with the dig, thank you. Was she interested in it? I didn't know. She didn't tell me if she was."

Isabel opened her mouth to push this question further when she felt someone standing behind her. She turned to see the large blond woman standing in the doorway. She hadn't heard her approach.

"Sean, what's going on?"

"It's nothing to do with you, Jennifer, don't worry about it."

Isabel stood and put a hand out to Jennifer. "Detective Superintendent Isabel Sayers. I'm looking into the murder of Moira Walsh."

Jennifer shuddered and stepped toward the chair onto which Sean had tossed his bag. "How terrible. I still can't believe it happened." She bent as if to move the bag out of the way, but Sean put a hand on her arm.

"You don't need to stay, Jennifer. This really doesn't concern you. Besides—" He glanced at Isabel. "I'm your teacher. I don't want you getting involved in a murder investigation. Not exactly healthy student activity, is it?" He tried on a smile, but when no one smiled back he dropped it.

"Professor Rourke, if there is any reason you think of why Moira might have been interested in your dig and what you found, you'll let me know?"

"Why would Moira be interested in the dig?" Jennifer asked.

"I don't know. No, it... no, there's no reason." Sean shook his head. "Now if there's nothing else? I have something I need to do."

Jennifer opened her mouth to speak, but glanced at Isabel and closed it again.

Isabel simply ducked her head in acknowledgement and stepped out of the office ahead of him. Sean turned away from her without another word. She watched him disappearing down the dark hallway and wondered who he was going to see and which of her questions had sparked this sudden need.

CHAPTER NINE

FROM HIS TABLE at the window, Adam could see the intersection where the pedestrianized street met the wide, curved road. To his right, crowds of shoppers, young and old, students and families, swarmed past the buskers trying to make a living or make a name for themselves on the cobblestone path. He was getting used to the mix of languages and accents of the people in this international city. This street alone housed not only this little coffee shop but a line of restaurants offering cuisine from China, India, Pakistan, Italy, and of course Ireland.

The iconic Spanish Arch squatted across the street, the history museum and tourism center just beyond it. As he admired the view, the movement of a hulking figure in front of the arch caught his attention. Conn O'Flaherty cut through the crowds like a bull through a china shop, not stopping to check on those who failed to move out of his way. He barged past the arch, passing the spot where years ago women from the Claddagh would gather for the weekly fish market.

Conn's destination wasn't of particular interest to Adam, until he saw Sean following in his footsteps a few minutes later. Unlike Conn, Sean wove his way through the crowd, flinching if he came into contact with another human being. He, too, passed the arch, heading toward the tourist center.

Adam considered what that might mean as he logged onto the cafe's free wifi to place a video call.

The phone rang three times before Pete answered.

"What took you so long, you asleep at your desk?"

"Nice. Very nice. Why're you calling, Kaminski? You got lost on your way to Galway?" Pete Lawler's eyes moved beyond Adam to look over his shoulder. "Where are you?"

Adam laughed, feeling a little more relaxed with Pete on the phone. Something about his partner always calmed him down, helped him focus on the case at hand. Though this time there was no case. "I'm at a coffee shop. Just calling to check in. We had a little trouble here."

"What kind of trouble?" Adam could hear the wariness in Pete's voice, see it in his eyes.

"Someone Sylvia's been working with was murdered. Last night."

"Crap. Sylvia's not a suspect, is she?"

Adam shook his head. "I don't think so. The police aren't exactly taking me into their confidence, but she seems to have a pretty good alibi. Actually, I'm more of a suspect than she is."

"Not again." Pete almost groaned the words, and Adam knew he was thinking about Adam's experience in Warsaw.

"Not really. Not like that. It's just that I found the body. So that automatically links me to the case."

"Makes sense. Will you be helping with the investigation at all? Professional courtesy?"

"Looks like not. Sylvia doesn't want me involved in it anyway — she's upset that I… well, she didn't know I was coming, you know? And she found out through a call from the police saying I'd found a body."

"Ah… not the best kind of surprise then."

"No. Exactly. So she doesn't want me any more involved than I already am. And the local detective superintendent shares her opinion on that. Which wouldn't be better if she knew I was a month back on the job after my ninety-day suspension."

"No kidding. So what're you gonna do?"

"I'm going to go on with my plan to see the area, dig up a few facts about my great-grandfather, then take a few days off with Sylvia to enjoy ourselves."

"Sounds like a good plan, buddy. How's life on campus?"

Adam grinned. "Brings back memories, I'll tell you."

He stared out of the cafe window at the historic, cosmopolitan town around him. The history of this city was embedded in every ancient wall, every blackened beam. He could picture the university courtyard he'd seen earlier within the slate gray quadrangle, its elegant architecture, the wooden bones of ivy, hints of green and red leaves still clinging in places, gracefully climbing the sides of the buildings. He could imagine himself at home in a place like this, spending his time researching history instead of investigating criminals, teaching young minds instead of catching killers.

"You could still go back to teaching, you know." Pete knew exactly how Adam felt about his career choices. And why Adam had left teaching in the first place.

"You know I can't. Not while... not yet." Even thinking about his students still caused him pain. The students who had been killed while he was their teacher. Nothing to do with him, of course. They had been victims of a random drive-by. Just innocent teenagers hanging out on their own front stoop. But Adam had been their teacher. He was supposed to protect them. Keep them safe. He had failed.

"I need to focus on what's important." He laughed, a grim, grating sound. "Once the world is safe for our kids, then I'll go back to teaching."

"So, when pigs fly, is that what you're saying?"

"Something like that. You know how important what we do is. We keep people safe, Pete, I can't give up on that." Adam looked out at the young people passing on the street, many of them most likely students. Some looked worried, stressed. Others carefree. They should all be carefree. "Listen, there's one more thing I need from you."

"And what's that?"

"I need to see the review. The final report."

Pete didn't answer right away, so Adam continued, "I know it's in, I got an email. But they won't email it to me. It's only hard copy."

"Would need to be encrypted, all that personal information, you know that." Pete paused. "Why do you want to see it now?"

"Look, Isabel, the detective here, is going to be looking into me. I just want to know what she's going to find."

"She won't get a copy of this report, though. That's private."

"I know, but the captain's seen it. And if she calls to talk to him, what's he going to say?"

Pete took awhile to answer again. "I don't want to read it. It's yours, for your eyes only."

"It's just a psych eval. It's no big deal. You know I don't believe half that crap anyway."

"No? Maybe you should. Look, it can't be that bad. They let you back to work, didn't they?"

"I know. But I want to see the final report. Will you help? Captain said he left it on my desk, in a blue envelope."

Pete would easily recognize the envelope used in their interoffice mail for sensitive documents.

Pete didn't take too long to decide. "Do you have a fax over there? I can send it to the police station."

"No, I don't want Isabel seeing it. Send it to the university. I'll text you the number as soon as I get it."

"I'll look for it, send it over later today. Might be nighttime your time zone."

"That's fine, I'll be here when it arrives. Thanks, buddy."

As he dropped his phone back into his pocket, a movement to his right caught Adam's attention. He saw a man out of the corner of his eye who seemed a little too interested in what Adam was doing. When he turned his head to look, the man grabbed up his bag and ran.

Adam had no idea who'd be watching him or why, but he wasn't going to let him get away. He took off after the fleeing redhead in the pale blue denim jacket.

He caught glimpses of the man through the crowd on the street, his trim red hair making it easy to follow him. Adam skipped and jumped his way through the crowd, but the other man was faster. He moved with youthful energy, jumping over a bench and skidding around a tight corner.

Adam did his best to keep up, but he had to take his eyes off his suspect to prevent himself from running smack into a pedestrian or tripping over a busker's amplifier. He dashed past brightly painted doors and square shop windows carved through gray, stone walls, the music of buskers chasing after him.

He lost the young man and stopped running, his breath coming hard now. He turned to look up every street at the intersection, his mind spinning as fast as he was. Who would've been listening to his conversation with Pete? Whoever it was now knew that Adam just got off suspension. Had a psych report detailing his shortcomings. That was information Adam preferred to keep private.

There, he saw a spot of red in the sunlight, a pale denim jacket. He ran in that direction, but it was too late. The man was too far ahead. As Adam reached the spot where he had seen the man, he knew he'd lost him. He spun around again, searching the crowd, but only strange faces stared back at him. Whoever had been eavesdropping on him was gone.

CHAPTER TEN

"CONN, THERE YOU ARE."

The hulking figure of Conn O'Flaherty didn't slow or change course when Sean called, and Sean watched as he entered Peig's office, pulling the door shut behind him.

"Damn." Sean stopped in his tracks and a young boy, no more than ten, walked into him from behind.

"Sorry, sorry." The woman, presumably the boy's mother, pulled him close to her as they maneuvered their way around Sean through the crowds of tourists that moved in and out of the tourist center.

Even though it was only March, too early for the tourist season to be in full swing, the sidewalks around the Galway City Museum and Spanish Arch teemed with visitors. Sean's frown deepened.

He could leave. Find Conn another time. But it had been hard enough tracking him down today. And he needed to know what Conn knew. He couldn't let Peig get in the way.

He pushed his way through the crowd in the small tourist office just off the museum until he stood outside Peig's door. He hesitated for only a moment, then knocked. Then knocked again when he heard no sounds from within the office.

Peig swung the door open after his second knock. "Professor Rourke." She seemed surprised to see him. "What can I do for you?"

"I'm here to see Conn. He here?" He kept his voice low.

Peig looked suspicious. "He is. Come in."

Sean followed her into the cramped office, where Conn O'Flaherty was already taking up most of the space. He leaned against one wall, cigar in hand, one arm leaning heavily on a bookcase that looked ready to topple over with the weight. Conn didn't look worried. He never did.

"Sean. Friend. What brings you here?" Conn's smile was expansive.

"It's about Moira. I thought... That is, I wanted to ask you..."

Sean glanced at Peig. She was tucked into the far corner of the office, leaning against the wall, probably aiming to look casual but instead looking like she was hoping she could simply be absorbed into the corner.

"It's a terrible thing." Peig shook her head. "Just terrible. And after we've worked so hard to build the image of our town."

Conn laughed and Sean shuddered at the sound. "Nice to see you have your priorities in order, little Peig. We did work hard, didn't we?" He turned to Sean. "And what did you want to ask me, then?"

Sean shrugged. He pulled a chair away from the wall and sat heavily. "I'm not really sure. The police came around asking questions. Asking *me* questions." He looked up at the other two. "I don't get it... do you?"

"Well, Sean, friend, you did make a bit of a scene yesterday morning, from what I hear." Conn was grinning from ear to ear. God, he was enjoying this, watching Sean squirm. What did he know?

"Right. True." Sean chewed on a lip and sank lower into his chair. "But they were asking me about the dig. They said you sent them, Conn. Why?"

Conn stuffed his cigar between his teeth and bit down.

Peig jumped up and into the conversation. "I can't

imagine what the connection might be, Sean. Unless Moira was helping you in some way?" She looked at Conn with interest, even though her question was asked of Sean.

Sean simply shook his head.

"Look, I just know she was interested in it. That's all I told Isabel. That she was interested." Conn directed a leering look toward him. "Maybe it wasn't the dig that interested her. Maybe it was the man doing the digging?"

Sean sat up straight, leaned forward. "Why not? We were getting to know each other. I thought we had a future together. Maybe." His voice failed as he saw the look of incredulity on Conn's face.

"You?" Conn actually had the gall to laugh. "I don't think so."

Peig moved to stand closer to Sean, one hand on his shoulder. "I'm so sorry, Sean. When someone dies, it's never easy. And this was so unexpected." She looked down at the floor for a moment. "But look, the police are on it, right? They'll find whoever did this. I'm sure they will."

"Are you sure you want them looking into it, Sean, buddy?" Conn's expression was inscrutable.

"Why would you say such a horrible thing?" Peig asked.

Conn shrugged. "I just wonder what else they'll dig up."

"Look." Peig moved back behind her desk, picked up a sheaf of papers. "Look how much good you've done for this town, Sean Rourke. And you not even Irish. You should be proud of what you've accomplished."

Sean nodded sullenly.

Peig continued, "I've been promoting the heck out of that find of yours. Galway, uncover your dreams." She held her hands out as she spoke, as if pulling curtains away from a sign in the air. "That sort of thing, you know. It's been very effective."

"Well, I'm glad someone has benefited from this."

Conn pushed himself away from the wall with some effort. "Doesn't look like young Sean here's too happy."

Conn lumbered toward the office door, patting him heavily on the shoulder as he passed. "I still don't know why you tracked me down, Seannie boy."

"I just thought you might know... Might have some advice." Sean mumbled his response.

"Oh, I've got some advice for you, all right." Conn bent at the waist so his face was close to Sean's. Sean could almost taste the scent of cigar that clung to his lips, feel the stubble that speckled his chin. He leaned back in his chair, but Conn kept pace. "Keep your head down. Focus on your work. It's all you got right now, isn't it?"

Conn grinned and left the office.

CHAPTER ELEVEN

"WHAT'S THAT, THEN?" The woman's voice carried down the hall as Adam approached. Low, strong, almost masculine, the accent not quite Irish, not quite English.

"An inspirational quote," a man's voice answered, then sniggered, destroying the authoritative tone he'd probably been going for.

Adam stopped where he was, not wanting to interrupt. From where he stood, he had a clear view of the woman behind the desk holding pride of place in the widened hallway, some sort of antechamber before the doors to the main offices, which remained closed. The other person who spoke was only partly in view, standing as he was in the far doorway. Adam could tell only that he was a tall man, big in size as well as height, who had a habit of speaking that involved raising his nose in the air and talking down his clean-shaven chin.

"I just posted a notice about the memorial service for Moira. Don't move that."

"Of course not, Nora. Why would I possibly want to confuse people about the appropriate time and place to sing Moira Walsh's praises?" The man stepped closer to Nora's desk and Adam saw he was dark in coloring, with hair cut short to his head, his hands thick and beefy. "I should think you'd be glad she was gone."

The woman made a strange, sucking sound with her mouth. "That's a terrible thing to say."

"Well." He inhaled sharply through his teeth, as if chewing on the thought he was about to spit out. "She did bring in some hefty grants, I'll give you that."

Nora looked around as if to see if anyone was listening. "Professor Dempsey, you shouldn't go around saying—" She cut herself off when she saw that Adam was, in fact, listening. "Yes, may I help you?"

"Hi. I'm Adam Kaminski. A friend of Sylvia Stanko's." He turned to Professor Dempsey, but the man simply glared at Adam, then stalked out of the workspace, down the far hallway.

"Pay him no mind," Nora said. "He's a man on a mission."

"Something to share with the staff or his students?" Adam asked with a smile.

Nora simply shook her head. "That's a very strange thing for him to do. But then, Liam is a strange one."

"Right. So… Sylvia said you might be able to give me a fax number where I could receive a fax?"

"Hm." Nora Kane's lips tightened even more. She stood and Adam saw she was dressed in a classic English style tweed skirt, just below the knee, sturdy brown walking shoes. Her voice might carry traces of the land that adopted her, but her style was pure England. As if she were making a statement.

"I suppose I can give you that. Why do you need to use our fax?" She'd asked the question only after agreeing to help, so Adam took it as curiosity rather than part of her decision making process.

"I need to receive a document that can't be emailed. You understand." His intention was to butter her up, but it didn't seem to work.

She clucked her tongue, her lips tightly sealed, producing the strange, wet sound he'd heard before.

He tried a different approach. "You do have a way with dealing with difficult faculty. I imagine you have to manage all types of personalities around here."

It seemed a little too blatant to him as he said it, but

apparently not to Nora Kane. When she smiled her whole face lit up.

"So what is your official role around here?" Adam persisted in his efforts. "You work for the deputy president, I understand?"

"I'm his executive assistant." She held up one pudgy finger. "Not a secretary, mind you."

"But you're not from Ireland, are you?"

Nora beamed even brighter. "Can you tell? I've been told my accent is quite Irish these days."

"I can hear a touch of the Irish in your voice, but you look like the perfect English lady to me."

"I'm from Yorkshire." Nora leaned toward Adam, eager to share more about herself.

"Beautiful there, I've heard. I've never been. Not yet, anyway."

Nora nodded. "Oh, you should go. It is wonderful land, friendly people." She frowned. "Not a lot of job opportunities, I'm sorry to say." She paused, her lips in a satisfied line, neither smile nor frown, as she looked Adam up and down.

She stepped around her desk, her wide hips wobbling over surprisingly small feet as she shuttled a set of files from her desk to a cabinet on the far side of the workspace. She chatted as she worked, and Adam listened politely as she explained her various moves from the University of York, where she started as an administrative assistant, to her first job in Galway, to the time it took her to work her way up the bureaucratic ladder.

"I've lived and worked in Galway for twenty years now," she concluded her story as she turned toward him, hands on her hips. "I'll write out that number for you. We're lucky we still have a fax." She gave Adam a resigned look. "Budget cuts, you understand. We're short on staff, making do with out-of-date office equipment. Repairmen who don't show up when they say they will…" She took a sharp breath and clapped her hands together. "But we make do."

"I understand budget cuts, same around the world."

"And what do you do, Mr. Kaminski? You said you were a friend of Sylvia Stanko? You're also with the delegation from Legg University?"

"Do you work with them much?" Adam asked.

"Oh, on and off. I help out with a number of projects, whatever needs doing. I support the administration of the Legg-NUI Galway exchange program."

"So will you be part of the big event this week?"

"Oh, no, not me. Moira Walsh, she's the public face of that." Her smile held for another second before she realized what she'd said. "Oh, dear, I shouldn't have said that. I wonder what they'll do now. Who will represent the university?" She looked up to Adam as if he had the answer.

"They'll figure something out, don't worry. I've spoken to the detective investigating Moira's murder. She seems very competent."

"Isabel Sayers, is that her?" When Adam nodded, she continued, "Yes, I've met her before. She was up here for some trouble earlier." She shook her head as she passed him a slip of paper with the fax number.

Adam waited for her to say more, but she simply stared at the ground, shaking her head. "Well, there it is then." She glanced at the clock on the wall, made a tut-tutting sound to herself and wobbled off down the hall, leaving Adam standing at her desk.

He realized he'd never answered her question about who he was and what he was doing there. Was he trying to stay incognito in order to avoid getting dragged into the investigation? Or was he keeping his identity close so that he could better be involved in it?

"ADAM, DARLING, there you are." Sylvia seemed to glide rather than run down the hall toward him, ever elegant, always sexy, even when in a hurry.

"What's wrong?"

"Adam, you must do something. You must." She threw her arms around his neck and buried her face in his shoulders.

He encircled her in his arms, holding her even closer. "What happened? Are you hurt?"

"It's not that. It's this murder. You must do something."

"I won't let anybody hurt you, don't worry."

"No, no." She leaned up from their embrace to look him in the eyes. "It's not that, I'm not afraid."

"Then what?"

She turned away from him. Took a deep breath. "One of my donors — a very promising prospect — just cancelled. He's not coming to the event because of the murder."

Adam couldn't help but grin. "Ah, I see."

She turned back to him just in time to catch his grin and responded by slapping him on the arm. "This is not funny. It's serious. This is my job we're talking about."

"But what do you want me to do?" Not two hours earlier she'd been chiding him for being involved; now she wanted him to "do something." He was at a loss.

"Adam, you must solve this. Solve this murder."

He took a step back from her, both hands in front of him. "I'm not part of the investigation. There's not much I can do."

"Darling." She returned her arms to around his neck. "You are a good policeman. We both know this."

"We do?" He breathed in her lavender scent and thought of their life in Philadelphia, momentarily losing his focus on the matter in hand. "Wait, I thought you didn't like my job."

Sylvia laughed. "I know, I don't. I am learning to appreciate it, you know that, right?"

He nodded, waiting for the "but."

"I do know that you're good at it. If you investigate,

you will find who did this. Then the police will announce it and no one else will cancel."

"And your fundraiser can go forward, a full success." Adam stepped out of their embrace and led the way down the hall back toward the front door. "You know I'll do anything for you, honey. I don't see that one cancellation is such a big deal, though."

"It is only the first, I am sure of it." Her voice was firm, her mind made up. "There could be others. If you don't solve this."

"Or if the police don't solve it. I would only be helping. If they even let me." He felt her relax next to him, hearing the acquiescence in his voice. "You can't be surprised. Your career is important to you; therefore it's important to me. If you want me to help, I'll help."

She took his hand as she followed him down the hall. "Thank you, Adam. I am sure you will solve this. And the sooner the better. Every hour that passes means more people might consider cancelling."

He laughed under his breath. "It will take more than an hour to solve this, honey. Murder investigations take weeks, months, even years. You know that."

"No." She gripped his hand even tighter. "You do not have weeks. If too many of the donors cancel, we will have to cancel the whole event. It can't go forward without a realistic expectation of success."

He stopped and looked at her. "But your event is in five days."

"So you see, you do not have much time. And perhaps I can help. I thought of something."

"What do you mean? What did you think of?"

"Something that happened with Moira that evening. It's probably nothing, I know, but…"

Adam raised his eyebrows, encouraging her to continue. "What is it? Even if it's nothing, I can take it to Isabel, let her know that I can be of help to her."

"Yes, that is what I was thinking." Sylvia nodded urgently, her face serious. "It was a note."

"A note?"

"Yes, a notecard. In an envelope. Very formal."

"And what about this note?"

"It came for Moira."

"Who sent it?"

Sylvia shrugged. "That, I do not know. But I saw her receive it."

"Who gave it to her?"

"One of the students who had been working at the front reception desk. It had been delivered, and this student brought it to Moira."

"What did the note say?"

"I am sorry, I do not know this either." Sylvia frowned and looked truly sad she didn't know more. "But it was after she saw the note that she changed her plan."

"Her plan to join you at the museum?"

"Yes. So perhaps this note was important."

"Sylvia, darling." Adam kissed her gently on the lips. "It is most definitely important. Thank you for telling me. I'll let Isabel know right away."

"Good." Sylvia smiled. "Then this case will be solved right away, too."

"Sylvia." He shook his head. "I love that you have this much faith in me. But I can't promise you anything. I can't even promise the police will let me help. I'm still technically a suspect to them."

"They will welcome your help." She tipped her head to the side and smiled up at him. "I am sure of it."

CHAPTER TWELVE

"ABSOLUTELY NOT. Out of the question."

Adam raised an apologetic hand. "I understand your situation, but Sylvia's so worried. I'd really like to help."

Isabel had the grace to look concerned. "Is she frightened because of the murder? I truly don't think she has anything to worry about, unless…" She frowned. "Well, unless she knows something she's not telling me?"

"No, no, nothing like that." Adam hurried to assure her. "No, it's her work. It's everything to her, you know?"

Isabel's face took on a knowing expression. "I know something about that, yes."

Adam didn't let himself wonder what that meant. It wasn't his place to pry. "The murder is hurting her efforts with the fundraising event. Looks like some of her big donors, people who'd committed to coming and all but agreed to hefty donations, are backing out."

Isabel nodded. "Makes sense. Murder is rarely good for business."

"So she asked me to help." He'd considered the best way to approach Isabel as he was looking for her, and had ultimately decided that the plain truth was the best way. He hoped he'd been right. Her abrupt response suggested he wasn't.

"Detective Kaminski" — she shook her head as she

spoke — "you cannot be part of this investigation. In fact, if I find out that you've been interfering… Surely you understand that, as a detective yourself?"

"I know. I do." Adam reconsidered his approach. "Let me tag along. Nothing formal."

"Bring one suspect to an interview with another? I don't think so."

"You know the expression, keep your friends close, your enemies closer. So, keep me close."

Isabel seemed to soften; she even laughed. "I don't think that applies here, does it? You're hardly my enemy."

"Glad to hear it." Adam smiled back at her, knowing that his dimples were on full display. He tried a different approach. "I don't know about you, but I can get more done with the help of my partner than when I'm on my own."

Isabel stiffened. "I'm doing just fine on this investigation, Detective. And if I need help, I have the entire staff of the Garda working with me."

"Do you?" Adam asked, pretty sure he'd picked up on some internal conflicts there. "I see." He looked down at the ground, avoiding her eyes, offering her the lead.

"I appreciate your offer. But there's simply no way."

"What if I get my captain to call your boss?"

"Hmph. Which one? I mean, no, that would only complicate things. Make them worse. I have enough problems."

"I see." He did. She looked at him and he could see the indecision in her eyes. He pressed on. "It would be good to have someone to talk things through with. Someone not involved in Garda politics, that is."

He'd hit the nail on the head with that one, he could see it in her eyes.

"I'll follow your lead," he promised. "And stay quiet when you need me to." He gestured gallantly with his arm. "After you."

"NORA KANE? HA! She'd like to think she knows everything. But I know better, don't I? *Níl saoi gan locht.*" The woman's dark eyes took on an almost evil glint, and Adam had a vision of one of the warrior Irish queens he'd been reading about.

Adam didn't understand the Gaelic phrase, but Isabel nodded. "Yes, we've all got our weaknesses. So what were Nora Kane's weaknesses?"

Colleen, the Queen Maeve look-alike, seemed to be enjoying this. She sucked on her lips and looked up at Adam and Isabel, both standing near her desk, with a sly grin. "Didn't she tell you about their little spat?"

"When would this have been, Ms. Hogan?" Isabel asked with exaggerated patience. She must have been just as curious as Adam, but she was doing a good job of hiding it.

"Oh, quite a few months ago. Might've been a year now? It was after Moira got back from her trip to Philadelphia."

"And can you tell me exactly what you saw?"

"Well, Nora lost it, didn't she? At Moira." She looked back and forth between Adam and Isabel, a confused expression on her face.

"Yes, but what exactly did you see?"

When the young woman didn't answer, Adam jumped in. "Did you hear them? Maybe you heard Nora talking loudly to Moira?"

"Talking loudly?" Colleen let out a breathy laugh. "Yelling she was, no doubt about that. Anyone about at the time could've heard."

"And you were about." Adam nodded his understanding. "So what did you hear? Where were they?"

"Just down the hall." She gestured with her head. "Standing next to Nora's desk there."

From where he stood, Adam could see where the narrow hallway opened up. Nora's desk stood just outside the office of the deputy president. From her desk, she had a view out to the quad in one direction, and a view down the hall to the narrow space that held the other administrative assistants in the other.

"She must have known you could hear her."

"I suppose." Colleen shrugged. "She would make her voice quiet, then it would get louder, then she'd start whispering, like. It was kind of funny to watch."

"So what were they arguing about?" Isabel asked.

Colleen shook her head. "I can tell you what they were saying, but I'm not sure that's what they were arguing about. If you know what I mean?" She looked up at Adam and he smiled. She was smarter than she was acting.

"Moira hadn't kept all of her receipts," Colleen continued. "She didn't have the right paperwork. Nora confronted her, explained that she needed these for the files."

"Sounds reasonable." Adam encouraged her to go on.

"Yeah, but Moira didn't like being caught in error in front of other people. She taunted her. Called her a secretary."

"I picked up on that earlier. Nora doesn't like that, does she?"

Colleen shook her head firmly. "Oh, no. Nora likes to be in charge, she does. And she expects us to show her the respect she deserves. Well—" Colleen raised a hand to cover a giggle. "The respect she thinks she deserves."

Adam's estimation of this young woman was going up every minute.

Isabel didn't look impressed. "So that was it? They called each other names?"

"Names?" Colleen laughed out loud. "Moira told Nora she was replaceable, while she, Professor Moira Walsh, was not. Nora got so upset, she tipped over her own tray of files, papers everywhere. I never saw Nora so upset. And I'll tell you what else. Nora and Professor Walsh didn't talk much after that."

CHAPTER THIRTEEN

ISABEL WAS GLAD to see the back of Adam and Sylvia as they walked out to University Road to catch a cab into town and the romantic dinner that no doubt awaited them. Isabel had doubts about the future of that relationship, but that was none of her business. She'd easily refused Adam's invitation to join them, not surprised to see the relief in Sylvia's eyes at her response.

She was, however, hungry. It had been a long day. She took the footpath in the opposite direction of Adam and Sylvia, heading back over the cable-stayed bridge. She stopped in the middle of the bridge, facing the lime kiln, the narrow path on which Moira's body had been found just ahead at the bend. She played with her ring, letting her mind run freely through what she knew. She turned the cold, smooth metal around and around her finger as she tried to imagine Moira passing through here.

The water was narrow and shallow here. It was a tributary of the River Corrib, nothing more than an access point, really. To her left, it opened up into the Lower Corrib. To her right, it branched off into the Eglinton Canal, the same thin stream that wound its way to Mill Street and the Garda station there. The River Corrib found its way through most parts of the city eventually, in some places as rushing water but more often in the ruined remains of industries that had grown up around the water when it flowed freely through the landscape.

She stepped off the bridge, walked past the old lime kiln, and followed the path as it curved to the right. Yellow crime scene tape still fluttered in the wind here. The techs had collected all the evidence they were going to get — after a full night and day exposed to the elements, anything they'd missed would probably be gone by now. But Isabel kept the scene roped off. She didn't want any curious onlookers gawking at the space, trampling over it.

She also liked to keep a crime scene available to herself for as long as possible after a crime.

There was no science to her method. She walked along the path until she came to the first line of yellow tape. She stopped here and looked over the scene before stepping into it. The air smelled fresh, clean. It should, washed almost daily as it was by the regular spring rains. Night had long since fallen, and the reds, golds, and greens of the bare branches and few stray leaves on the bushes along the path all blended into a dark brownish-grayish hue. It would have been lighter when Moira was killed, though darkness would have been falling.

That mysterious, dangerous stretch of twilight. Was Moira looking at those colors when she walked this way last night, Isabel wondered. Was she looking where she was going at all?

Isabel ducked under the tape into the scene, taking small steps, her eyes on the ground. She could see the flattened dirt where Moira's body had lain, just under the bushes to the far side of the path. Amazing that Adam had seen her at all, really, hidden as she was. He was observant, she'd give him credit for that. Divots and holes created by the crime scene technicians as they'd scoured the ground searching for evidence scarred the area. There had been no telltale signs or prints beyond a set probably left by a child playing football. Isabel saw nothing new.

She stopped where she stood, next to the spot Moira

had seen last, and looked out over the water, toward the city center. Lights were on across the river. People moved in swarms across the Salmon Weir Bridge. It was an hour later than the time Moira had been killed, but even so, there must have been people out at that time of evening, too. Isabel was once again struck by the brazenness of the killer, to commit murder in such a public place, at such risk of being caught.

Was the killer so bold as to not care about the risk? Or was it unpremeditated, the killer caught up in an emotional storm, not stopping to consider the risk? Isabel closed her eyes and tried to get a feel for the space. Definitely not scientific, but every space had a feeling. A scent. She let her mind roam over the few facts they had. The way Moira had been killed… her interest in the archeological dig… her involvement with Conn O'Flaherty… Her phone rang, pulling her out of her meditation.

"Sayers, just calling to check in. How's that murder investigation of yours coming on?" The voice of Detective Chief Superintendent Alex Coughlan, the man she'd served under while working in Dublin, brought her up short.

"Sir. Good to hear from you again. I sent in a report two hours ago, I could forward that if you're interested."

"I saw it. But two hours is a long time. And it went through Mill Street, through Garda channels. I was wondering if you had anything else you wanted to share with me. With NBCI. You understand."

Isabel gritted her teeth. Despite her former boss's expectation, and perhaps his practice, she did not keep secrets from her colleagues at Mill Street. That simply wasn't how she worked. "I've nothing to add, sir, not really."

"Not really? So what is it?"

"An interview I just finished. With a secretary at the university. Seems Nora Kane had a run-in with the victim."

"Recently?"

Isabel shook her head. "A year ago. But it was quite emotional. And very out of character for Nora Kane. Our witness says they've been on the outs ever since."

"Good, good. Keep pursuing that. I'll get someone on our end to dig into Nora Kane's background, see if there's anything of interest there. No reason not to include this in your next report, Sayers."

"Yes, sir." Isabel could barely get the words out. Glad to know she had permission to include all of her findings in her reports. If the reports only went through NBCI it would be different, but knowing that they were shared with all gardaí working the case, Detective Chief Superintendent Coughlan would assume she'd keep some information out. How little he knew her.

"You need more, though, Sayers. It's gone twenty-four hours."

"I know, sir." She did know. She knew how important those first twenty-four hours were in any murder investigation. And how little she knew at this point. "We're still waiting on more results from the techs. We've talked to everyone who knew or worked with the victim. I'll go back through those statements again to see if we missed anything, maybe revisit some in person, if the gardaí's reports warrant it."

"Good, good. Did you say we? Who are you working with on this?"

"Oh, no, I just meant the other garda, sir." Isabel saw no point in complicating her relationship with her old boss any more than it already was.

"Well, careful what you share, Sayers. If you need help from our team, give me the word. I can pull a few lads off the Declan case if you're not comfortable relying on local support. Now you get onto reviewing those files. I'll check in with you again in the morning."

Isabel took another deep breath, but the moment had gone. She felt nothing more from the scene. She followed the path around to the cathedral then turned left to cross the Salmon Weir Bridge, glancing back as she walked. The patch of grass where Moira had been killed was in almost total darkness. Even if anyone had been crossing this bridge at the time of the murder, it was highly unlikely they could have seen anything.

She glanced at her watch. She'd grab something to go from the Banner's Dig, then settle down in her office. It would be a late night.

CHAPTER FOURTEEN

THE PEDESTRIANIZED STREETS were already getting crowded with people out for the evening and it was only March. The smell of beer competed with the sweeter scents of kebab and seafood coming from the many small restaurants and pubs that dotted each street. The ever-present music from the street buskers blurred the sounds of voices from others walking the streets. Isabel hated to think what June, July, and August would bring. No question, tourism was looking up for Galway this year. She supposed that was good for the town, but for her it was nothing but headaches. More crowds meant more accidents, more trouble, more danger.

Stepping around a cluster of students, Isabel spied one of the people responsible for the upswing in tourism. Peig Browne stood staring into a shop window, bundled against the chill night air in a brown frilly sweater that wrapped around her like a blanket, a silky scarf trailing down from her neck. Isabel shivered in her standard business suit and admitted the pang of jealousy she felt. It would be nice to be able to dress like a woman, for a change.

"Peig. How you keepin'?"

Peig hadn't seen her approach and jumped at the sound of Isabel's voice. She saw the flash of surprise on Peig's face reflected in the window in front of her.

"Oh, Isabel, hiya. Just looking, you know."

Isabel glanced down at the jewelry displayed in the window in front of them. "Some pretty things. Something in particular there you're looking at?" Isabel grinned as she asked, knowing what it felt like to want something that wasn't really within reach.

"You could say that." Peig's answer surprised Isabel. "But it's not what you think. I made those."

"Those?" Isabel looked back at the collection on display more carefully. Thin, intricately woven strands of silver ran through and around glittering beads, shimmering stones. Each piece was unique, each carefully designed and created. She looked back at Peig. "Very impressive. I didn't know you made jewelry."

Peig smiled, clearly proud of her work but unwilling to look proud. "Thank you. I do enjoy it, you know."

"Is that one of your own creations, then?" Isabel indicated the necklace around Peig's neck, a heavy brown stone hanging low on her chest, held aloft by intertwining bands of silver and gold. "Can't be easy to make something like that."

"I suppose not. I started slowly, you know. Simple pieces. That didn't require a lot of tools. Beadwork, thin strands of silver." She looked toward one particularly simple but elegant necklace on display. It was one Isabel would have chosen for herself if she'd been shopping for a necklace.

"But your more recent pieces take more work?" she asked Peig.

"Oh, yes. I have a workshop at home, in a shed out back. I've been experimenting recently with different precious metals. Learning how to shape them, move them, control them." As she spoke, she twisted her scarf in her hands, as if demonstrating the technique she used to twist the metals in her creations. Peig may have had gold and silver on her mind, but to Isabel it was too much of a reminder of Moira's gruesome death.

She averted her eyes, turning back to the window display. "I'm impressed."

"I was so excited when Paul offered to carry these in his store. This is what I've been waiting for. Hoping for."

"I'm sure they'll sell well, Peig. They're beautiful. And I think they're attracting attention." She nudged Peig as another woman stopped to glance in the window.

"I hope so."

"So do you want to do this full-time? Make jewelry, I mean? I thought you enjoyed your job."

Peig's eyes darted around the display, as if drinking in everything she saw. "Sure, sure, I did. I mean, I do. I've enjoyed the past two years working with the tourism board. It's certainly better than my old job."

"You were in marketing, yeah?"

"Well, you could say that. I was a secretary in a marketing firm. Not exactly the same thing. When the tourism board offered me this job, it was my big break. My chance to make it in public relations on my own. I was so grateful to Conn for giving me the chance when I probably didn't deserve it."

Isabel shook her head as she looked over Peig's creation. "You're a true artist, you know that?"

Peig glowed with the praise. "I just have this need to be creative, you understand? To produce something interesting and beautiful and inspiring."

"That's quite different from your job, then."

"Oh, I don't know. There are creative aspects of my job. And Galway is beautiful. I don't mind selling Galway as a destination, getting the chance to tell people how much they can see here, what they can do here. It's just the people. Well, you know, the bureaucracy." She shuddered. "I hate having to deal with the reports, the paperwork, the details."

"I agree with you there." Isabel laughed. "You've been doing a good job, though. With promoting tourism, I mean. Things have really been busy and everyone says we're expecting a banner summer."

"Oh, that wasn't only me. That was the necklace. The

other necklace, I mean," Peig clarified when Isabel pointed to the necklaces on display, a question on her face.

"Right, of course. Sean Rourke's discovery."

"Everyone is so excited about it." Peig turned away from the window and Isabel walked up the road next to her. "I knew it would be big as soon as I heard about it last fall."

"I thought the results of that dig were still under analysis."

Peig shrugged, frowning. "They are. And I waited, at first, before promoting it. Just in case it turned out not to be such a big find. But then I said to myself" — she turned to Isabel, her hands open wide — "what are you waiting for? The man just found a historic necklace. It might matter to him if there's more or if it's part of a larger encampment. But that doesn't matter to me. Sell the necklace, Peig," I said to myself. "Sell the necklace."

"Sounds like you took that advice in more way than one." Isabel smiled.

"That's right. It was karma. I'm sure of it. And it worked, too. That necklace has been a boon. The press is lapping it up. The tourists are coming." She rubbed her hands together, though the wind had died down and Isabel felt warmer now. "This could make my career, Isabel. If I can boost our numbers enough, this could be great for me. Finally get me out of—"

Peig stopped, swallowed. "I mean, finally give me a chance to try working on my jewelry full time."

"But what about your jewelry business while you're pursuing this big break?"

"I can do both, don't you worry. Just like I said about the necklace: it represents possibilities. Dreams. We don't know much about it yet, it's still relatively unknown. But we can dream about it, can't we?"

"I suppose we can. And people are coming because of that? Because of something they don't know?" Isabel found that hard to believe.

Peig shrugged again. "Sean assures me it's the real thing. He believes there's more, a whole Roman encampment buried under there. Once he starts exposing that, then things will really pick up."

Isabel pictured Stonehenge and how much that had changed over her lifetime. Or the Blarney Castle. She shuddered at the thought of the tourists trampling over it.

"And it's good for Galway, right?"

"Yes, it is." Peig answered as if she'd answered that question before. "I know, I get it. Not everyone likes tourism. I'm pushing the Aran Islands, too, and there are some eco groups out there telling me I shouldn't do that. Let the islands be on their own, they say. They're too small. Too fragile, they can't handle the crowds. Well, maybe so, but the men and women who run the stores out there, the boats, the restaurants, they can handle the crowds. And they need the income. That's why it's important, Isabel."

Isabel nodded. She understood, she did. She was about to tell Peig that when her phone rang.

"Detective Superintendent Sayers... Yes. Yes, I understand. I'll be there as soon as I can."

"You okay?"

Isabel shook her head, unable to answer that question. "I just... I have a family emergency I need to take care of. Sorry to run off."

"No worries. I'll see you soon enough."

Isabel shoved her phone back in her bag and took off toward her car at a trot. She would not get sucked into this again. Not now, not in the middle of a case. Not this time.

CHAPTER FIFTEEN

THE ROADS WERE DARK, too dark to be safely driving the speed she was. But they were empty, thankfully. Surprisingly so, really.

The publican had told her she didn't need to come. He knew her father well enough; he could send him on his way. He'd find his way back to the house eventually. Surely.

It was Michal's absence that drove her. Where was he? He was supposed to be watching out for their father. He lived with him, worked fewer hours than Isabel. So why wasn't he answering his phone, stepping in to help Da out? Worse, she'd been told this was the second night Da'd found himself in this condition, and the second night Michal hadn't answered the phone.

Her anger pushed her foot harder onto the gas, her little car careening around the dark curves of the road. Only once did she run into traffic, a farmer late getting his equipment back in from the fields. Her anger got the better of her as she waited impatiently behind him, her attempts to take deep breaths failing to calm her. She passed him in a gap in oncoming traffic that she would not usually consider sufficient, said a small apology to the traffic fairies, and hit the gas.

She made the three and a half hour trip in under three hours, pulling up to the pub as a group of locals emerged, shaking hands and calling good nights.

"Isabel, that you?" One turned his smiling face toward her. "Fabulous to see you, child, you've been away too long."

"Mr. Montgomery." She pecked him on the cheek. "My da still in there?"

"He is, dear, he is indeed. Charlie's taking care of him, never you fear. Managed to trick him into drinking some water, if you can believe that."

The group of older men all laughed at this as they slowly made their way in various directions, heading back to the cottages and farmhouses scattered around the village center.

Isabel pushed the dark wood door open and scanned the interior of the small pub. Her father was propped on a stool at the far end of the bar, his head lolling against his arm on top of the bar. The barman, Charlie, saw her.

"He's okay, Isabel. I told you on the phone, no reason for you to drive all this way."

"Still no answer from Michal?" she asked as she put an arm around her father, trying to straighten him up

Charlie shook his head. "Lost in one of his books, most likely. Doesn't even hear the phone ring."

Isabel nodded grimly. "Hiya, Da. Coming home now?" She shouted her question into his good ear.

The old man grunted, turned his watery eyes toward his daughter. "Sibéal, that you?" His voice was strong, as strong as the whiskey fumes that escaped with his words.

"It's me, Da. Let's get you home."

She half-carried, half-dragged him out to her car. From there, it was only a two-minute drive up to the cottage her father shared with only her brother now.

She hated coming to this cottage. Too many memories. Happy memories. Of growing up here, playing with friends, playing with Michal. It had been such a good time, then. Her mother's ring felt cold against her finger, but she wouldn't let herself touch it.

She turned lights on as she helped her father into the

cottage, lighting a path for him to the worn kitchen table. A heavy cast iron pot sat on the cooker, no doubt holding leftovers from the day before. Or the day before that. Isabel lit the hob and placed the pot over the flame to heat up.

It was just bubbling when she heard the front door open.

"Sibéal? What are you doing here?"

Her brother Michal had stopped in the doorway, looking confusedly around the room.

"Check your phone, Michal. You're supposed to answer it when it rings, you know?" She walked over and gave him a quick kiss on the cheek, then returned to spooning out the food, adding one more plate for her brother.

He pulled out his phone and grabbed a seat next to their father, who once again had his head lying on the table.

"I'm sorry, Sibéal, I didn't hear it ring. But you didn't need to drive all the way out here." He looked up at her, his eyes serious. "You really didn't."

"I know. But I'm here now. Here, eat this."

She dropped a plate in front of him, then carried over hers and her father's. At the smell of the food, his head lifted up and he sniffed.

"What's for supper then?" His words were terribly slurred, but she was used to interpreting them by now.

"Leftovers. Eat up." She gestured to Michal, and he reached over to help feed the old man.

"Aren't you on a case, then?" Michal asked.

"I am, actually."

"Then why'd you come down here, Sibéal? Really?"

Isabel shook her head. If only she knew the answer to that.

"My case seems to involve a local archaeologist," she said instead, knowing it would interest Michal. When his face perked up, she continued, "Sean Rourke. Found a Roman necklace last summer, hopes to find the whole encampment this summer."

"Sure, sure, I read about it. I'd love to visit the site, see what he's doing there." Michal stopped to wipe his father's mouth and the spittle that dribbled down his chin.

"Do you believe it?" she asked her brother. "That he found an encampment?"

Michal shook his head. "Not likely, is it?"

"Hm, no." She considered telling him more about the investigation, seeking out his advice as an expert on Irish history. While the museum where he worked focused exclusively on the history of this little part of Ireland, she knew his education made him an expert on much more.

"Even if it is true, it's bad luck to be digging it up the way he is, selling Irish history to promote tourism." Michal scowled as he spoke, and Isabel clamped her mouth shut. She did not want to have this argument again.

She stood and grabbed her plate, dropping it into the sink with a clatter. "I gotta get back. Get back to work."

"You're not driving at this hour?"

She glanced at the clock. Almost midnight. She grimaced but grabbed her coat, wrapping it around her as she walked out. It would be closer to morning than night when she got back, but she had no choice.

"D'you get the letter, then?"

"What letter is that?"

Michal moved his head to indicate the well-worn basket on the counter. Isabel felt her lips tighten into a firm line at his laziness as she stepped toward the basket and started digging through it. It didn't take long. The letter practically jumped out at her.

She didn't touch it, pulling her hands away sharply as if burned. She felt for her ring and twisted it around her finger. The ring her mother had given her. The ring she'd once thought she'd pass on to her own daughter.

"What's this, then? When'd it come?"

Michal shrugged, but he'd stopped eating and was watching her. He knew what the letter was. "They called a few times, too, you know? Did Da tell you?"

Isabel shook her head. Pushed her thoughts and emotions down with her hands deep into her jacket pockets.

"Take the letter, read it," Michal urged her. "Where's the harm?"

"Don't talk to me about harm." Isabel answered him through gritted teeth, pulling the door open. "You know I don't want to think about it."

"You have to deal with it at some point, Sibéal. You know you want to." He grabbed the letter and pushed it into her purse before she could stop him. If she really wanted to stop him.

"Take care of Da, Michal." Her voice softened. "And listen for your phone, right?"

She could see Michal standing in the doorway, watching her as she pulled away.

CHAPTER SIXTEEN

THE OFFICE WAS QUIET. Too quiet. Something about the shelf-lined hallway muffled the morning sounds that should have carried throughout the otherwise modern building.

Adam pushed the desk drawer closed again and turned his attention to the low shelf that ran along the wall. Book after book on archaeology, Irish history, Irish mythology. Nothing unexpected. He paused to glance down at the open courtyard below, crowded with students, a line of bikes securely locked up along a thick planter.

The fairly new glass windows were perhaps a little too well made. Adam could see students passing across the paved square below, running to their early morning classes, but their voices didn't carry to where he stood watching them. Did Sean find this quiet comforting, he wondered. An appropriate atmosphere in which to carry on with his studies? Or was he as discomfited by it as Adam was?

"I thought I saw you coming down the hall. You're getting an early start."

Adam spun around at the sound. Jennifer stood in the doorway. Her footsteps coming down the hall hadn't carried into the office. He tried to act nonchalant instead of startled. As if he hadn't been taking advantage of Sean's absence to poke through his things.

"Jennifer, hi. Were you looking for me?"

"I saw you in here. I thought… I don't know what I thought."

Adam leaned back against the windows, the glass cold on his back, and crossed his arms over his chest, his feet crossed at the ankle. As casual as he could look, inviting her to relax with him.

"What did you think of Moira, Jennifer? I'd love to hear your take on her."

"My take on her? What does that mean?" Her voice held a note of caution, but she stepped farther into the room, one hand resting on the back of a chair.

"Did you like her?"

A smile flitted across her face and she looked down as she shook her head. "No, not really. I suppose I shouldn't say that…"

"You can say anything you want. No harm in talking."

Jennifer nodded, and Adam could see from her eyes that she was thinking. Planning out her next words.

"I guess I didn't like her because she said things about Sean. Things that couldn't possibly be true."

"Like what?"

She shrugged. "About his work. About the dig. She was hardly trustworthy." She blew the last word out through her lips as if laughing it out. But she didn't look amused.

"How do you mean?"

"Moira? She could do magic with statistics. And she knew it. She used to say, give me a number, I'll give you the answers you want."

"Meaning?"

"She could manipulate any statistics to come up with whatever result the people paying her wanted."

"And she hired out her services?"

Jennifer shrugged again, and her eyes dropped to a backpack that lay on the floor next to the desk. "A bit, I guess. Not so much. You might be interested… it's about our work…" Her voice trailed off and she leaned forward to grab the bag.

Adam took a few steps across the room toward her as she opened the bag and rifled through the papers shoved into it. She paused with a manila folder in her hand. "I don't know if I should be showing you these, not all of them are published. Yet."

"Ah." Adam leaned back against the desk, again striving to make her feel relaxed. Calm. Whatever it was that Jennifer wanted to share with him, it wasn't in that folder. At least not all of it.

She walked past him to the window where she toyed with one of the dead plants.

"Why does he keep those plants in here?" Adam asked.

"How would I know?"

He shrugged. "You seem to know Sean pretty well."

Jennifer smiled, as if pleased that her familiarity with Sean had been noted. "I guess I do. But I don't know why he hasn't got rid of these yet. Too busy, I suppose."

"I imagine there must be a lot to do. With the great discovery and all."

She put her head to one side, her dangling earring catching the gray light through the window. "Not so much right now, really. Still writing up our finds from last summer. Cataloging photographs." She waved the file she held with the last words and a loose piece of lined paper came free and floated to the floor. Adam saw handwriting on it, but couldn't read it. Jennifer bent to scoop it up and stuff it back into the folder.

"Is that what those are, photographs?"

She came over to Adam and perched on the desk next to him, the flowery scent of her perfume trailing after her. He wasn't entirely confident about the desk's ability to hold both their weights, but he wasn't about to shatter any confidence he might have built with her.

"These are copies. I was going to shred them, but the bleedin' shredder..." Her voice trailed off, but Adam got the point. She glanced at him. "I took a lot of these.

Some Sean took himself. Some Garret."

"Garret? I don't think I've met him yet."

"No? Garret Doyle. Another grad student here. He's working the dig, too. He hasn't been around much recently."

Adam watched as she flipped through the photos, giving him just a glimpse of each one. As she turned the pages, other notes and cards slipped free. She'd catch them with a finger or thumb, sometimes shoving them back into the folder, sometimes pulling them loose and dropping them into the pocket of her shirt. Another lined paper of handwritten notes, a small snapshot showing smiling faces, a folded notecard.

"Why did you want to show these to me, Jennifer?" He put his hand on one of the photos, preventing her from flipping past it. "What am I looking at here?"

"That's an overview shot. Of the whole site, not just the successful dig."

"You dug in a few places?"

"Of course," she laughed. "It's a long process, you know. First you have to assess the site — walking over the surface, looking for anything unusual, like hills or gullies that could indicate something below the surface."

"And you did this with Sean?"

She nodded vigorously. "Sure. There were others on the team, too."

"Like Garret?"

She nodded again. "And a couple of engineers who helped us survey the land. Then some laborers who helped with the initial dig. It's a big team."

"And what are these trenches running across the landscape? Did you make those?"

"Once we found the artifact, we knew there had to be more around, so we marked out trenches to cover as much space as possible, focusing on likely areas."

"And what were you looking for?"

"The encampment." Jennifer shook her head as she said it. "I never believed it, you know?"

"Never believed what?"

"Sean had faith." She shook her head as she spoke, her eyes caught on the image in front of her. A photograph of a long, rectangular hole in the ground, about six feet deep. Too long to be a grave, but Adam shivered anyway.

"Faith in what?"

"That it was there." She turned her head to look Adam in the eye. "Sean was so sure, so I went along with it. But I never expected to find anything. I guess I still doubt myself, my abilities. But you understand that, don't you?"

Every muscle in Adam's body tensed. "Why do you say that?"

"Oh, sorry." A small smile flitted across Jennifer's face as she waved her thought away with her hand, "Just something Garret said. Don't worry yourself." She squinted as she peered more closely at the photograph. "I still don't know how I missed that."

Adam forced himself to relax and look at the photo. All he could see was a dirt trench cut in the grass. "Missed what?"

"That. There." She pointed at the image. "That different coloration along the bottom."

Adam leaned in and saw what she was talking about. A line of reddish dirt cut across the path of the trench. It was subtle, but the dirt was definitely a different color than the rest of the trench wall.

"And what is it? Why is it important?"

She laughed again. "It's the proof, isn't it?"

"Proof of what?"

"That there's something else there. That discoloration shouldn't be there. It's not in the other trenches. There's no natural cause for it that we can see."

He looked again at the picture. "Is this one that Sean took?"

She shook her head. "That's the thing. I took this photo. So how did I miss that? It's so obvious now."

"Well." Adam stood. "He is the professor, after all. I guess he has a little more experience seeing things like that. It's really not that obvious."

She chewed on her lip. "It should've been to me." She shook her head, clearly still frustrated.

"Look, tell Sean I was looking for him, okay?"

Jennifer nodded absentmindedly without looking up. "Sure." As Adam left, she was still staring at the photograph, chewing on her lip.

CHAPTER SEVENTEEN

"DETECTIVE SUPERINTENDENT Sayers? Oh, Detective Superintendent!"

Nora's voice carried down the long hallway; it truly wasn't necessary for her to raise it to that pitch. The workspace was empty and quiet, only the muffled sounds heard in any office: the hum from the overhead lights, the white sound of a shredder in the distance, clicking from the printers as they put themselves to sleep. Isabel gritted her teeth and put on a smile. "Ms. Kane, I was looking for Professor Rourke."

"Were you? I wonder why." Nora's expression of curiosity made it clear she'd be all ears if Isabel wanted to confide, but Isabel had no intention.

"Do you know where I might find him? He's not in his office."

"No, he wouldn't be, dear." Nora smiled sweetly. "He left earlier this morning. With the other American, Adam Kaminski."

Isabel nodded, working double time to prevent her frustration from showing on her face. "Do you know where they went, then?"

"They went to look at the great archeological dig." She clucked her tongue, her lips tightly sealed.

Isabel shuddered at the odd sound but smiled brightly. "That seems like a good idea. I'd've been interested to see it myself."

"Oh? Something going on there, then?" Nora's face dropped some of the dissatisfaction it had gained when she talked about the dig. "I would need to know that, if there is."

"And why's that?"

"I manage almost all of the university's grants. Surely you know that."

"I'm sorry, I didn't realize." Isabel tried not to grin.

"Oh, yes. When faculty get a grant, the funds are given directly to the university. I open an account and the faculty member can then spend the funds from that account." Nora held up a chiding finger. "With appropriate justification showing that the expenditures were directly related to the purpose of the grant, of course."

"Of course," Isabel agreed. "So they went to see the dig… Who else worked on that with Professor Rourke? His students?"

"Oh, yes." Nora's chest seemed to expand as she told Isabel about Jennifer and Garret. "Garret is doing very well. Jennifer is a good student… now."

"But not before?"

"Well, you know…"

"If there's something you know about Jennifer, I'd appreciate it if you could tell me, Nora."

Nora seemed to appreciate the coziness of the question, the implication that her knowledge was useful. "Well, there was that scene, about a year ago. Jennifer was… well… she was hurt."

"Hurt? How?"

"And that's the thing, isn't it? She did it to herself."

"She tried to hurt herself?"

Nora shrugged and made her odd clicking sound. "Who knows what happens in the darkness of someone's mind. But she was found and taken to the hospital before any real damage was done. She left the school for a few months, went back home, I think, then came back, and we all pretended nothing had happened.

Oh!"

Nora's mouth snapped shut as Jennifer appeared out of a room up the hall. Isabel realized the sound she'd heard earlier had stopped.

"Well, at least that's the shredder fixed," Nora said, busily tapping a sheaf of papers straight against her desk, their conversation apparently over.

Jennifer left the building without giving either of them so much as a glance. Had she heard Nora's gossip about her?

Isabel considered this information about Jennifer. Someone involved in the dig trying to kill herself; that could be connected. If Moira's death was really connected to the dig at all. She only had Conn O'Flaherty's suggestion that it was, and she knew what his word was worth. She turned to go.

"Oh, Detective Superintendent?" Nora called after Isabel's back was turned.

"Yes?"

Nora held thin, curling white paper in her hand, two or three pages. "This came. For Adam Kaminski." Nora's expression made clear her opinion of someone not being immediately available to receive a fax.

"What is it?"

"Well I don't know, do I? I told him he could receive it here, but the least he could do is have the courtesy to be here when it arrives. What am I supposed to do with it?"

Isabel shrugged and tried on her more pleasant smile. "Couldn't you just keep it on your desk until he comes for it?"

The complete and total absence of clutter from the surface of Nora's desk made clear enough the absurdity of that suggestion. Isabel didn't need to see Nora's pained expression to know it wouldn't fly.

"Here, I'll be seeing him soon enough, I'm sure. I'll get it to him."

Nora's lips straightened into a thin line, an

improvement over the frown of a moment before, and she nodded with satisfaction as she handed Isabel the papers. "I was hoping you'd say that. I don't see why he didn't just have that sent to your headquarters, anyway."

CHAPTER EIGHTEEN

DRIVING QUICKLY PAST the lights and glitz of
Salthill, Adam and Sean made their way more slowly
through the towns of Barna, Spiddal, and Rossaveal. The
road heading north from Galway took them through a
series of quaint villages, each more picturesque than the
next. Some names Adam recognized, others in Gaelic
were beyond him.

Between each town, the landscape around them
opened up, but as they passed through the towns, the
road would narrow, lined on either side by stone
buildings gray with age. From the grates of the houses
and pubs they passed, Adam picked up the smell of turf
fire, so elemental he could taste it, taste the feelings of
earth and home it evoked.

The drive took less than an hour. They pulled off the
main road just past Rossaveal, past the sign for the ferry
that carried tourists by the hundreds out to the Aran
Islands every day. The rain of the morning had burnt
off, and it promised to be a sunny, if chilly, day, perfect
for a ferry ride followed by a hike or bike around the
striking islands.

From the main road, they drove along a short
peninsula toward the ocean, Inishmore, the largest of the
Aran Islands, visible through the clear morning sky.

As they drove north, the landscape hardened into
beautiful desolation. Low hills and gullies, still covered

in the purples and greens of winter splintered with the shocking yellow of early spring daffodils, ran out as far as the eye could see. The air was crisp and clear. Adam thought he could've seen for miles if the rise and slope of the hilly landscape hadn't interfered.

Sean pulled the car off onto a path that was no more than a dirt track, gears shifting, tires grinding and bumping over the uneven surface.

He finally parked tight up against a hedge. Adam had to push the door deep into the branches to get out of the car. He followed Sean's gaze over the uneven field that lay before them.

"So what am I looking at?"

"This is it." Sean waved his arm in front of him, capturing the entire field in one gesture. "The famous dig."

His voice carried a tinge of sarcasm, but Adam let it lie, not wanting to pry too much too early. He'd be pushing for the information he needed in good time.

"Show me around?"

Sean lifted a shoulder in acquiescence as he nodded. "It's why we're here, isn't it? Though I still don't understand why you wanted to come out here. What does this have to do with the murder?"

"Probably nothing," Adam answered as he followed Sean along a barely visible trail toward a large blue tarp spread out over part of the field.

Patches of ground around the tarp were scraped bare of grass in regular, oblong shapes. Other areas were covered in similarly thick tarps, held in place with metal stakes.

Sean lifted the edge of one of the smaller tarps, and Adam bent to peer underneath it. "It's a hole." He straightened his back.

"Yes, it is." Sean laughed. "That's what we do, you know. We dig."

"So is there anything special in this hole?"

Sean shook his head. "I don't think so. We excavate

along a trench, you see." His finger pointed up along the straight line of the hole. "To get a sense of what might be under a certain area."

"And how do you identify these areas?"

Sean dropped the tarp, then bent down to reaffix the metal stake, making sure the tarp was pulled taut over the opening. "Fairly straightforward surveying, really. Evaluating the surface of the ground to look for any telling swells or dips. Then using ground penetrating radar to look under the ground. Noninvasively, you understand."

"And that will tell you if there's anything metal under there?"

Sean shrugged. "It will tell us if there's anything we don't immediately recognize. So we dig, and more often than not, it's nothing. But we also identify our dig locations using other sources — history, stories, even myths."

"Legend has it a fearsome soldier was buried on this hill, that sort of thing?"

Sean grinned. "Exactly. I've always been a fan of Irish legends. Since finding the necklace, I've been focusing my research on the stories of Queen Maeve and Queen Boudica."

"Yeah, I've heard of them."

"Really? I'm surprised. Well, yeah, so legend has it Boudica wore a necklace somewhat similar to the one I found."

"But she was just a legend, right? Not a real person?"

Sean shrugged again and gave Adam a sly smile. "Perhaps both. A real woman surrounded by legend."

Adam pointed to the largest of the blue tarps. "What's under that one?"

"Same sort of thing. I don't want to pull that tarp up; it would be harder to pull it back into place."

Adam nodded as he let his eyes scan over the area. "It's a big area you covered. That's a lot of work. I mean, especially with no guarantee of a payoff."

"It's a gamble. Archaeology always is. You do your homework first. Only dig when you know there's a good chance that you're in the right place and there will be some evidence left to find. Bones, artifacts, traces of buildings."

"And that's what you found last, right? Traces of a building?"

"Maybe." Sean frowned, looked down at the ground, his shoulders hunched. "Jennifer and Garret were working with me on the dig, Jennifer with me the day I recognized the stratum. I can't really take credit for the find."

"Oh." Sean's description didn't match Jennifer's recollection of the day. Why were they each so eager to give the other credit for the find? "And how about the necklace, did they find that, too?"

"It was a team effort."

"You're a good teacher, Sean, letting your students take credit for their own work. I get the impression that's not always the way it's done."

Sean grinned and shrugged, but didn't let any hint of pride come into his expression.

Flashes of a classroom came back to Adam, the feeling of working with a group of teenagers, helping them find the answers to his questions, helping them think through puzzling stories. But something else was buried within Sean's words, a meaning Adam could sense but not fully understand.

"Come on, look at this." Sean led Adam closer to the edge of the field, and Adam realized they were at the top of a cliff abutting the ocean. The grass cut away sharply and the rough rock face sloped straight down toward the swirling water below, wet, salty air rising up to them with the crash of each wave.

"Awe-inspiring."

"Yes, and also ideal for an invading army." Sean's enthusiasm, which seemed to have waned while they were discussing the specifics of the dig, had returned.

"How so? Looks like it would be hard to land here. Plus you'd have your back to the water if anyone attacked."

Sean shook his head and pointed to the south. Adam finally saw what he was talking about. An inlet, not more than sixty feet wide, cut into the rock, creating a calm tidal pool.

"They could beach there, unload. It's completely invisible from the land, no one would see them coming. And it's protected from the weather. They'd have plenty of time to come ashore safely."

"Then why build a stable encampment right here?"

"It's a headland."

Adam turned his back to the ocean and saw what Sean meant. The piece of land on which they stood, which stretched out into the ocean like a thick finger, was raised, rising at a gradual slope as it stretched away from the land and toward the water. As if an ancient God had tried to build a bridge out over the water but stopped partway.

"You could see anyone coming from any direction."

Sean nodded vigorously. "And the Romans weren't afraid of the Celts. Not at that point. Their armies were far superior. Their weaponry, their technology." Sean scanned inland briefly again, then turned back to the water. "This would have been the perfect place to land and set up camp."

"Did local legend support that theory?"

"Indeed." Sean nodded absentmindedly.

"So you weren't surprised to find what you did? You were expecting it?"

Sean shrugged, looked down at the ground. "But no one else was. I'm sorry to say that, if true, this discovery changes what we know of Irish history."

"Why would you be sorry to say that? That's huge."

Sean seemed to be chewing over the words he might otherwise use to answer him, his jaw working but nothing coming out. Adam tried a different tack. "Why was Moira Walsh interested in this dig?"

"What makes you think she was?"

"She told Conn O'Flaherty she was. She told him there was something interesting about this dig and that he should pay attention to it."

"Ha!" Sean's laugh came out more like a bark. "She said that, did she? Well, bully on her. I should've known."

"Should've known what, Sean? What did Moira know about this dig?"

"Nothing." He shook his head and picked up a rock, shifting it between his hands, then tossing it at Adam.

Adam caught it and looked at Sean with a question in his eyes.

"Exposed bedrock. That's a hard sandstone. We know the Romans used that to build fortresses in England."

"Why won't you talk about Moira now? You seemed eager to confront me about it yesterday morning."

"It's not about me anymore. This dig affects so many people. Not just me."

Adam said, "You have a responsibility toward your students; I get that. I know how important that is." He toyed with the rock, then tossed it over the side of the cliff into the water.

"You shouldn't do that," Sean chided him.

"Do what?" Adam asked, confused.

"Don't move things around like that. You should've dropped that back where I found it. If everyone who came here tossed a rock into the ocean, the landscape would degrade even faster than it already is. We need to do everything we can to preserve it."

Adam looked back at the scarred field, brown, green and blue. "But you're digging into it."

"With respect, Detective, always with respect. Come on." Sean headed back toward the car. "I'll take you to a few other sites that show promise. We haven't tried digging at them yet, but our initial studies and surveys indicate they may have some hidden secrets."

"I'm surprised you're still looking. I thought you hit the jackpot here."

Sean shrugged. "You never know. We always need to have the next site staked out, the next grant application in. Just in case."

CHAPTER NINETEEN

"THIS IS STILL PRELIMINARY, you understand."

"Of course," Isabel agreed, eager for any insight into this crime, regardless of how preliminary.

"Confirms time of death, provides limited new information," Tadhg O'Regan said as he handed her the file. "You can read it for yourself."

Isabel nodded, already scanning the pages of the report. That was one thing she knew she could always count on. Tadhg, a doctor in the coroner's office, understood the importance of timing in a criminal investigation. While others might wait until they had double and triple checked all their facts, Tadhg was willing to share preliminary information. A habit that had in the past got him in trouble with the coroner.

"This supports the report on the circumstance of death we sent him." Isabel was talking to herself more than Tadhg, and he seemed to realize that. She looked up at him. "He knows you're sharing this?"

Tadhg nodded. "The coroner is releasing an Interim Certificate of the Fact of Death. No question this was not a natural death. Clearly violent. He's fine with sharing this preliminary report. The full postmortem will take time."

Isabel returned her attention to the report in front of her. It didn't really say much she didn't already know.

"You found epithelials on the scarf?" she asked

without looking up from the report.

"That's right." Tadhg settled into a chair in front of Isabel's desk. "Might be some DNA, if we're lucky, but it will take awhile for those results to come back."

"And hope it's not just the victim's."

Tadhg nodded. "If there is a second donor, then we need someone to match it to."

"Limited alcohol in her blood. No drugs, no excessive bruising…"

"Other than you'd expect from a strangulation." He finished the sentence that Isabel had left dangling.

"Funny, that."

"What's that?" Tadhg leaned forward in his seat.

"Her ear's not torn. I'd assumed her earring had been ripped out. Though I've lost enough earrings myself to know how easily they can fall out. Perhaps, if she was struggling…" Isabel pictured the scene in her mind, working around the limited information she now had.

"I can only confirm what's in the report. The rest is up to you."

Isabel sighed as she closed the file and looked at him with a sad smile. "Of course. So this time around, preliminary really does mean preliminary."

He shrugged apologetically. "I'm afraid so. This murder is remarkably straightforward. Nothing new to find about the victim or cause of death. It was exactly as it appeared."

"A healthy, sober young woman, taken by surprise and strangled with her own scarf." Isabel pursed her lips, biting back her disappointment. She wasn't sure what she'd been expecting, but she'd come to rely on the forensics in her investigations. The tiniest clues, invisible to the naked eye, that could lead to a killer.

"This is just from the autopsy, mind you," Tadhg added. "There's still the analysis from the scene. MacNulty is handling that one." He made a wry face.

Isabel understood. "So no preliminary report on that. I'll need to wait until he's done."

Tadhg nodded.

"That's fine. He likes to be certain, I can understand that. But..." She looked at the ceiling, then over Tadhg's shoulder to the window and the mill wheel beyond.

"You don't have that luxury. I know."

She offered him a weak smile. "Just give me something I can use. Anything."

"Well" — he sucked on his teeth for a moment, thinking — "your killer was relatively strong."

"Makes sense." Isabel pictured the scene. Moira off to the side of the path. Her scarf still wrapped around her neck. "Strangulation. It's not easy, usually means a male killer."

Tadhg leaned forward in his chair, ready to return to his lab. "Statistically, that's true. Though I wouldn't rule out a woman attacker just yet."

"Hm." Isabel thought about that. "To be fair, Moira wasn't particularly big."

Tadhg stood. "Sorry I couldn't bring you more. But I wanted you to know what we had now, rather than wait."

"I appreciate that, I do." Isabel stood as well. "Sometimes knowing when you don't find anything is as important as knowing when you do. Let me know if you hear anything from the scene analysis, right?"

"Of course. Who knows, maybe your smoking gun will be somewhere in that collection of debris they're still sorting through down in their lab."

Isabel laughed. "A smoking gun would be nice, but for now I'll settle for some good old-fashioned physical evidence." She cut herself off when her phone rang.

She listened to the quick message, thanked the caller, and looked back at Tadhg. "Well, now, turns out I might just have that physical evidence."

ISABEL STOPPED AT the hospital entrance to confer with the garda at the front desk. He'd called her in once he realized who the two new arrivals were. And Isabel's interest in them.

"Doc's almost finished with him, I understand," he explained as they walked. "Wasn't a serious injury."

She followed him to an exam room through two double doors and down the long hall, leaving him standing in the hallway as she went in to talk to Jennifer and Garret.

Garret sat on the small bed in the center of the room, curling forward as he held his injured hands in front of him. He looked more like a teenager than a graduate student to Isabel, though she admitted that could be the effect of his round, clean-shaven face or trim red hair. He glanced up at her, and the forlorn look in his baby blue eyes reinforced the youthful impression.

The doctor wrapping Garret's hands perched on a tall stool in front of Garret, Jennifer hovering not far behind him. The doctor looked up at Isabel's entrance.

"Detective Superintendent Sayers," she introduced herself. "I'll need to talk to your patient, if you don't mind."

"I'm finishing up here as it is." The doctor stood, giving Isabel a cautious look. "Do you need anything from me, Detective Superintendent?"

"I might at that." Isabel nodded as she answered. "But for now, I'll just be talking to these two."

"Right then." He faced Garret. "Keep the bandages clean and dry. Change the wrapping if it gets wet. And keep your hands raised as much as possible for the first 24 to 48 hours to decrease swelling. I'll see you here again in three days time, yeah?"

"Sure," Garret mumbled.

The doctor cast a worried glance over the three of them, then left the room.

Isabel stood with her hands in her coat pockets, taking stock of the situation. Both of Garret's hands were wrapped in white gauze, a condition that would make it hard for him to do... well, anything, for a few days at least, it sounded like. Jennifer didn't look injured, or even particularly worried about Garret.

"D'you hurt yourself at your lab, then?" Isabel asked him.

Garret shook his head but didn't answer. Jennifer's mouth stayed in a firm line.

"You were at home?" Isabel tried again.

Garret shrugged.

"And what's your role in this?" Isabel looked at Jennifer.

Jennifer shrugged. "Garret came home, his hands were burned, I brought him right here. What else was I to do?"

"I didn't realize you two lived together."

"Live together?" Jennifer laughed. "Don't get the wrong impression. We share a house. With one other archaeology student. We're in the West End, just beyond the university."

Isabel nodded, understanding the costs of living that encouraged students to house together. "So how d'you hurt yourself, Garret?"

"Just an accident." He was still mumbling.

Isabel crossed the room to perch on the stool the doctor had vacated. "What kind of accident?" She ducked her head so she could look up at Garret, try to meet his eyes.

He looked at her, then looked away, first at Jennifer, then around the room. "It was stupid. I was trying something new. It didn't work. I burned myself."

"That's a pretty bad burn, looks like. What were you doing?"

Garret shrugged. "Just messin' about."

Isabel waited, expecting more, but Garret wasn't in the mood for sharing. "You need to tell me what you were doing, Garret."

"Why?" He finally looked directly at her. "I'm working on a project with some friends. It's work related. Nothing to do with you."

"Can you confirm this?" Isabel directed her question to Jennifer.

"Me?" She shook her head. "This's nothing to do with me. I just saw that he was hurt and brought him here." She held both hands up in front of her in a gesture of denial.

"And you can confirm Garret was burned?"

"Confirm? What the…" Garret's confusion was turning to anger.

"I can't confirm anything," Jennifer answered firmly. "His hands were clearly hurt. He said it was a burn. I didn't examine him, if that's what you mean."

"All right." Isabel stood. "I can talk with the doctors about that, it's not a problem." A blatant lie, since she had no expectation the hospital would be eager to share their patient records.

"I can go, then?" Garret stood with difficulty, first placing his hands on the bed, then jerking them back in pain.

"The more you tell me about what happened, what you're working on, the more helpful it will be for my investigation. You do want me to catch the person who murdered Moira, don't you?"

Garret shrugged. "What does my accident have to do with Moira?"

Isabel let a patient smile cross her face. "When something unusual happens to people who are involved in a murder investigation, it does tend to catch the investigating detective's attention." She gestured to his hands. "And I'd say this is something unusual."

"Not that unusual. People hurt themselves all the time." He gingerly tucked his arm under the denim jacket lying on the bed next to him. "You coming?" he asked Jennifer.

She nodded, glanced at Isabel, and followed Garret out of the room.

Isabel stopped next to the garda who still waited in the hallway. "Did you hear anything else when they came in? Was it really a burn?"

He shook his head. "I'm sorry, ma'am, I didn't hear. You think he might have hurt his hands strangling her?"

Isabel shrugged and frowned. "Would be nice, wouldn't it? But not likely. That was two days ago now, he would've come for help before now."

"Could be." The guard shrugged. "You never know. If someone's willing to commit murder, he's not exactly right in the head, now, is he?"

CHAPTER TWENTY

ADAM'S PHONE RANG. He glanced over at Sean in the driver's seat, then down at the phone. Pete. He grimaced at the charges the call was going to rack up, but he answered it. It was Pete, after all.

"Partner, did you get the fax?"

"Shit, no." Adam let the words escape before he could stop them. He had to be more careful to keep his end of the conversation simple, not too interesting for Sean's eager ears. Sean kept his eyes on the road, but Adam knew the signs well enough to know when someone was listening. He did it often himself. In Sean's defense, he didn't have much choice.

"I sent it a few hours ago, buddy. Thought you'd have it by now. I'm sorry it took me so long to send."

Adam glanced at his watch. It would've hit Nora's desk after he and Sean had left for the day. He wondered what Nora would do with it. "It would've been picked up by a woman at the university, Nora Kane. Hopefully, she'll hold onto it until I get back."

Sean picked up that part of the conversation and snorted. "If whatever you're planning depends on being able to trust Nora Kane, you're out of luck, friend."

Adam ignored Sean's comment but bit back his words even more. "Things good on your end? How's Jules?"

Pete laughed out loud. "Same as always, buddy. She's got another exhibit coming up and it's all she can focus on right now."

"What, she's not missing her big brother?" Adam smiled.

"If she's missing anything, it's her sanity."

"Then it's good she's got you around." Adam meant it. He hadn't been happy when his partner had started dating his sister, but it didn't take long for him to realize he didn't really mind it at all. He felt better knowing Pete was there to watch out for her.

"The last thing that woman needs is someone to take care of her, buddy. She's got that well under control," Pete said, cutting into his thoughts. "You need to stop thinking of her as your little sister."

Adam glanced at Sean and bit back the retort he would otherwise have made. "Maybe so. Not so easy to do, though, is it?"

"Anyway, just wanted to let you know I sent the report. Keep an eye out for it."

"I will, and thank you, buddy."

When Adam tucked his phone back in his pocket, Sean was staring straight ahead at the road.

"So tell me, how did you get into archaeology?" Adam asked, hoping to turn the conversation toward something useful to his investigation.

"I've wanted to be an archeologist for as long as I can remember. From the first time I watched *Raiders of the Lost Ark*." Sean grinned.

That would explain the safari jackets and long hair, Adam thought.

Sean was still talking. "From the time I saw pictures of a dig in Africa, that discovery of the new humanoid species around the turn of the century. My parents supported me, buying books on the topic, sending me to archeological summer camp."

"There's a summer camp for student archeologists?" Adam's voice betrayed his skepticism.

"There's a summer camp for everything under the sun, Detective. You should know that." He shook his head, tossing his hair in what, to Adam, was a decidedly feminine gesture. Perhaps the strength of his jaw and his broad forehead alleviated any concerns on his part that he might look weak.

Sean prattled on, about the university he'd attended, his years studying anthropology, archaeology, history, languages. Adam coughed, in the hopes of staunching the flow of irrelevant information in order to bring him back to the present-day dig. Sean glanced at him, completely misunderstanding Adam's intentions.

"I wasn't the slowest in the program, you know? I didn't spend the most time there, compared to other students. Hell, one of the students who started with me is still there, still All But Dissertation. But I took my time, it's true."

Adam didn't reply, intrigued by the level of Sean's emotions on the subject.

"It started to show." Sean let out a low sound, almost a growl. "To affect the way I was received during conferences, by other institutions. I used to be the golden boy." He shook his head. "Six years into the graduate program with no discernible movement toward a dissertation, rumors started flying. That I wasn't as bright as I'd claimed. That I'd already burnt out before I'd even started."

"I'm sorry to hear that," Adam responded quietly.

"So I finished. Quick." Sean's voice shifted. "I was rushed, damn it, it wasn't my fault. Sometimes people just take time. My dissertation could have been better. Much better."

"Was it not well received?"

Sean shrugged carelessly. "Well enough, I suppose." He looked up, his eyes lighting for a moment. "I loved Irish history. My family was all from Ireland — I can feel it in my blood. The same way I feel archaeology."

"And now you have your own dig, your own research, right here."

Sean took a breath, his eyes on the road but his

mind's eye obviously back at the dig site. "We dug the first trench in May. I couldn't possibly put into words the excitement I felt at that moment. The first cut of the earth in my first dig. *My* dig, not somebody else's."

"Your dig." Adam nodded, wondering if Sean had more to add and not wanting to stop him. But he seemed to have worn out his enthusiasm for the topic and now sat silent behind the wheel.

Adam considered what he'd learned about Sean from his soliloquy. This was his dig, he'd made clear. To manage, to control. To claim credit for. Perhaps to rekindle some past glory.

But Adam was left with the question, if this was his dig, why wasn't he claiming more of the credit?

CHAPTER TWENTY-ONE

THE SUN HAD long since set when Adam and Sean pulled into the university car park behind the science building. Most of the windows were dark, but the tall windows on the ground floor, which housed the main reception room, shone brightly. Figures moved back and forth in front of the windows in silhouette and Adam thought he could make out Sylvia's familiar form.

"Thanks for the archaeology lesson, buddy." Adam's words were quick as he jumped out of the car.

"No problem, but then… did I have a choice?"

Adam was already walking away, his mind on finding a phone to make a quick call to Isabel, let her know what he learned that day, then finding Sylvia and giving her all of his attention for the rest of the night.

He found Nora Kane's desk after only a few false turns, its surface barren, swept clean. No fax anywhere visible. The lights that spotlighted the desk during the day were turned off, and it was lit only by a few dim night lights along the base of the wall. Adam's own movement along the hall created mini shadows that scuttled along the floor ahead of him like mice retreating from the sound of his footsteps.

The running shadow mice disappeared at one open doorway as a stream of light broke into the gloom of the hallway. At first, Adam thought someone had left a light on. Then he heard the voices. Then he heard the laughter. He'd recognize that laugh anywhere.

"Sylvia?" he asked as he turned into the room.

Sylvia and the other occupant of the room were in motion as soon as he turned through the doorway. Were they moving away from each other? Or had they simply been pacing around the table? He focused on the lessons of his mindfulness training, watching his breathing, calming his anger.

"Adam." Sylvia's smile was broad as she moved toward him, her arms outstretched. She saw the expression on his face and her step faltered. "Adam, you remember my colleague from Legg, David?"

"David, right, sure."

The other man stepped forward, his right hand extended. "Adam, good to see you again."

Adam pushed down the mistrust and fear he was feeling, took another mindful breath, and shook David's hand.

"Darling, we were finishing up a last few things." Sylvia smiled. "Can you give me another few minutes?"

Adam thought of the call he'd been going to make to Isabel. He could go make that call, leave Sylvia here with David to finish whatever they been doing.

Somehow, that didn't sit right with him.

"That's fine," he said. "I've had a long day. Do you mind if I grab a chair here and wait?" He moved as he spoke, dropping into an elegant armchair along the wall.

"Oh... I see." Sylvia looked back at David, but he gave no indication of his thoughts. "Well, of course, that's fine."

She walked back over to the table, gesturing for David to follow her. "So the seating for Mr. Kilkenny?" She looked up at David.

"Ah, yes." David cleared his throat. "We just need to be certain he doesn't engage with Sharon Rameros, right?"

Sylvia laughed, a nervous sound. "Exactly. And who was it who had the shrimp allergy?"

Adam watched them as they continued their discussion about seating, meals, and caterers. It all sounded legitimate and boring. It sounded like work. Though Adam couldn't help but notice there were no papers on the table. You'd think they'd want to write some of this stuff down.

He settled lower into his chair. He should've trusted her. God, what an ass he was for his suspicions. They were to be husband and wife, and he didn't trust her. What kind of basis was that for a marriage?

It was going to be a long night.

ISABEL GLANCED AT her watch. Kaminski should've called her by now. When she moved, she felt the stiffness of the papers of the fax folded into her jacket pocket. She was going to have to talk to him about that. At some point.

"Isabel." The city councilman nodded and raised his wine glass in greeting as he passed, though Isabel couldn't miss the questioning look he gave her.

She had to join the party. She took a breath, raised her chin, and smiled at the room in general. The buffet dinner had been set up along the far wall. A few hungry looking folk still gathered at that end of the room, but most of the participants were now circulating, chatting, networking, as was the whole point of the exercise. To Isabel, it was all as pointless as the rest of her day had been.

She'd spent the rest of the afternoon doing her job, the dreary drudgery that was police work. Reviewing the reports that came in, one by one, from the gardaí working the case. Comparing those results with what she knew of the victim and the suspects. Wishing MacNulty would hurry up with his analysis of the evidence found at the crime scene. Revisiting the scene of the crime and establishing parameters to assign gardaí new jobs of canvassing the neighborhood. Reviewing those reports when they came in, hoping for a clue. Hoping for a lead.

Her only glimmer of possibility at this point lay in the other guests at tonight's event. It was a gathering of the town's literati and glitterati — civic leaders, members of the city council, faculty and staff from the university, large and small business owners from the town and surrounding communities. The purpose of the event was something to do with a current proposal to renovate the harbor, Isabel couldn't remember exactly what. But for her it presented an opportunity, an opportunity to talk to people who knew and worked with Moira Walsh.

Nora Kane hovered near the deputy president and president, smiling nervously at seemingly inappropriate moments. Not far from that cluster, Conn O'Flaherty held court with a group of apparent admirers. To Isabel's surprise, Peig Browne was not one of those admirers, but rather involved in a conversation of her own with a group of faculty from the university. As Isabel watched, Sean Rourke made an awkward, late entrance and shuffled over to Peig's group.

Isabel moved that way herself, taking the opportunity to grab a glass of white wine from the bartender.

"Yes, but we all know the Irish tribes did not have queens." One voice was raised above the rest. Apparently Isabel had walked into quite a heated discussion.

"I realize that." Sean kept his voice at a normal level, but the tension in the words was evident. "But the story has to generate from somewhere, doesn't it?"

"Tara. It must be a confusion of Connacht and Leinster. You know Medb was, in fact, the tutelary goddess of Tara in Leinster. The early writers simply erred in their attribution." The speaker's words were nasal, his eyes settled on an area above Sean's head, as if he couldn't be bothered to look at the man who was arguing with him.

"I believe it's simply a myth, you know," another man in a tweed jacket chimed in, a smile on his face. Trying to lighten the mood perhaps. "We can interpret the myth as a conflict between the father dominance of the Celtic-Aryans and the mother dominance of the pre-Celtic inhabitants."

"Hmph," the nasal man intoned. "You and your psychology."

"Isabel." Peig stepped apart from the group of debating men to put a hand on Isabel's arm. She seemed genuinely pleased to see her. "And how is the investigation going?" She almost whispered the question, as if talking about someone who had passed away. But of course, she was.

"It's early days yet, isn't it?" Isabel smiled at the group. "We're still hard at work, confident in solving it and bringing a killer to justice."

A few in the group looked at the ground or around the room, shuffling their feet. Not everyone was comfortable discussing murder, Isabel knew. "I don't think I've had the pleasure of meeting you all." Isabel smiled again. "I suppose I don't spend as much time up at the university as I should."

"Not much call for you to, though, is there?" The man who spoke kept his chin lifted as he addressed her, his words traveling through his nose, then dripping disdainfully down his chin. "I am Professor Liam Dempsey, and these are my colleagues in the maths and sciences." He indicated his colleagues simply by gesturing with his wine glass, as if they were not worthy of individual introduction.

Isabel nevertheless took the time to greet them each and learn their names. Other than Professor Dempsey, they were friendly and welcoming. She turned to face Sean, thinking to start her questioning with him, but just as she opened her mouth, his phone rang.

"Ah, excuse me." He held up a finger as he answered and turned away from the group.

"So you all worked with Moira, then?" Isabel watched as Sean's posture straightened and he made a beeline for the exit.

"Aye, we did." A tall thin man with sad eyes started to answer, but Dempsey cut him off.

"This is hardly the place for you to conduct an interrogation, Detective Superintendent."

"No? I am sorry if I offended."

He sniffed, and when he spoke, his words were as nasal as before. "Hardly. I simply think—"

"Isabel, darlin'. So glad you could make it out tonight." Conn's arm landed so heavily on her shoulders she almost spilled her wine.

Dempsey did not look happy to have lost the spotlight. Isabel felt a perverse pleasure in turning her back to him to face Conn.

"I hope this evening is proving to be a success for you?" She did her best to smile through her exhaustion and frustration.

"Oh, it's grand. It's a good group of lads here, I expect we'll all reach agreement tomorrow at the council meeting."

"This is about the harbor freight?"

"Yeah, that too."

"And I heard someone mention the youth camp you've been championing."

Income from the national lottery went to support a number of good causes around the country, but Isabel knew Conn's pet project — and one he somehow managed to direct an awful lot of funds toward — was a youth enrichment camp just outside the city. All nonprofits were struggling to make up for shrinking income from the lottery and other government support, and this camp was no exception.

"I've heard good things about that camp, it's a good thing you're doing there. I'm sorry to hear they're facing another difficult season, funding-wise."

He nodded, his eyes roving over the room, stopping whenever he spied a woman in a low-cut dress. "Sure, yeah."

"Maybe I should go out there myself this summer. See if the Garda can be involved somehow."

His eyes turned to her. "Now why would you do something like that?"

"We're always looking for a way to keep our officers engaged with the community. It's a natural fit." Her old boss in Dublin wouldn't agree, that was for sure, but it was something her local boss might jump on.

"You just keep your focus where it needs to be, Sibéal." She blinked at his use of her Irish name. She didn't know he even knew of her background. Perhaps Galway was a smaller town than she realized.

"What do you mean?"

"You've got a murder to solve, don't you? Work on that. Leave my work alone. I'm doing just fine without Garda involvement."

"I thought we could help, Conn, nothing more."

"Help yourself, why don't you? All this talk about improving the harbor, but that eco group — whatever they call themselves — have made another threat. D'you know that?"

"I'm sorry, I hadn't heard."

"Then you need to pay more attention, Detective Superintendent. They claim they're going to stop us before we can damage the harbor ecosystem, or some such nonsense. Or better yet" — the smile he gave Isabel with these words sent shivers down her arms — "solve Moira's murder. You haven't been doing much there, have you? I might just have a quiet word with Chief Superintendent McManus. He's a good friend. Very good."

Isabel found that hard to believe. Or did she?

"If I drop a word to him that you're busy playing around with my business instead of focusing on your case, what would he think about that?"

Isabel took a step forward. "Are you threatening me, Conn O'Flaherty?"

Conn laughed, his arms spread wide. "Of course not,

darlin'. Who would have the balls to threaten a Garda? No, I'm trying to help you out, that's all. Have you had that talk with Professor Rourke, as I suggested?"

Isabel nodded. "What do you have against Sean Rourke?"

Conn shrugged. "Nothing, yeah? I saw him that night, though. Did I tell you that?"

"You saw him? Where?" Isabel could have slapped herself for not hiding her interest, but it was too late. She saw the glint in his eyes.

"He was hanging around the cathedral. Alone. Why d'you suppose he might have been there?"

With that, Conn tipped his beer to her and moved across the room. She watched him go, patting people's shoulders, backs, and sometimes bottoms as he went. His presence caused laughter, red faces, and flinches, in equal measure.

ADAM GLANCED at his watch. "Almost done over there?" He saw the annoyance in Sylvia's glance at his interruption, but tried to ignore it.

"Just a little bit longer, darling. If you are hungry, you could run out now and I will catch up with you."

"That's fine, I'll wait." Adam shifted in his chair. It had looked comfortable an hour ago, but man, his butt was hurting now.

"You know this is important, darling, or I wouldn't ask you to wait." She walked over and planted a quick peck on his cheek. "You know my work is important to me," she whispered into his ear. "I love you."

"I love you, too." Adam resisted the urge to point out that she wasn't asking him to wait.

The sound of footfalls promised a welcome interruption. Sean burst into the room from the gloomy hall, talking even as he entered.

"Good news. Well, good news for me that is maybe not for — what are you doing here?" Sean's smile faltered when he saw Adam, Sylvia, and David.

"Looking for anyone in particular?" Adam asked. "What's your good news?"

"I just thought Nora — well, never mind. Yes, it is good news." His grin returned as he looked at the gathered trio.

"Adam, perhaps you and Sean…" Sylvia gestured toward the open doorway expectantly.

"Right, sure. I'm all ears, Sean, if you've got something to share." Adam had taken three steps toward the doorway, where Sean still waited, before he realized Sylvia was no longer at his shoulder. He glanced back to see Sylvia and David bent close over the table.

"It's a job offer." The excitement had returned to Sean's voice.

"Here at the university? But you already have a job here."

"Not here." Sean's tone dismissed the idea. "It's back at home. In the States."

"But why would you want to leave Galway? I thought you had this great discovery here."

Sean waved Adam's concern away with his hand. "Someone else can carry on that dig. Jennifer probably. Or Garret, it doesn't matter. This is a fabulous offer, one I've been hoping for."

"Huh." Adam considered this turn of events. "Just surprises me. Congratulations. If you're looking for Nora Kane, I think she's at that shindig downtown."

"I didn't see her there."

Adam shrugged. "I think that's where everyone is. The building seems pretty deserted."

"I suppose you must be right. No matter. I'm not going back over there, that call was my get out of jail card." He laughed at his own joke. "She can hear my good news tomorrow."

"And will she be as happy about it as you are?"

Sean's grin turned downright evil. "Probably not, Detective, probably not."

Sean practically floated out of the room, a dramatic change from his urgency when he entered. Adam shook his head. No question that man was hiding something. He just needed to find out what. He turned back to look into the room. Sylvia's head was bent low over the table, close, too close, to David's.

CHAPTER TWENTY-TWO

SEAN LEANED BACK in the hard wooden chair. It creaked with his weight, but he didn't care. Raising his arms to link his fingers behind his head, he let out a contented sigh. Finally, a way out. The end was in sight.

He closed his eyes and listened to the muted groans and creaks of the building at night. As far as he knew, he was the only one left. Most of the faculty and staff were at that awful reception. The people planning the absurd fundraising event had finally left. Leaving him alone with his dreams.

He slid even lower until his head rested against the hard wood back of the chair. He closed his eyes. Everything he wanted, everything he dreamed about. It was so close he could almost taste it.

He took a deep breath. Then another.

She came to him through the darkness of the hallway as his mind drifted into the cool mist of sleep. Flowing wild black hair, emerald green eyes that sparkled with emotion. Was it rage? Love?

Queen Maeve, surely it was she, infamous for her beauty and her sexual prowess. Love goddess, war goddess, all in one beautiful woman. In his dream, he was one of her many lovers, warriors who fought bravely on the battlefield in exchange for her sexual favors.

She approached him, leaning low over him, so close

he could smell the scent of Irish rain that suffused her hair, the peaty musk that clung to her skin. She raised a hand to run her fingers gently along his face and he groaned. But another man approached from the hall. Sean heard his heavy footfalls. He tried to stand, to run, but Queen Maeve held him tight. He couldn't move.

King Ailill, royal consort to the queen, barged into the room, growling as he came, sword aloft, eyes ready for battle. He grabbed the queen's arm, tearing her off of Sean and throwing her across the room. But Queen Maeve was nobody's slave, she gave as good as she got. Sean watched, terrified, as she returned his strikes, blow for blow. Two giants of Irish mythology battling it out in front of him.

But something wasn't right. This couldn't be the queen he'd uncovered. For all of her beauty, for all her prowess, she was not the woman of his dreams. She was not his queen. In front of his eyes, Ailill faded away, disappearing into a deep fog that vented into the hallway.

Maeve stood straight and turned toward him, but her appearance had changed. Hair that had been raven black now glowed red and gold like a burning flame. Her eyes showed sadness and rage instead of love. Eyes that had seen far too much. And around her neck: the necklace. That awesome necklace.

Surely this was his queen, the woman whose truth he was about to uncover, the woman whose story would make him famous. He raised a hand to shield his eyes from the glow of the stones in her necklace. As she approached him where he sat, he felt his fear grow. This was a woman who had killed so many. This was a woman who would not die.

He kept his eyes trained on the necklace. That was his salvation. That was his great discovery.

But still, it made no sense. The woman standing before him was Boudica, warrior queen of the Britons. She wore a bejeweled torque, twisted strands of gold used to ornament the Celtic warrior chieftain, symbolizing a warrior's readiness to sacrifice his life for the good of his tribe, hers encrusted with precious stones. Only Boudica the warrior queen was bold enough to wear a necklace worn by warriors. She had fought the Romans, Sean knew. On occasion, she had won. But she was queen of the Britons, Celt though she was. Her encampment would not be here on the west coast of Ireland.

As his unconscious mind worked through the problem, the necklace she wore faded into a simple gold torque, then she too faded into mist.

And as the mist cleared, one more woman stood before him. He raised his face to look into the surprised, scared eyes of Moira Walsh.

Sean gasped and jerked in his sleep, knocking himself out of the chair. He looked around the dark office, startled. It had been a dream, just a dream, nothing more, he reassured himself.

He pushed himself up off the ground, leaning heavily on the desk. The muted creaks and groans of the building no longer sounded comforting. He saw warrior ghosts jumping out of every shadow as he hurried down the long hallway, pulling the exterior door closed tight behind him without looking back over his shoulder, afraid of what might be following him.

CHAPTER TWENTY-THREE

"PROFESSOR DEMPSEY." Adam jogged to catch up to the other man ahead of him on the sidewalk, still relatively empty at this time of the morning, even out here near the Spanish Arch and tourist office.

"Ah, there you are." Dempsey's greeting was a nasal as Adam expected.

"Thanks for meeting me, I appreciate you taking the time."

"Hm, yes." Dempsey acknowledged his agreement as if it were an extraordinary contribution to the investigation. "I have to admit, I find this whole thing quite fascinating. It's good you were able to meet me so early, before I get swamped by work."

"Not at all, I always get an early start. Tell me, Professor, how well did you know Moira?"

"How well did I...?" He shrugged. "How well does anyone know anyone else? I suppose only a mother could truly know a person. But I'll tell you this." He held up a well-manicured finger to make his point. "Moira was a liar."

"Because she fudged numbers." Adam nodded.

"Well… yes… I suppose in a way she did."

"Then what?"

Dempsey picked at a loose thread on his tweed jacket, carefully wrapping the offending string around his finger before pulling it taut and snapping it. "The things she said about me — that I..." He cut himself off with a shudder, his eyes closed.

Adam waited for him to work through whatever he was about to say, though he wondered briefly if he should invite Dempsey to continue this conversation inside the coffee shop instead of on the street in front of it. Adam didn't mind getting an early start, but the aroma of coffee taunted him.

"We worked together on a project. Fascinating thing, really," Dempsey finally continued. "Using mathematical and statistical models to resolve questions surrounding early Irish literacy rates." Dempsey's eyes looked past Adam to the water beyond, his mind clearly still in early Irish history, not on a modern street in Galway.

"And what did she accuse you of?"

Adam's question brought Dempsey back to the present with a start. "Of getting it wrong. Of making an error in my numbers."

"Did you?"

"What kind of question—" Dempsey sniffed and looked down at his feet. "Well, as it turns out, yes. There was one small error. As soon as she mentioned it, I corrected it."

"So she was right? Just pointing out something that was true."

"But you don't go around saying things like that, Detective. A quiet word to me on the side would have sufficed, wouldn't it?"

Adam wondered if Moira's decision to share her findings publicly had more to do with Dempsey's personality than Moira's, but saw no benefit to sharing that thought with Dempsey.

"We've all done things we're not proud of," Dempsey continued. "We simply don't go around telling people."

A black Peugeot pulled up along the curb where they stood.

"Kaminski? Got plans for today?" Isabel leaned across the narrow car to call to Adam through the passenger side window. "Adam?"

"That's my cue." Dempsey stalked off without a word to Isabel.

Adam cast a longing glance at the coffee shop, then walked toward her car.

"Detective Superintendent. Is there something I can do for you?"

"Just wondering if you wanted to come meet Moira's parents with me." As she spoke, he leaned down to rest his forearms on the open window and Isabel leaned back, lowering her voice. "I know I said I didn't want you to be part of the investigation, and that hasn't changed."

"Then why invite me?"

"It's her parents. I suspect they may be more in your line than mine."

He pulled the car door open before she could change her mind, asking as he slid into the passenger seat, "How so?"

She checked her mirrors as she pulled back into traffic. "They lived in America for a number of years. Moira was born there, in fact."

"Moira was American? I had no idea."

"Not really. They moved back home when she was still a baby. But they'd spent a good twenty years there, at that point."

"So you think they may be more American than Irish? That's a stretch."

Isabel shrugged. "I looked into their situation a bit after Conn's remark about her family situation. I suspect he's not far off. They won't be easy to talk to. Any edge I can use, I'll take it."

Adam watched as the car pulled onto a highway. "You know I'm happy to help, and I'm glad you asked, but where exactly are we going?"

"Moira's folks live in Dingle, you probably haven't heard of it."

"We're going all the way to Dingle?" Adam asked as

he settled more comfortably into his seat, given the long ride ahead. He meant the question to be casual, but he couldn't keep the excitement out of his voice and Isabel gave him a look.

"Meeting with Moira's family is my priority today. It's worth the drive."

"Hasn't someone spoken with them already?"

"The local guards did, yeah. But I want to talk to them myself. Face to face. Now tell me, how do you know about Dingle?"

Adam laughed out loud. "All roads lead to Dingle, don't they? I've heard it's a wonderful little town."

SEAN TOOK THE few stairs at the southeast corner of the main Quad two at a time, his enthusiasm driving him into the museum's entryway at a run. As always, students and researchers milled about, waiting for their opportunity to access NUI Galway's hidden gem, the only remaining gallery of the former Natural History Museum.

He hurried past the harried receptionist, busy checking in tourists and visiting scholars, skimmed over the exhibits of rocks, minerals, and fossils. He stopped short, however, when he recognized the rotund form standing in front of the exhibit that was his goal. His exhibit. His necklace.

Nora Kane turned when she heard his footsteps. "Ah, Professor Rourke, so nice to see you. Coming to look at the exhibit?"

Her smile might have seemed friendly to anyone else, but Sean saw the jealousy and greed it tried to hide.

"Actually, I've come to take the exhibit." He smiled back, oh so sweetly. "I need to run a few more tests on it."

Nora straightened, as if trying to stand taller. A futile effort. "I don't think so, Sean. The exhibit is finally complete. It just opened to the public yesterday. I was told all tests had been finished."

"Right, sure. But I had a few more ideas and I need to take a closer look, that's all. This is a creative science, as you know."

"Well, it's alarmed. You'll need to get the curator's help to even open the case."

Damn, he hadn't thought of that. Something so simple. Where was his brain these days? He pictured the image of Queen Maeve that had come to him last night and realized where his brain was. Still in dreamland, unfortunately.

"Right, of course. I know Aiden, I'll call him."

"He's not free to simply open this up, Sean, and you know it." The tight brown curls that covered Nora's head were shaking as she tried to control her rage. "The deputy president will have something to say about it if you jump in and mess things up."

"Always worried about tying everything up in a neat little bow, aren't you, Nora? What's the big deal? I just need to take it for a couple of hours, compare it to some other photographs. It's part of the job."

Nora's eyes narrowed. "And why wouldn't you have made those comparisons in the fall, when you had the necklace in your lab?"

Sean shrugged, stuffed his hands in his pants pockets. "Like I said, a new idea came to me."

Nora sniffed and shook her head. "You'll need to fill out an acquisition form like everyone else. You can't simply walk in here and take it." She smiled. "And of course, that will require the deputy president's signature. He does supervise the museum director, as you know."

Sean felt his lips tightening into a thin line. She was right, of course, he couldn't simply walk in here and waltz out with the necklace. Which is exactly what he'd intended to do. There were security measures in place, measures to protect the museum's and university's collections.

But what if there was some truth to his dreams? What

if the necklace really was connected to Boudica? Or Queen Maeve? Or Moira Walsh.

"You know what, Nora? You have an amazing ability to annoy the hell out of me. There, I said it."

"Is that right?" Nora smiled sweetly in return. "What a surprise. I never would have guessed it."

"I have some news, Nora, I was going to share with you. But I don't think I can even talk to you right now." He spun on his heel and stalked out of the gallery with as much dignity as he could muster, fully aware of the petulance of his last statement.

"That's fine, dear. I'll wait to hear your big news." Her voice trailed after him.

THEY PASSED AN easy hour in silence before Isabel spoke again. She spent the time trying to figure out how best to handle the approaching interview. As far as she could tell, *he* spent the time admiring the peninsula they drove along. They wound their way between green hills and rocky valleys, catching occasional glimpses of blue water sparkling in the sunlight. He kept his window open just enough to let the clean air in, occasionally taking a deep breath.

"We've got over an hour on the road still. Want to tell me why you're so eager to get to Dingle? It is a beautiful town, I know, but I have the feeling your interest isn't just tourism."

Adam pursed his lips, waiting a moment before answering. "I've been in touch with a man. Someone who knew someone who knew my great-grandfather. It's one of the reasons I came to Ireland."

Isabel laughed. "That's a rather tenuous connection, isn't it?"

Adam slumped lower in his seat and she regretted laughing at him. "Right now, it's all I have. He's the son of a German artist, an artist who painted my great-grandfather's portrait."

"And why do you need to speak to him?"

"It may be a wild goose chase, I don't know. I've heard conflicting stories about my great-grandfather, stories about why he left Poland, how he left Poland. The artist painted his portrait right before he left. I thought he might… well, he might know something. Maybe my great-grandfather said something to him."

"And maybe he passed that information on to his son? That's a long shot, Detective."

Adam gave a small laugh through his nose and looked out the window. "No kidding. But if it's all the same with you, I'll give him a call, let him know I'm in town. I can meet with him once we're done with Moira's parents, if that's all right."

"It's your time to waste." Isabel realized she was running a finger over her ring and tightened her grip on the steering wheel. "Why are you so interested in your family's past?"

"Aren't you? It's a way for me to figure out who I am."

"Hmph." Isabel didn't bother to hide her cynicism. "I have plenty of information about the past. More than I want, frankly."

Adam ducked his head to look at her. "Seriously? If you ignore the past, how do you know where you fit in now? Today?"

Isabel felt her ring under her thumb as she glanced at Adam. "We should make sure we're on the same page for this interview, before we get there."

Adam nodded his agreement, so she continued. "Moira's parents aren't exactly fans of the Garda, from what I've gathered. They were very short with the local team that went to interview them."

"What do they have against the police?"

Isabel shrugged. "I haven't figured that out. No record, either of them, that I could find. Could be some experience in the past."

"Something the police did to them… or something

the police weren't able to do for them."

"Something like that. You know how it is, everyone becomes a suspect when there's an investigation, any investigation. Not everyone takes it well."

"I do know." Adam laughed again, but this time with a smile. "I've been on that end of things myself before."

Isabel grinned. "You still are, friend, don't forget. You, Sylvia, her colleagues… just because you're American doesn't mean you're above suspicion."

Adam opened his mouth to reply, but Isabel didn't give him a chance. "What do you know about the Warriors for Nature?"

"The what?" Adam's confusion at the change in topic seemed genuine enough.

"Your fiancée didn't bother to mention them? When she was asking you to get involved in my investigation?"

Adam turned in his seat to look directly at her. "I have no idea what you're talking about. Want to fill me in?"

Isabel kept her eyes on the road ahead of them. "We received a threat."

"What kind of threat?"

"Legitimate, as far as we can tell. They're a group of troublemakers who use the environment as an excuse for their vandalism."

"Ah." Adam sat back in his seat. "Yes, I've seen the group. Outside the tourist office. What are they threatening?"

"Something to disrupt tourism in Galway. It's the same old thing."

"What made you think I'd have heard about it?"

Isabel shrugged. "Seemed the sort of thing Ms. Stanko would be all over. Given the date of their threatened action."

"Are you saying it's the day of the fundraising event? Are they trying to stop it?"

Isabel shrugged again. "They didn't say so. Could be a coincidence. Or could not. We don't know what they're proposing to do. All gardaí are on high alert."

"Good. That's the last thing Sylvia needs now."

Isabel considered the man in the seat next to her. A man willing to travel around the world to talk to a stranger who probably knew nothing of use. A man so in love with his fiancée he failed to see that she was less than excited by his surprise visit to Ireland. A man who tripped over a murder victim and seemed perfectly willing to not get involved in the case until asked. A man who understood the importance of the past. It didn't add up. Either she really didn't understand him, or there was something she didn't know.

"Tell me about your job, back in Philadelphia. What's police work like in the U.S.A.? All guns and violence, like we see on television?"

Adam grinned. "Yep, that's it. It's just one big Wild West shootout, every day."

Isabel had the grace to laugh, though from the news she watched, it seemed like that description wasn't so far off.

"I'm sure it's a lot like police work here," Adam continued. "A lot of drudgery, a lot of reports, files. We're bored when we're not on a case, but we spend all our time praying nothing will happen, no case will come up. Because when we have a job to do, it means someone else was hurt."

"And you don't like it when people get hurt." Isabel's voice was low as she remembered the fax she hadn't yet shared with him.

He looked at her quizzically. "Do you?"

"No, of course not. But I know it's not my fault, either. I'm here to help. I don't feel guilty when other people get hurt."

Adam shifted in his seat, facing her directly. "Is there something you're not telling me?"

"There's a lot I'm not telling you. But for now, I'm just trying to get a sense of you. To figure out if I trust you or not, Detective."

"Hm." Adam sat back in his seat. "I can't help you there. Either you trust me or you don't. Hell, our job depends on our ability to assess people, doesn't it? The grieving parents we're going to meet. The old man I'm going to see. We need to not just listen to what they tell us, but evaluate it. Consider it from all angles. Use our judgment to get to the truth."

Isabel nodded her agreement. "Very well said."

She bit her tongue before voicing her real concern out loud. Her concern that neither of them seemed to be showing good judgment these days.

CHAPTER TWENTY-FOUR

THE VIEW FROM the sitting room into which they were ushered was just one of the many charms of the Walsh's bed and breakfast. Situated on the street leading out of town, facing the harbor and the hills beyond, the house offered guests an elegant simplicity of design as well as an ideal home base for touring this end of the peninsula. And sumptuous breakfasts, if the scone Adam was eating now was any indication.

Sarah Walsh smiled at Adam's expression as he finished the last of it and held the plate toward him, tempting him with the scent of fresh baked goods. He reluctantly declined.

"I still don't understand what else we can say." Colin Walsh repeated the concern he'd been expressing since Isabel first introduced herself and Adam. "Why don't you have any more news for us?"

"We have some leads we're pursuing, Mr. Walsh, but we're still looking for more." Isabel was stretching the truth a bit, Adam thought. "Leads" was a strong word.

"*Is minic bréag ar aonach*," Colin muttered.

Isabel seemed to sink back into her chair at his comment. "I'll only be honest with you, Mr. Walsh."

"I understand you both went to college in the States?" Adam asked, trying to change the tone of the conversation.

Sarah nodded, her chubby face deepening into a thick

smile. "It's where we met," she gave her husband a wicked glance. "Where we…" She let her words fade away, no doubt remembering the activities that had led to the birth of their first child. Their only child.

"Tell me about Moira," Adam said to her. "What was she like?"

"Oh, Moira was… well, she was special, wasn't she, Colin?"

"You could say that." Colin's response held a gruffness absent from Sarah's voice.

"In what way?" Adam asked.

"She was a bold child. Always bold. But always told the truth in the end. Always did the right thing."

"How d'you mean, Mrs. Walsh?" Isabel leaned forward in her seat, creating a closeness between her and the other woman.

Sarah leaned back into her chair. "Just what I said, that's all."

Isabel kept the sympathetic smile plastered to her face, but her eyes shifted toward Adam.

"What was she like growing up?" Adam asked. "Did she have many friends?"

"Oh, yes." The impish smile came back to Sarah's face. "Didn't she, Colin?"

Moira's father nodded, though his expression stayed firm, a scowl having taken permanent residence on his forehead. "Sure, she did. I'll agree with you there."

"As I said, she was bold. She stood up for her friends, Moira did."

"How so?" Adam pressed her.

"Well, there was that incident with little Billy, wasn't there, Colin?"

Colin looked at his wife but didn't answer.

"Billy had a bit of a problem with the bigger kids. He was quite small, you see," Sarah continued. "Kids will be kids, I always say."

"Good to learn to stand up for yourself," Colin added.

"But Moira had a different opinion?" Adam asked.

"We found out later, of course. No idea anything was going on, at the time."

"Now that's the truth of our Moira," Colin interrupted his wife. "Never knew what was going through her head."

"Nonsense." Sarah waved a dismissive hand toward her husband. "I always understood her. When she thought she could help, she would."

"So what did she do?" Adam prompted her.

"Well, I don't really know, do I? All I know is that one of the bigger boys… what was his name?"

Colin frowned, the furrow across his forehead deepening even more. "Liam, was it?"

"Could've been." Sarah nodded. "Anyway, whatever his name, he was expelled from the school."

"Because of Moira?" Adam asked.

"That's the thing, isn't it? No, it was because of Billy. Billy somehow found out that Liam — or whatever his name — had been running some kind of cheating scheme."

"Pretty creative, you ask me." Colin chuckled, smiling for the first time since Adam had met him. "He played the middle man, getting kids to pay him, then getting another kid to write the exams."

"And Billy told the school about it?" Adam asked.

Sarah and Colin both nodded.

"So what did Moira have to say about it?"

"She was tight-lipped about it, not surprising. But she told me later—"

"Made up a story later, more likely." Colin once again interrupted his wife.

"She told me later," Sarah said firmly. "She knew about that cheating scheme. She wasn't going to tattle on them."

"She wouldn't, either, not my Moira." Colin nodded proudly.

"But she told Billy, you see," Sarah explained to

Adam. "She told Billy. Let him do what he wanted with it."

"Whatever happened to Billy, Mrs. Walsh?" Isabel chimed in once more.

"Thick as thieves they were, for the longest time." Sarah's eyes took on a faraway look. "Friends for many years after that. But" — she shrugged as she stood and picked up the plate of scones — "time passes, doesn't it? Now, you're sure you don't want another?"

She held the plate once more toward Adam, but he shook his head. "Perhaps another cup of tea?"

"Of course." Sarah left the room with the plate.

"I suspect Moira's changed quite a lot since childhood," Isabel said after Sarah left the room. "We all have."

Colin shrugged but didn't respond.

"So what took you to college in the States?" Adam asked. "That's a long way to go."

"My parents worked hard to send me there." Colin's voice took on a defensive tone. "And why shouldn't they? Our own president studied in the United States, d'you know that?"

"I didn't, no," Adam admitted.

"Oh, yes. It was tough, I admit. A big change. But then I met Sarah."

"You two had a lot in common, I imagine. Both being from Ireland."

"We surely did," Sarah answered, reentering the room with two cups of tea. She handed them over to Adam and Isabel. "What a time we had there. Our Moira was born there, not long after we graduated."

"You returned home to raise your family?" Isabel asked.

"We did, Detective Superintendent. And I'm glad for it. At least, I was. Now..." She looked down at her hands in her lap. Her husband reached over and placed a protective hand over hers.

"Our Moira, she was a good girl, Detective

Superintendent." Sarah looked up and Adam saw tears in her eyes. "She didn't deserve this."

"No one deserves something like this," Adam answered her. "We will find out who did it. I promise you."

"My little angel." Sarah's lips quivered. One tear fell loose from her eyes and rolled down her face.

They weren't going to get anything more out of her, not now. Adam and Isabel saw themselves out, leaving Colin and Sarah holding hands in their sitting room, their minds on the past. On death. Their eyes blind to the remarkable view in front of them.

They hadn't learned much they didn't already know. It was clear the Walshes had no fondness for the Garda, though not clear why. But they had learned something about Moira. Adam let Sarah's words roll around in his mind, testing them out to see where they might fit into this puzzle. Moira always told the truth. One way or another.

CHAPTER TWENTY-FIVE

AROUND THE LAST BEND, the sky opened up before Isabel. From her car, she could see the green landscape of the Dingle Peninsula, beyond that the sparkling blue of the water, and within that the giant stone outcroppings that were the Blasket Islands. Home to her people for so many generations. Home until they were chased out. Removed. Forced to leave the islands for the mainland, to give up their way of life, their language, even their history. Thank God.

Ahead she could see the modern outline of the History Museum of Western Ireland, home away from home for her brother Michal. Or perhaps this was his real home, their house simply a place he went when he had to.

She found him on his knees in front of an exhibit built into the floor.

"Sibéal, what brings you here?"

He didn't even look up from the round electronic display that showed scenes of Blasket Island history and populations. Or at least was supposed to. Clearly, it wasn't working correctly. Michal was kneeling, facedown like a penitent begging his digital gods to reawaken, his fingers moving expertly among the bowels of the machine.

"I came down to talk to the parents of a woman who was murdered."

"That's the case you're working on, then? Anything I would've heard about?"

"If you paid any attention at all to the world around you, probably, yeah. But I know you don't."

Michal ignored her tone. Or maybe he didn't hear it. He only seemed to hear what he wanted to hear. "So how did that go? Talking to her parents? That must be tough."

At least he appreciated that. "It was. And it was pointless. Very nice people, destroyed over the death of their only daughter. No one should have to live through that."

"No, I suppose not. Hard enough watching Da slowly die. And he's had a good life."

Isabel glanced at her brother in surprise. That was the first time she could remember his acknowledging the difficulty of taking care of Da. "I'm sorry you're stuck with him, Michal."

"What?" He sat up straight. "What are you talking about? I'm not. I love living with him."

"Oh." She took a step backwards. "Of course, I'm sorry, I didn't mean..."

She took a few more steps away from him, her hand drifting over the rails that held informational signage about each of the exhibits on the wall.

"You've found peace here, haven't you Michal?"

He didn't answer, but when she glanced at him out of the corner of her eye she saw him nodding, back to work on the exhibit on the floor.

"I'm a little bit jealous of that, I have to admit."

Again, he said nothing, but continued to nod. Had he even heard her?

"Michal?"

"Yes?" This time he stopped his work to look at her.

"My case keeps coming back to Irish history. That archaeological dig I mentioned, up near Connemara. Sean Rourke. Found an old necklace. Signs of a possible Roman encampment."

"Hmph." Sean made an odd sound as he turned back to his work. "No signs, I'll wager. And if you don't mind, not an 'old necklace.'"

Isabel laughed for the second time that day. "Sorry, didn't mean to offend. Tell me, what do you know about that dig? Why are people so interested in it?"

"Sibéal." He sighed as he leaned back on his haunches, hands on his knees. "Don't you remember anything we learned in school?"

"I remember enough." She felt as much as heard the whine in her voice and bit her tongue. "Remind me."

"The Romans never invaded Ireland. They came as far as Britain. Maybe even landed on our coastline, but never invaded. We're not sure why; there are several theories."

"So if he finds proof of a Roman encampment, up by Connemara, that would change our history?"

"It would. It would indeed."

"But again, so what? I mean—" She held up a hand to forestall the argument she saw forming on his face. "I understand why it's significant. But would anyone kill over it?"

"Oh, I shouldn't think so. It matters to historians and archaeologists. And people who love Ireland or love our history. It's big news. But it's not something that would attract a criminal element." He grinned widely. "No money in it, you see."

Isabel nodded. "But if someone had money that depended on it."

"I don't see how that could be."

"Someone involved in tourism, maybe?"

"Then that someone should be very happy. It will surely be a great tourist draw."

"But what if you're right, and it turns out to be fake? Not an encampment at all?"

"First of all, I never said it was fake. I wouldn't accuse someone of that. Just a misreading of the evidence, that's all. Far too unlikely to believe. Wishful thinking, more likely. And if it is a misreading then, still, I don't know..."

"No, I don't know either."

"Christ." He stood, throwing down the cables he'd been trying to connect to the display. "This isn't going to work." He glanced at his watch. "Look, do you need anything else from me? I need to run back to the house, get a flash drive I have there. I can just reload the whole program and be done with it."

"Sure, fine. I need to head back anyway."

"Why don't you take a look around, Sibéal, while you're here?"

"You know I don't like this place. Gives me the creeps. Staring at faces of the dead." She looked around the images that surrounded her — groups of people, old huts and farm equipment — and shuddered. Exactly the type of place Adam Kaminski might enjoy if he really did like studying history as much as he claimed. Even now, he was off chasing a figment from the past.

"Just look around," Michal advised her as he gathered his tools.

She toyed with her ring as she watched Michal walk away and wondered if he and Adam had the right idea about learning from the past. To her, it seemed to bring nothing but pain.

IT WAS COOL but not cold, not as cold as it would have been back in Philly at that time of year. Adam walked along the quay in Dingle, looking out over the few boats gathered at the dock. Recreational boats, mostly. The working fishing boats were gradually making their way back to the docks, laden with the day's catch.

A cool, salty breeze whispered against his face. Adam pulled his scarf out of his shoulder bag and wrapped it around his neck. A few tourists and residents walked along the promenade, couples holding hands strolled by, families with kids chased after the seagulls.

One man sat on the rocks looking out over the water, bundled up tightly in overcoat, scarf, hat, and gloves. Dressed more warmly than the weather seemed to warrant.

Adam approached him. When he didn't turn around, he said, "Konrad Rupiewicz?"

The man waited a beat before turning his face toward Adam. Watery, pink-tinged eyes looked up at him from a face lean with age, worn by time. He nodded, gave Adam an appraising look, then turned back to the water.

Adam settled on the rock next to him. "Thank you for agreeing to meet with me. I'm sure this isn't an easy topic for you."

"Sure, I don't mind talking about my father." Konrad spoke with a strong Irish accent. If he'd ever had a German accent, it had long since been replaced through his years in Ireland. Or perhaps through conscious effort.

"As I told you when we spoke before, I'm hoping you have something you can tell me about Marek Kaminski, my great-grandfather."

The old man nodded, his eyes still on the bay. "So you said."

Adam waited.

"Why do you believe I would know anything?"

Adam tried to hide his impatience. "You told me on the phone that your father kept notes. Records of his work. He painted my great-grandfather's portrait. It's possible he has some notes about it."

"I have spent many years moving away from the legacy of my father. He was a Nazi, you know." The man turned his watery eyes on Adam, and Adam was surprised by how piercing they were, bright baby blue in a sea of tears.

"I understand. And I'm sorry. But I need to know."

"I looked up my father's diaries from the time period you described. It was a very difficult time."

An angry seagull screeched overhead and the old man stopped talking. A group of kayakers docked, and Adam and Konrad watched them drag their boats out of the water, peel off their wetsuits. Adam shivered.

"I found the notes you were interested in."

"You did? What did they say?"

"I just started reading them, skimming really. Your great-grandfather was a prisoner when August Rupiewicz painted his portrait."

"Yes, I figured that."

"He was a prisoner of the Nazis. They arrested him on accusation of helping Jews escape."

Adam took a breath and held it, letting those words sink in. His great-grandfather had been a hero, of sorts, doing what he could in dangerous times to help those who needed his help. He smiled.

Konrad was watching him.

"He didn't say much, you understand. Just a notation — the date, the name, the reason he was in the camp."

"Why did Rupiewicz paint the portrait? Why was he allowed to?"

"That's a difficult question. I'm afraid I don't have the answer to that yet. I'll read through more of his diary, perhaps he says." Konrad sat silent for a moment. "I know my father looked for interesting subjects. He wanted to capture emotions in his work, whether in faces or landscapes. It could be something in your great-grandfather's face caught his attention?"

Adam thought about this. "Perhaps. Perhaps."

Konrad shook his head. "Why do you want to pry into something that's done? A time that deserves to stay in the past?"

Adam smiled to himself, knowing he had no answer to the question. He didn't know what drove him to find the truth, whether about his own family or about the murderers he chased. Or about the victims. Victims like Moira Walsh. "I don't know. I just want to know."

"THAT ADAM KAMINSKI'S certainly very interested in what's going on around here," Liam Dempsey said pointedly. "Nothing to do with me, of course, but I do find it curious. None of his business, really."

Sean bit back the questions that sprang immediately to mind. He didn't want to appear nervous about the investigation. Fortunately, Garret asked the questions for him.

"Why would Adam Kaminski care about what we're doing? What would we have to do with Moira's murder? It must be completely unrelated to the university, surely." Garret glanced back and forth between Liam and Sean, a question in his eyes.

The three of them had the faculty lounge to themselves that afternoon. Which in itself was unusual. But not as unusual as Liam deigning to share his infinite knowledge with people like Sean and Garret, people who, he made no secret, he felt were below him. He must really want to talk, Sean thought, to sink to this level.

Liam raised an arrogant eyebrow. "Nothing for you to be concerned about, is there, Garret? He came to me for information, of course."

Sean sniggered and Liam glared at him. "He came to you because you like to hear yourself talk, Liam."

"Hm." Liam sniffed and faced Garret, turning his shoulder to Sean.

That was fine with Sean. He bent forward over the table, filling out the ridiculous forms he had to file to gain access to the necklace. His own damn artifact, for crying out loud. He gripped the pen and tried to focus on the information he was being asked to provide, but Liam's nasal voice carried easily across the small room.

"He wanted to know my opinion of Moira."

"What did you tell him?" Garret's voice came out high and tight, and he coughed a little, as if embarrassed by his own nervousness.

"The truth, of course."

"The truth as you see it," Sean interjected without turning around.

"I told him that Moira was fixated on money. On those bloody grants she kept going on about. Too busy churning out cogs for our great economic machine to worry about things like academic standards. Intellectual integrity. She had no idea how to fit in here, to adhere to our standards." He paused, but Sean refused to turn around to see what he was doing. He turned his head slightly to catch Liam's and Garret's reflection in the window. Liam had leaned closer to Garret, conspiratorially.

"Frankly, I told him she was a liar."

Sean laughed again.

"Why are you making that racket, Rourke?"

"Basically, you lied." Sean stood to face the other two.

"Aren't you taking over one of Moira's grants, Professor Dempsey?" Garret asked, his voice calmer now. "The departmental grant?"

"Well... yes, of course. I'll probably be responsible for a number of the projects she was funding through the Economics and Statistics faculty. But that's not the point."

"Oh?" Garret's voice was growing stronger. "What's the point?"

"The point, young man, is that Moira was not a true mathematician."

"She was a statistician."

"Exactly." Liam snapped his fingers. "She didn't care about true maths. About what the maths can teach us about the world around us. Oh, no." He chuckled. "She cared only about how much her students could earn once they graduated."

Garret smiled. "That's not such a bad thing, is it?"

Liam frowned. "I disagree. We are not here to churn out cogs. We are here to educate young minds. She didn't know what was good for her, good for her career."

"So your dislike for Moira had nothing to do with her calling you out a few years ago? When you made that mistake in the study you were involved in on early Irish literacy?" Garret shocked Sean by asking the question. He didn't think Garret had the balls to confront Liam so directly.

Apparently neither did Liam. He spluttered for a minute or so, then pranced out of the room without saying another word.

Sean sniggered again. He knew Moira better than either of them; he didn't need to listen to Liam's bluster or Adam Kaminski's intrusive questions. Moira always knew exactly who she was, where she stood, and what she wanted. His pen stopped moving for a moment as he wondered if that's what had got her killed.

SIMPLE PICTORIAL EXHIBITS lined the walls. Images of people gathered in front of their humble homes, working the fields, or bringing in the latest crop from the sea. Groups of old men and women, groups of fewer and fewer people as the images progressed through time, the Blasket Islands community changing from a small but vital community to a smaller and smaller, older and older hamlet.

Isabel recognized none of the faces. She was related to some of these people, she knew. The island community was small. Everyone was related to everyone else in some way or another.

She'd passed through three rooms of exhibits and artifacts before a photograph low on the wall caught her attention.

She'd been fine up to then. Skimming her eyes over the photographs of people she was sure Michal would know but weren't familiar to her. Ignoring the pain in her side that arose whenever she thought about the insults of her youth.

Féarach Bó, the tiny village where she'd grown up, was a small community. Sibéal, as she was still called at the time, excelled at her studies, earning top honors in all of her courses. This didn't come without some struggles, however.

At school, everyone knew her story. Other students, their parents, their grandparents, all knew the Sayers family descended from the Blasket Islanders. Not directly from the most famous Sayers, but surely indirectly related to her. While such a known ancestry might provide a strength to some, to Sibéal it proved a burden to shoulder.

By the time she was in school, the people of the Blasket Islands were already entering into the local mythology, a people who had lived a life of hardship, who spoke their own dialect of Irish, whose way of life had died when they were finally forced to leave their island home and settle permanently on the mainland. Her ancestors were relics of a different time. A different place, even though that place could be seen from the back of the schoolyard if one looked out into the bay at the rocky outcropping visible through the mist that seemed to rise with the sun over the waters each morning before Principal rang the bell for first summons.

She read stories about her ancestors in class, the other students poking each other behind her back and making faces they thought she couldn't see. Or perhaps they didn't care if she saw. She wanted nothing to do with the stories of the challenges of the fisherman's life, the beauty of the rugged landscape of the islands, the poetry and literature that remained as a permanent reminder of a long-gone community. A heritage that brought pride to her parents brought her nothing but embarrassment.

She denied any connection to the islanders when teased at school, but her denials only fueled the bullies, for they all knew she was lying. The town was too small to get away with making up stories.

When she made the transition to post-primary school, she promptly changed her name to Isabel and dropped the baggage of her family's past, leaving it like lost luggage at the three-way intersection that marked the boundary of Féarach Bó. Though she couldn't keep her ancestry secret — she was still on the Dingle Peninsula, a small, isolated countryside — she finally got the chance to define herself by herself. She was finally able to fit in. To be normal. That's all she ever wanted.

From school, she headed off to Dublin and the east coast, leaving her family, her childhood, and her west coast ancestry far behind her. And her innocence. Part of her heart and soul.

Yet there it was. A small photograph, tucked into the corner of the lowest exhibit on the wall. She knelt to get a better view, her right knee on the ground, her right hand tracing the face that had caught her attention. Her eyes moved from the image on the wall to the ring on her finger. Her mother's ring. She balled her hand up into a fist, leaning against the wall.

Why? Why did that young girl look so familiar? She must look like her mother, that must be it. Any reminder of her mother always brought back the pain of her loss. But as Isabel looked closer, she knew. She knew the young girl didn't look like her mother. The eyes were too wide apart, the nose too long.

It wasn't her mother she could see in that young girl's face. Tears pricked at her eyes as she tried to stand but failed. She let her other knee lower to the ground, her hands to her side, mimicking the position in which she'd found Michal earlier.

The face looked like her. Like her daughter would no doubt look. The young girl in the photo looked just like a young Sibéal.

She stayed for a moment where she was. Feeling the energy of the museum in a way she never had before. Finally understanding what it was that Michal found here, why he kept coming back here, why he'd made his life here. These were answers. Answers about who she was, where her family had come from, where she belonged.

She didn't know how long she knelt there. She heard footsteps of other museum patrons passing by, whispering as they saw her. She felt the tears coursing down her cheeks.

Eventually, she took a breath. Shook her head as she stood.

She couldn't do this. It might be good enough for Michal, but not for her. Her life was out there. In Galway. In Ireland. She would not hide away in a museum. She would not live for the past, but for the future.

CHAPTER TWENTY-SIX

"PEOPLE DON'T ALWAYS tell the truth." Isabel's voice carried a level of bitterness Adam couldn't ignore.

"Of course not. You didn't really expect the meeting with Moira's parents to go well, did you?"

"Bah," Isabel coughed out the word as she downed the last of her coffee. "How could it? They just lost their only child and the detective in charge of the case is coming to them for answers."

"I get it." He did. He'd been there enough times, he knew how hard it was. "But I believe this guy, Rupiewicz" — he continued the story he'd been sharing before Isabel had interrupted. "My gut says he's telling the truth."

"Yeah, maybe. But so what? History can be fudged. Just say the same thing often enough and others start to believe it."

"You thinking of something in particular?"

"I watched a film a little while ago." Isabel leaned forward over the cafe table conspiratorially. "A documentary. There were two Nazi families living happily outside Galway for years. Decades. Never arrested. In fact, they were ignored by the Irish authorities."

Adam nodded. He'd watched the same film when he'd learned his search for the truth about his great-grandfather was sending him to Galway. But he didn't know what was bugging Isabel so much. If he hadn't seen her enter the cafe, watched her order and drink the coffee, he would've sworn she'd had something stronger to drink.

"But that film just exposed a handful of criminals, all of whom were either dead or captured by the time they made it," Isabel said to make her point. "There was no story about a Nazi artist living out Dingle way. Why were you so eager to believe it was true?"

"The film may have hit on the big names, but surely that must mean there were also some smaller fry hanging out near them, using the same means of escape from Germany to Ireland." Adam toyed with his empty cup. "It fits. And like I said, I believe him."

"So is that the end of your journey? Are you satisfied with what you know?"

"I said I believe him. That's why I need to verify it."

"I don't understand."

Adam shrugged. "If I had doubts about what he was saying, it would be easy enough to walk away and take what he said as gospel. But I'm sure it's true. I'm sure my great-grandfather didn't leave Poland like the coward his family in Poland think he was. If this guy has letters, diaries that prove it, I want to see them."

Isabel dipped her head in acquiescence. "If you need to make a call, use my phone. Then we gotta get back. It's almost four."

Adam thanked her and got up from the table. He kept his eye on her as he placed the call to Konrad, but she didn't move. Just sat staring morosely down into her empty cup. Once he'd finalized his arrangements with Konrad, he returned to the table.

"What is it you need right now, Isabel?"

She smiled at him, and the movement of her lips only emphasized the sadness in her eyes. He could tell she'd been crying, but wouldn't invade her privacy to ask her why.

"What I need? I need to see someone, that's what I

need. But I can't."

"Why not? What's stopping you?"

"Well, for one thing" — she stood and threw a few bills on the table — "this case. We need to get back, it's getting late."

Adam didn't know Isabel, not really. He didn't know her story or her secrets. But he recognized a cry for help when he saw one.

"Come on." He stood next to her. "Let's go."

"Good, back to Galway." She turned on her heel.

"No." He stopped her with a light touch on her arm. "Wherever it is we need to be to see this person you want to see."

"Adam, there's not time. I'm in the middle of a case. We need to get back. Besides, it's not appropriate. This is personal, I shouldn't even have mentioned it."

"Isabel, we need to do this *because* you're in the middle of a case. Whatever this is, it's affecting you. Affecting your judgment. Come on. I'll go with you. People in Galway can wait one extra hour. Give me your phone again."

Sylvia's cell phone went right to voicemail. After leaving a message, he tried calling Nora Kane's number in the hopes that Sylvia would be nearby. No one answered, so he left another message, then turned back to Isabel.

"Now, who do we need to see?"

NONDESCRIPT FOUR-DOOR sedans were parked in each drive, each leading up to a standard-built stone house, lace curtains in the front windows, patches of grass in the front yard. Adam watched the street pass by as Isabel slowed, the letter with the address loose in her hand. She pulled the car up in front of 251.

"I thought you were looking for 256?" He counted the houses to find the house they were looking for, then saw what Isabel had already seen.

A little girl, no more than eight, crouched in the yard, her focus on the stuffed animals that surrounded her. She played alone, but Adam could see her lips moving, talking, no doubt, to her furry playmates. One of the animals took an unexpected leap into the air and Isabel laughed out loud, then covered her mouth with her hand as the laugh turned into a sob.

She leaned back in her seat, her eyes glued to the little girl. As the child lifted her arms, Isabel would raise her chin; as the child squatted to the ground, Isabel's brows would drop. Like a marionette controlled by the movements of the child.

Adam sat silent, giving Isabel the time she needed.

The sky darkened as he watched, though the girl didn't seem to mind. It must have been hard for her to see her toys. Eventually, a woman came out of the house. She waved her arm toward the girl, who gathered up her toys and followed her into the house.

The white painted front door closed behind her.

Isabel shook her head. "I couldn't keep her. I was too young."

Adam nodded his understanding. Though he knew he couldn't really understand.

"And now it's too late. I can't get her back."

Adam found he had to clear his throat before speaking. "Do you know the adoptive parents? Could you reach out to them?"

Isabel let out a low laugh. "They already reached out to me." She flicked the letter she still held, then dropped it. It slid down between the seats of the car. "It was supposed to be an open adoption, but I haven't gone to visit her yet. They've invited me."

"So… why…?" Adam wasn't sure what he wanted to ask. Or what Isabel wanted to share.

He stole a glance at her. Tears streamed down her cheeks, her hands in her lap furiously turning the gold ring she wore. He turned away again.

"I could. I know… I should. It's just…" She shook

her head and ran a hand roughly along her cheek. "I don't know how that would work. I don't know."

She turned the key in the ignition and the car started up again.

"Your life is in a different place now, isn't it? You have something to offer her. You still can." He knew it was none of his business, but he saw how much she hurt. He couldn't sit there and say nothing.

"I'm afraid…" She let the word hang there, and Adam was about to ask what she was afraid of when she continued. "I'm afraid it's too late."

She pulled away from the curb.

"OF COURSE SHE'S already cut out for the day." Sean glanced at his watch. Apparently Nora Kane didn't believe in burning the midnight oil.

"We can talk to her about it tomorrow, Sean. No big deal," Jennifer said.

Garret nodded, his gloved hands held up in front of him like a priest offering a prayer to his savior. "No problem."

"I just would've liked to get the paperwork signed today, that's all. Get an early start on it tomorrow." Sean chewed on the inside of his lip and looked around Nora's workspace. His application to remove the necklace from the exhibit was nowhere to be found. Had she even started processing it? "Fine, you two come back here first thing, right?"

"Yeah, sure." Garret took Sean's words as a cue to leave and took off back down the hall.

Jennifer moved a little more slowly, touching Sean tentatively on the arm and giving him a warm smile before following in Garret's footsteps.

Light shone from an open door down the hallway, voices carrying a note of laughter. Sean took a few light steps and stopped in the doorway to see who was still at work. Sylvia Stanko and a few of her colleagues from

Legg University stood gathered around the mantle in the ornamental office.

Sylvia glanced at her watch, then looked over at the man Sean had seen her with before. Sean recognized the look in her eye. He'd know that look anywhere. Any man would. "I expected Adam back by now. I'm not sure what's taking him so long."

The man walked over to her, leaning his head close to hers. "Didn't he call?"

Sylvia pouted and raised her eyebrows, an expression of mockery as much as sadness. "I'm afraid my phone is completely dead. I can't even check my messages."

The man grinned and stepped even closer to her.

"All right, folks, I think we're done for tonight. See you all in the morning?" The man who must have been leading the meeting walked around the room gathering some loose folders and papers that remained from whatever they had been working on.

"Anyone up for a late dinner?" one young woman asked. "Happy to take you to my local, introduce you to the best pub fare Galway has to offer."

A man and a woman accepted her offer and grabbed their coats. Sylvia hesitated by the mantle. "I think I'll wait just a little longer to see if Adam returns."

"I'll wait with you," the man next to Sylvia jumped in. "We'll try to catch up with you if we can."

The others said their goodbyes, nodding to Sean on their way out of the room. As Sean turned to follow them, he caught the man's words, "If you don't hear from Adam, why don't you and I go somewhere quiet?" followed by a low murmur from Sylvia.

Sean shook his head. No doubt where that quiet evening was headed. He almost felt bad for Adam. Almost. A man that sanctimonious deserved a little pain in his life.

He strode back down the hallway, the flashing red light on Nora's phone indicating a message marking the beat of his steps.

CHAPTER TWENTY-SEVEN

PULSATING BLUE LIGHT filled the air, thrumming off the dark stone walls and into the sky's blackness. The sight always filled Adam with dread. He had his door open before Isabel had fully stopped the car in front of the Quad, running out to the nearest garda in uniform.

"What happened? Is anyone hurt?"

"Please step back, sir." The young man held both hands out toward Adam, as if pushing him away from a distance, then his eyes shifted to Isabel as she approached.

"Detective Superintendent. They're inside."

Isabel nodded and gestured for Adam to follow her. The garda stepped aside.

"Why didn't I get a call sooner?" Isabel muttered under her breath. Adam had no response. The news of the break-in had reached Isabel while they were on the road. She'd driven as fast as she could to get here, but it had still been over an hour since she'd taken the call.

They followed the sound of voices across the courtyard and up the stairs at the southeast corner. Adam could see the cluster of people in a pool of brightness at the end of the hall in the grand stone exhibit room.

Isabel spoke as they entered, all eyes turning to her. "What happened?"

The deputy president stood with the college dean and

museum director, Nora Kane's curls just visible over her superior's shoulder. They turned to her as one, but didn't speak. To their right, a glass display case sat on a pedestal. Its steel frame remained intact, but the glass that had been protecting whatever was inside lay in shards on the floor.

Another officer in uniform trotted over to her, and Adam listened as he reported. "It was a break-in, ma'am. Display case was smashed. An artifact stolen. Couldn't have been much more than two hours ago."

"Bloody hell. I should have been here." Isabel's words expressed regret, but her face showed no emotion, the tears of earlier in the evening long since rubbed away. "What was taken?"

The young man checked his notes. "A necklace. A fairly recent addition to their collection, apparently."

"I told you I needed to get back, not hang around moping over lost chances." Isabel almost walked into Adam, pushing him aside roughly, venting her anger on him.

Adam ignored her. He pulled his phone out, punched out Sylvia's number again. Again, it went straight to voicemail. "Damn it, Sylvia. Where are you?"

CHAPTER TWENTY-EIGHT

"WHAT ARE YOU doing here, Kaminski?"

"It's a public meeting," Adam whispered back at Isabel over his shoulder as she slid into the bench behind him. "Nothing stopping me from being here." He turned his attention back to the presentation Peig was giving to the committee that morning.

"As long as you're not getting involved in police business..."

Adam wasn't surprised to hear the warning in Isabel's voice. Things had not gone well after they'd returned to the university the previous evening.

Isabel had been furious at him, in that bizarre logic women sometimes seemed to have. Like it was his fault she'd wasted time in Dingle, instead of being there, at the university museum, lying in wait for the criminal to appear.

She was still upset about seeing her daughter, he knew that. He could even understand that. But understanding someone's anger and putting up with it were two different things. She'd had the nerve to tell him, once again, to keep his nose out of the investigation. Even though she'd been the one to drag him back in that very morning.

He'd left her fuming at the university only to find Sylvia not at their B&B when he returned. Isabel was right about one thing; they shouldn't have spent as much time as they did in Dingle. Served him right for trying to help her. He should've been back here keeping an eye on Sylvia.

When Sylvia finally did get home, well past midnight, their conversation had been brief and tense. She'd had no explanation for her whereabouts — out for drinks with the team, she said. Her phone had died, she said. He didn't believe her, and hated himself for not trusting her. She was his future, he'd committed himself one hundred percent to her. He needed her to be a part of his life.

All he wanted was to drop this investigation, abandon Isabel Sayers, and focus on Sylvia and their future together. But Sylvia begged him to keep on with the investigation. Another big donor had pulled out and she was beside herself with worry.

So that was two unhappy women he had to worry about.

At least focusing on the investigation gave him something he actually knew how to deal with. Just like in any other murder investigation, he needed to get back to basics. Isabel had the resources to track down the evidence, to canvas the neighborhood, to double-check alibis. He needed to focus on his strength: he needed to understand Moira Walsh.

That meant starting with the people who knew Moira Walsh best. As far as he could tell, these days that was Conn O'Flaherty and Sean Rourke.

The committee was meeting in a nondescript hall, located in the center of town just off Eyre Square. Peig stood at a half lectern, which itself squatted on the long table around which the council members had gathered. Adam was one of only a handful of members of the public who had chosen to attend the meeting about promoting tourism to Galway. Sean sat across the aisle from him, no doubt interested in the committee's opinion on crime and its connection to tourism.

He focused his attention on what Peig was saying.

Despite the theft of Sean's famous necklace the previous evening, and despite the doubts that continued to circulate around the find, Peig was still using it as the centerpiece of the new marketing campaign she was there to unveil.

"Find your own dreams... Uncover the possibilities..." She read the slogans off the poster boards lined up behind her, animatedly describing the images that could accompany the slogans, doing her best to sell this newest idea to the committee. They seemed to be lapping it up.

"Aren't they even worried that the centerpiece of their campaign has been stolen?" he said over his shoulder, knowing Isabel was still leaning forward in her seat.

"Perhaps they simply have great faith in the Garda that it will be found and returned soon." The sarcasm in her voice was not lost on him.

He laughed, then considered Peig's position. "Or maybe that really is why people come to Ireland."

"Well, either way, this theft has given the murder investigation a new direction."

"You're not serious?" He turned in his seat to face her, and a young woman a few seats away shushed him loudly. He dropped his voice. "You don't really think they're connected, do you?"

"You don't? That's a sight too much coincidence for me if they're not."

"Okay, okay, connected, yes. But how?"

"Maybe the murder was the first attempt, gone wrong?"

"That makes no sense." Adam pictured the dark, barren path on which he'd found Moira's body. She'd left the meeting about the fundraising event, but where had she been going? Could she have had the necklace on her?

"No way," he said out loud. "No one would expect Moira to have the necklace on her person."

"Maybe the thief thought he could steal her faculty ID to get into the department? Look, I don't entirely disagree with you," Isabel added as Adam started shaking his head, "but that's the direction my leadership wants me to follow. The Galway Division's working the robbery angle, and my colleagues in Dublin thinks it's worth pursuing, too."

A smattering of applause brought Adam's attention back to the meeting in front of them. He hadn't heard the comments from the council members about Peig's plan. He wondered if they agreed with her. Her smile suggested they did.

"So what are you doing here?" he asked Isabel.

"I need to have another word with Conn O'Flaherty."

CHAPTER TWENTY-NINE

"THAT WAS A waste of time."

Adam agreed with Sean's sentiment, though he suspected for different reasons.

Isabel had been invited to give an impromptu presentation on the ongoing investigation into the theft the day before at the museum, which led into a heated discussion about what more could be done by council to provide security for the university and a unanimous decision that it was not this committee's responsibility.

"I don't know," Adam said to him, "must make you feel good that everyone's so interested in your discovery, doesn't it?"

Sean shook his head and looked across the room, where Isabel had cornered Conn O'Flaherty.

"Of course it does," Jennifer answered instead. "And our work this summer will be even more significant."

"Yeah, of course." Sean nodded, his eyes now following as Isabel and Conn worked their way back to the front door, a path that would bring them past Adam and the archaeologists.

"Sean, listen to me." Adam stepped closer to him and tried to keep his voice down. "Isabel thinks there's a connection between the theft yesterday and Moira's death. Can you think of how they might be connected?"

"There's no connection." He twisted his mouth with disdain as he answered. "How could there be? Moira wasn't involved with that necklace in any way."

He kept his eyes trained on Conn and Isabel, still moving toward them across the room.

"I know how important Moira was to you, Sean. I saw how upset you were when she died. I'm sorry to have to ask this again, but have you thought of anything else that might help the investigation. Anything at all?"

"Even if he did, why would he tell you?" Jennifer insinuated herself into the conversation and Adam realized she'd been inching closer as they spoke.

"You need to talk to him." Sean gestured to Conn with his chin, his hands shoved firmly in his pants pockets. "He was up to something, I'm sure of it. Moira said she was helping him with a special project." His voice rose an octave as he referenced the special project, making it clear what he thought of it.

"Let it go, Sean." Conn spoke as he passed by, barely slowing his stride. "Your involvement with Moira meant a lot more to you than it did to her. You were just a man passing in the night to our Moira, that's all you were."

Adam felt as much as heard Jennifer's sharp intake of breath. Conn and Isabel continued their way to the door and out of the hall.

Sean's face had crumpled as Conn spoke, and he turned to Adam now with anger. "That's not true. She was helping me because she wanted to, not because I bullied her the way he did. She liked spending time with me."

"You were involved in a romantic relationship with the victim," Adam said. "You must realize that makes you a suspect. Particularly if we find that she decided to end the relationship."

"What if we were? No crime in that. And she didn't end it." Sean glowered again. "It wasn't enough of a relationship to have an end. At least not yet."

Adam turned away from Sean to see Jennifer sitting in one of the chairs they had just vacated, her face a deep shade of red.

ISABEL KEPT CLOSE to Conn, almost pushing him forward with her presence behind him. The last thing she needed was for him to get into a fight with Sean Rourke.

"Over here." She pulled his arm as they left the hall, doing her best to get him out of the room and off somewhere they could talk privately.

She did not succeed.

"Mr. O'Flaherty." Nora Kane's voice was shrill with disapproval. "I do not appreciate your insinuation that we are not sufficiently capable to manage our own security."

"I don't think you need me to insinuate anything, Nora. You're the one who had the break-in, aren't you?"

"It is not unreasonable for us to rely on a modicum of support from our local guards." Nora glared at Isabel as she spoke. This could go nowhere good.

"Why did you have to antagonize Professor Rourke, Conn?" Isabel turned her back on Nora and tried to keep walking.

Conn stayed where he was. "That knucklehead? It would be asking too much of me not to rub his face in it, darlin'. He's just begging for it, isn't he?"

Nora hadn't walked away, but was standing only a few feet distant, clearly listening to them. Conn raised his voice, probably to make sure she heard. "He's moping about after Moira, when she had no interest in him."

"Then why did you direct me to him at the beginning of this investigation?" Isabel asked with real curiosity.

Conn shrugged. "Because she talked about that bloody dig, Moira did. I don't know why."

"Talked about it how? When?"

Conn draped a heavy arm over her shoulder. Isabel took a step back to move away from it, but just as quickly stepped closer to Conn. She would not let him intimidate her.

"Pillow talk, darling. You know about that."

Nora Kane inhaled sharply. "I never."

"No, you probably never did, did you?" Conn grinned.

"And is that all your relationship with Moira was? I was under the impression she had done some work for you."

Conn shrugged again. "Yeah?"

"If she was working for... for... *him*," Nora stressed the last word, "then it was fishy, for sure."

"So she ran some numbers for me, so what?" Conn glared at Nora.

"Ran them? Or fudged them?" Isabel asked before Nora could respond.

Conn raised an eyebrow, his head tipped to one side. "What do you want from me, Detective Superintendent?"

"That is too much. Simply too much." Nora looked like she was about to explode, standing with her legs apart, her hands on her hips. "All of this, it is simply dragging our faculty into something bad, something... evil."

"Take it as you will, darling."

Nora narrowed her eyes, redness spreading across her face and down her neck.

"Nora, why would you think Moira was involved in something fishy, as you said?" Isabel asked. "Have you heard these accusations about her before? About her being willing to fudge numbers?"

"I would never sit back and let anyone make such terrible accusations about the ethical standards of our faculty." Nora's words seemed to defend the faculty, the university, but she looked at the ground as she spoke, her tiny feet shifting her weight.

"No... but you knew, didn't you?"

"If I had any proof of it, I would have reported her immediately. The damage such behavior can do to the university is immeasurable." As she spoke, her posture weakened, her head dipped. "Of course, I had my suspicions. I knew her type. I had an idea of what she was capable… but that she had actually crossed that line? I couldn't prove it." She turned her glare on Conn. "And you, an advisor to our city council."

She gave one last huff and stormed back down the hall.

"Nora," Conn called after her. "You won't go spreading slander now, will you? Because then I would have to sue you and your employer."

Nora's face turned even redder and she practically ran away from him, past the door to the hall and out into the street.

"So you're not admitting anything?"

"I admit nothing, Detective Superintendent. Just trying to help your investigation in any way I can."

CHAPTER THIRTY

EVEN IN THE MARCH CHILL, crowds gathered in Eyre Square. A brave young man played guitar through cut-off gloves while a juggler set up shop along the sidewalk near the flags that marked the northeast edge of the square. The greasy smell of fish and chips and cheap meat pies carried from the pubs on the corner.

Sean kept his head low, his eyes on the pavement in front of him, trying to ignore the fact that Jennifer was trotting along next to him. With the desire to talk, apparently.

"I saw Isabel talking with Conn. Wonder what she's looking for?"

Sean felt her eyes on him, and when he didn't respond, she continued. "You seemed to point them in that direction."

"Bah, they're not really interested in Conn. I was just... never mind."

"Why not?" she asked. "Why wouldn't they be interested in Conn? He seems like a swindler to me."

"Well, for one thing, he was with Nia O'Keenan that evening. I saw them, right around the time Moira was apparently..." He shivered and swallowed the words he was about to say.

He made the mistake of sliding his eyes toward her as he answered and she gave him a funny look. "How do you know that?"

"Doesn't matter what I know, it's what the cops care about that matters. And right now they seem more interested in that damn necklace than in what happened to Moira."

"Don't talk like that. That necklace is important. To both of us. This is your big break, Sean. I'm glad people are paying more attention to it. Even if it did take the theft for it to happen. Maybe you should be grateful for that theft."

She reached a tentative hand out to him and he jerked his arm away. "I know that, Jennifer, I just… the police are looking in the wrong place, that's all. You know that as well as I do."

"So you know."

Sean's feet stopped moving, almost on their own. "Know what, Jennifer?" He turned to face her. "What are you talking about?"

"Oh… well… you know what happened to the necklace?"

Sean shook his head. He spoke slowly, enunciating each word. "Of course I don't. It was stolen. That's all I know."

"So you don't want me—"

Sean cut her off before she could make whatever inane offer she was about to make. "I don't want you to do anything, Jennifer. Let the cops handle this."

Jennifer chewed on her lips for a moment, and Sean tried to read her mind through her eyes. Their pale blueness gave nothing away. Though he was reminded what he'd seen in her to begin with. He softened his tone and moved closer to her. "What's got you so upset?"

He wrapped his arm around her waist, enjoying the feeling of her curves as she bumped against him. Thoughts of his dreams — those great, Irish warrior queens — came unbidden to mind, and he pulled Jennifer even closer.

Jennifer shrugged. "Just that Moira said some things.

About the dig."

Sean narrowed his eyes, all romantic thoughts vanished. "What kinds of things?"

Jennifer screwed her lips into a tight ball and looked at him, as if trying to keep the words in her mouth.

"Never mind," Sean said. "Whatever it was Moira said, it was crap. Don't listen to it." He resumed his forward march, then stopped again. "And don't repeat it, right?"

They walked up to the street. The Browne Doorway loomed behind them, once the grand entrance to a Galway mansion, now an architectural remnant, a reminder of times past. Tribal flags snapped in the air above them. Jennifer was silent the rest of the way, and Sean was grateful for that. But she broke her silence as they waited for the bus that would take them back to the university.

"She didn't care about you, Sean. Not the way I do."

He didn't know if he should laugh, scream, or kiss her, as she clearly wanted. He did the only thing he could think of. He kept his mouth shut, nodded to her, and turned to walk the rest of the way, leaving her standing at the bus stop, staring after him.

CHAPTER THIRTY-ONE

ADAM HEARD THE shouting even before he turned the corner off the pedestrianized street into the wide intersection. Father Griffin Road curved before him. To his left, customers at his favorite coffee shop gathered on the front step, watching the drama unfolding across the street in front of the tourism center.

It was a small crowd, but loud. A handful of uniformed gardaí shooed the group away from the main entrance to the tourist office, pushing them back to the banks of the river.

Adam stayed where he was, on his side of the street, not wanting to get involved in the skirmish. One garda stood in front of a group of about a dozen straggly-looking young men and women. If the men had looked meaner, Adam would've been worried. But they stood with shoulders sloped, long hair blowing in the breeze, the occasional dreadlock swinging over their faces. Even from where he stood across the road, Adam caught a whiff of cannabis on the otherwise salty air.

Peig stopped next to him, watching with him. "They don't understand the importance of what we're doing."

"What are they protesting?"

"Who knows. It's always something." She shook her head sadly.

"You must have some idea."

She shrugged, dipped her head. "They're an eco

group. You know… as far as they're concerned, everything we do is some kind of violation of our environment."

"But why are they protesting in front of the tourism center?"

She looked sideways at him. "Clearly, they think something we're doing is threatening the environment. They're wrong."

Adam wanted to push her farther, to ask about the group, when a head of trim red hair caught his eyes. He'd recognize that head anywhere.

With a quick "excuse me" to Peig, Adam dashed across the street, pushing his way through the protestors, his eyes on the redhead.

His quarry saw him coming. It took a few seconds for recognition to kick in, a few seconds of confusion as Adam drew closer. Then it clicked. The red-haired young man moved in the opposite direction.

Adam ducked and wove his way through the crowd, but the other man moved faster. In his rush, Adam pushed one of the protestors out of his way.

"Hey!" A skinny man with dreadlocks grabbed his arm and pulled him backwards.

"Sorry, sorry, man," Adam mumbled an apology. He didn't want to get into a fight now, not with the redhead in his sights.

The skinny man kept his hold on Adam and called out. "Garret? What's going on? This man bothering you?"

The redhead turned and Adam saw his two bandaged hands. So this was the infamous Garret.

Garret shook his head but didn't come closer, instead backing away. Backing directly into one of the garda. As the burly officer locked onto Garret, Adam pulled free from the skinny man. "Garret," he shouted over the crowd. "Why're you following me?"

"I never did. Don't know what you're talking about," Garret's response came floating back.

The group of protestors, who had been focusing their attention on the tourist office, now turned to watch the drama being played out within their own ranks as Garret struggled to pull free of the guard and shouted at Adam, while skinny guy made another lunge at Adam.

"Damn it." Adam didn't have time for skinny guy, who had a surprising amount of energy for someone so obviously high. He stepped away from his grasping hands, grabbed his left arm, and spun the man around, twisting his arm behind his back. "Leave me alone, got it?" he whispered in the man's ear.

"Dara! Dara!" Adam heard calls from others in the crowd. He felt the crowd surging toward him, felt other hands on him.

He pushed Dara away from him, toward the bulk of the crowd, and took a step back. He saw a garda coming at him from the right and turned to face her. She did not look friendly. Adam put both hands up in front of himself, to show he wasn't violent or dangerous, but just as he did so, someone shoved into him from behind, pushing him directly into the garda. She caught him, spun him around, and reached for the plastic cuffs on her belt.

"Calm down, sir. You need to calm down."

"It's not me," Adam answered her through gritted teeth, watching as Garret slipped away through the crowd. "I'm not involved in this."

Dara chose that moment to step up close to Adam. "Who do you think you are? What're you doing with Garret?"

A second garda trotted over and Dara stepped back, melting into the crowd of protestors.

Adam felt his arms being pulled together behind him. It took all his strength and patience not to fight back. To let himself be cuffed. "Come with me, sir," the garda said.

Adam let himself be turned, marched toward the street, where a marked police vehicle waited. He tried to breathe. Forced himself to stay calm.

He'd be taken to the station. He'd talk to Isabel there. She'd explain everything, set things right. She'd want him to be released immediately. Wouldn't she?

"Adam. Wait."

Adam let his breath out as he heard Peig's call. "Garda Simmons, please." Peig caught up with them, catching her breath. "Please, this is a friend of mine. He was just trying to help me."

Adam chose not to correct her. This was not the time.

"Maybe so, Peig, but he shouldn't be brawling on the street like this. Even with good intentions."

"I understand that, officer, and I'm sorry," Adam tried to sound as contrite as he could.

It didn't sound good enough to his ears, but perhaps Peig's connections were stronger, because he felt the cuffs being cut and pulled his hands free. The garda kept her grip on his arm.

"I am sorry, officer, I'll stay away next time, I promise."

"You better. I'll be keeping an eye on you, and your friends."

Adam laughed. "These are not my friends, believe me." He watched as the other gardaí broke through the protesting group, dispersing them back to the street, the bridge, the waterfront.

Finally free of the garda's grip, Adam turned to thank Peig, but she was already jogging across the square toward her building.

By the time he got inside, Peig was behind the main desk, organizing the small staff there. He gave her a few minutes to finish giving them their instructions, then cornered her near a bookshelf in the back. Rows of brochures from all local destinations lined the shelf.

"Peig, does that protest have anything to do with the new campaign you're proposing? Promoting Sean's dig?"

"It might." She straightened the piles of brochures as she talked, keeping her back to Adam. "Certainly there are people who think we shouldn't spread the word about all we have to offer here in Galway."

Adam considered the position. He saw the logic: the more people that came and tramped over a site, the more it would be destroyed, degraded. He thought of Sean's objection to Adam throwing one rock into the sea. What impact would hundreds of tourists have?

Peig interrupted his thoughts. "It is important to boost tourism, they just don't understand the economics of it. At least Moira understood that."

"What do you mean by that?"

"She knew the importance of what we were doing — me, Conn, the tourism board. She saw the value and offered her services to help. I'll miss her."

CHAPTER THIRTY-TWO

ISABEL'S HAIR STUCK up in clumps around her ears. She didn't care. She ran her hands through it one more time, grabbing onto it and squeezing, as if trying to squeeze an insight out of her brain.

She'd spent the rest of the morning back at her desk, just as she'd spent most of the night. Going through all the reports, all the witness statements, all the evidence found at the crime scene. Though to call it evidence might be stretching things a bit. All MacNulty had done — all he could do — was provide her with a list of all the things found at the scene of the crime, things like a wadded-up candy wrapper, an empty envelope, a few footprints, a single earring. It was up to her to figure out what it all meant.

She still had questions, questions she would've asked of MacNulty if she'd been here when his report came in. How could she have wasted a full day, driving to Dingle? And how could she have let that man, that Philadelphia detective, convince her to lose her focus on the case and waste time on her own personal needs?

The knock at her door made her jump. "Come in."

"The annual reports you asked about." The junior clerk left the pile of hardbound books on the edge of her desk and backed out of the office, probably correctly interpreting Isabel's mood from the condition of her hair.

"Finally," she said out loud, though the clerk had already closed the door.

Conn had been so eager to stop Isabel from helping out with his summer camp. An innocent comment she'd made in an effort to build rapport had ended up with a threat. Which meant she needed to dig more into that camp.

The council's annual report included brief summaries of all the social services supported by the town. A paragraph on the youth camp was buried on page twenty-two of last year's report. It was short and sweet. Described as a clear success, the camp brought in kids from all over the country each summer. They'd spend a few weeks learning Irish language, Irish history, rambling over the countryside around Connemara. The only downside was the reduced income from the year before.

Isabel flipped open the previous year's report to find a similar paragraph. All programs a success, a waiting list of needy children hoping to attend, funds reduced from the year before.

She went back another year, then another year before that. Each said the same thing. A well-run organization doing its best with reduced funds. All campers were happy and satisfied. If only the income wasn't being reduced each year.

She closed the books and dug her hands back into her hair, resting her head heavily on her arms. All social services were facing the same problem. Reduced government income, reduced donations from those well-off enough to donate back to the community. About the only thing that wasn't suffering was the national lottery.

Isabel laughed out loud at this. All these poor families struggling to get by, but wasting a dollar a week on those fantastic odds. The tax for the poor, she called it. Because that money came in to the government.

She raised her head and looked over at the annual reports. Something didn't add up.

A few more clicks on her computer brought up a

different report: the national lottery's annual report posted for the past several years. Income was good. Steady. Even increasing occasionally.

So the reduction in funds wasn't coming from a reduction in the profits from the lottery.

She went back to the city council annual reports. Income from the lottery was stable. Council voted each year on how to divvy up the funds, by a percentage, based on those organizations that demonstrated both a need and an ability to use the funds to the advantage of the community. The funds were there.

So why was the camp receiving less and less each year? The amount the city council set aside for the camp was reduced by the time it reached the camp.

The council's records showed only "administrative fees" being charged. And each year, those fees were going up. So who was charging those fees, and for what?

She had no doubt she knew the answer.

Conn O'Flaherty was a man who had friends in all the right places around town, including the chief superintendent. If he was skimming a profit from the funds that were supposed to be going to the camp, that explained the little project he had Moira working on for him. A statistician who could fudge any numbers to make them look legitimate.

Isabel took a deep breath. Smiled. She shook her head and ran a hand over her hair to flatten it.

Now this was a real motive. Not murky hints about some archaeological dig. Not tenuous connections to a stolen necklace. Embezzlement, pure and simple. Greed.

If Moira was covering up for Conn but got greedy herself — maybe she wanted a bigger cut of the action — Conn could've killed her for it.

CHAPTER THIRTY-THREE

ADAM FOUND SYLVIA with Nora Kane. She'd assumed a typical Sylvia pose, hands crossed in front of her, fingers tapping on her arms, one foot tapping impatiently on the ground. The look on her face made it clear that whatever she was waiting for from Nora Kane was taking too long.

"Hey, have time for lunch?" he asked with a smile and a peck on her cheek.

"If I can ever get my receipt from the university," Sylvia answered, glaring at the back of Nora's head.

Nora had her back turned to them, her not insubstantial bottom sticking out as she bent over an open file cabinet, rifling through the papers. Adam was surprised something as simple as pulling a filed form would take any time at all for the normally meticulous Nora. Perhaps she was trying to prove a point with Sylvia.

Sylvia turned her back to Nora to address Adam, making a point of her own. "That was terrible, no? About the necklace? Who could have done such a thing?"

Adam shrugged. "I don't know about the necklace. I'm still focusing on the murder."

She started to purse her lips in an expression Adam recognized, so he continued quickly, "Like you asked me to."

"Thank you, darling." Her lips curled into a narrow smile. "And have you found anything new?"

He wanted to tell her he'd solved it. He wanted to tell her that her event could go forward without any more complications now. That he'd fixed her problems. Taken care of her, like he'd promised to.

"I… no." He looked at the ground. "Nothing new. I'm focusing on the people who knew Moira best, trying to learn more about her. I figure that's my best bet right now."

"Here we are, then." Nora approached with her hand out, propelling an envelope toward Sylvia. "Your receipt."

"Thank you." Sylvia smiled sweetly. "Come, Adam, perhaps that lunch you mentioned?"

"Nora, I've been looking for you." Sean clattered down the hall toward them, bursting into Nora's work area.

"I'm right where I always am, Professor Rourke. What can I do for you?"

"I wanted to tell you before, but I didn't have a chance. I'm leaving Galway."

"Really?"

Adam couldn't be sure; it happened so quickly, and he was looking at Sean rather than Nora, but he had the distinct sense Nora's face lit up for a moment with Sean's news before closing down again into her normal irritated expression.

"Is this your last semester here, then?"

"It is. And I'll need you to manage the paperwork to get my grant shifted to my new institution."

Nora's face turned pink and then red. "Oh, wait a minute. It doesn't work like that, and you know it."

"I don't care how it works, or what you need to do. I'm leaving, I'm taking the grant with me, and I'll be glad to say goodbye to this dump."

He spun on his heel and stomped down the hallway, almost colliding with Jennifer, who had stepped into the space while Sean was speaking. When Sean stormed past her, she cast an apologetic glance toward the others.

"Well, I never," Nora said.

"So sorry," Adam said awkwardly, feeling like they were being used as an audience for someone else's play. "We, uh, we're just on our way out."

Jennifer tried to stop them. "This isn't like him, really it isn't. I don't know what's got into him."

"It seems a perfectly typical reaction to me," Nora said, focusing on the papers on her desk, avoiding eye contact with anyone else in the room.

"He just… he's got a lot on his mind. I'm so sorry about that." Jennifer ducked out to follow Sean.

"SEAN? WHAT'S going on?"

Jennifer trotted down the hallway after him. Not helpful when he was trying to storm out of Nora's workspace.

"D'you overhear what I told Nora? Then you know what's going on," he said.

"I didn't… I didn't hear, not really." Her voice faltered as she spoke and he stopped to face her.

"What's going on with you, Jennifer? Are you following me around?"

"Well… no, I… it's just…"

He shook his head at her and continued his march down the steps into the open quad. Clusters of students gathered around the benches and the chalky odor of the ivy-covered limestone walls only emphasized the picture-perfect atmosphere. He harrumphed.

"I can't wait to leave."

"Leave? Where are you going?" Jennifer put a hand out and grabbed his arm. "Sean, what's going on? What did you tell Nora?"

"I'm leaving, Jennifer. I got a job. In the States. This is my last semester here."

"What?" Her shriek carried across the quad and all

the other students turned to look at them.

"Shush." Sean ducked his head and pulled her down next to him on a wooden bench, as if trying to hide in plain sight. "Calm down, what's wrong?"

"What's wrong?" Her words came tumbling out, her face growing redder and redder as she spoke. "You're leaving. Without telling me. What am I going to do? Why would you do this?"

"You're going to finish your degree. You'll keep working on the dig, see what else you can find."

"The dig? But..." She stared off into the courtyard, clearly not seeing the building in front of her, her mind miles away.

"You'll be fine, don't worry about it. Now look, I gotta go."

He patted her on the shoulder as he took off, leaving her gaping on the wooden bench.

"HE MAY THINK he's getting away with this, but he's got another think coming, let me tell you."

Adam was pretty sure Nora wasn't talking to him or Sylvia, still hovering awkwardly near the door.

"Adam, we should go," Sylvia said under her voice, her hand on his arm.

"Sure, yeah. Just give me a minute, okay?" He stepped away from her touch, toward Nora. "Nora, everything all right?"

"Hm? What?" Nora turned to him as if seeing him for the first time, her hands still moving quickly over the surface of her desk, clearing away everything, even straightening the cord that ran from the brass lamp on the desk to the wall.

"You seem a little upset at Sean's news. Surely this happens all the time. Faculty come and go, right?"

"Oh, yes. Oh, yes, indeed." She nodded vigorously as she spoke. "But the nerve of that man, thinking he could just... Well." She looked back down at her desk, but there was truly nothing left there for her to tidy. She stood and straightened her skirt.

"Why is it so bad he wants to leave?" Adam pressed her.

"He can go wherever he wants. Better if he does, far away from here." She finally stopped fussing and looked at Adam. "But he won't be taking any of his grants with him. That's not how it works. Not around here."

"But surely if he is awarded a grant, he takes it to his university, no?" Sylvia asked, coming closer to Nora and Adam.

"No," Nora said firmly. "All of the grants I manage — Sean's, the grant that supports the exchange program with Legg University" — she nodded a recognition to Sylvia as she mentioned the exchange grant. "With any of these, the funds are given directly to the university."

"Right, but if the grant holder moves on, he or she takes the grant with them," Sylvia said. "I know that's how it works."

"Oh, no. Our Mr. Rourke must be under the same misimpression. No, the university is now the holder of the grant, the recipient of all funds. If he leaves, we'll have an opportunity to reapply. We'll be expected to, in fact. That's part of the agreement the faculty sign when they hand over their grants for me to administer."

A thought flashed through Adam's mind, then was gone just as fast. A memory, gone before it solidified. "Nora," he asked, "did Moira have any grants with the university?"

"Moira? She surely did. She was one of the highest ranking faculty, based on the funding she brought in."

CHAPTER THIRTY-FOUR

THE WIDE GLASS doors slid open as Isabel approached. She walked in, sidestepping a crowd of students surging out. She followed the airy hallway to the top of the stairs, where the space opened up in every direction. Arrows on the wall pointed straight ahead for experimental physics or chemistry, to the right for the biology faculty. Other signs directed her to turn left for the O'Flaherty Theatre. She suppressed a shudder and turned away, down the stairs that led to the student cafeteria.

The place kept up a steady stream of customers at this time of day, students running in for a snack, a lunch, or a main meal. She cast her glance around the small tables and green plastic chairs that filled all open spaces, the queues forming along the counters that offered quick, if not gourmet, service, the crowds that gathered near the entrances, as students came here to socialize as much as to eat.

Tracking down Conn O'Flaherty was never an easy job. The man had his hands in everything around the town, it seemed. Though she'd been surprised by the call from a garda that he'd been spotted here, at the university. Somehow, it was the last place she expected to see him.

And the student cafeteria was the last place she expected to see Liam Dempsey. She worked her way through the maze of tables toward the spot where Liam had for some reason stopped to chat with Adam Kaminski. An unlikely pair if she ever saw one.

They stood underneath one of the tall glass cut-outs that invited light into this underground eatery, a spot popular with all the cafeteria's customers on a sunny day like this one. As she got closer, she realized they were not having a friendly chat.

"When you asked me about Moira Walsh, I was considerate enough to offer you an honest response," Liam said. "The least you could do is treat me with the same courtesy."

"I'm not trying to be rude, Liam—"

"Professor Dempsey, if you don't mind. We" — he waved his hand back and forth between himself and Adam as if there might be some confusion as to who he was referring to — "are not friends."

Adam laughed out loud. "No, I can see that. It doesn't change the fact that your dislike for Moira is well known. Despite her clear success at her field. At bringing in grants."

Kaminski was up to his old tricks, goading witnesses into saying more than they otherwise might. Isabel still hadn't decided if she admired his technique or despised it.

"Her success?" Dempsey almost spit out the words. "That woman was a scoundrel. And a cheat. But the fact that I did not like her does not mean I killed her."

Dempsey spun around, in his anger spilling some of the coffee he held. He cursed, bending down to wipe away the offending drops from his tweed jacket. He passed Isabel with his head still lowered, not even registering her presence.

"That's quite a skill you have, Kaminski."

Adam recognized her and smiled. "Thank you. What skill?"

She shook her head and sighed. "I was being sarcastic, Adam. I meant your ability to drive everyone to anger."

"Ah." Adam dropped his smile. "Sometimes I get under people's skin. I know. But sometimes that's the best way to get them to admit the truth."

"The truth about what? You think Liam Dempsey strangled Moira?"

"Maybe." Adam shrugged. "Why not? And if nothing else, he can help me understand Moira a little bit better. That's what I was trying to do."

Isabel held her tongue for a moment, trying to figure out why Adam's words were angering her so. "You say you want to get to know Moira, but Moira is dead. The person we need to get to know is the man who killed her. And that's looking more and more like Conn O'Flaherty."

"Why, because he's a bully? Because he had an affair with her? Those aren't necessarily motives for murder."

"No? I've found a paper trail of his embezzlement." Isabel bit her tongue as soon as the words were out, but it was too late. She'd let her anger at Adam goad her into saying more than she intended. Perhaps that really was his skill. Or perhaps she was letting her fear that McManus knew exactly what Conn was up to affect her judgment.

"Embezzlement? Of what?"

She walked away from him as she answered, not caring if he could hear her answer. Hoping he couldn't. "He skimmed profits from the council funds, from the national lottery. It's money that's supposed to go to help disadvantaged youth. What a bastard."

She wove her way through the plastic chairs, back toward the main entrance, Adam keeping pace behind her.

Jennifer Hughes tripped lightly down the stairs into the cafeteria. With an unspoken agreement, they both stepped back, out of her line of sight, and watched as she approached the closest line for food and picked up a plastic tray.

"Now there's someone who knows more than she's

saying," Adam said.

"Jennifer? Now you're just floundering." She glared at him, hands on her hip, desperately trying to regain control. "What would Jennifer know about Moira? Isn't that what you're looking for, people who knew Moira?"

"Maybe she didn't know Moira well. But she's certainly keeping a secret. And I'd like to know what that is. So" — Adam looked around the room — "where's her partner in crime?"

Sean entered on cue, clattering down the stairs from the main building. He saw Jennifer immediately and trotted over to her.

"Thought I'd find you in here. You're supposed to be working on your paper."

"I know, I got hungry. So what? What do you need now?"

"Jennifer." Sean put his hand on her back, lowered his face toward her. Adam and Isabel stepped closer to better hear their conversation.

"Are you still mad?" he asked.

She almost laughed out her words. "That you're leaving? Yes, Sean, I am."

"Well, you should be happy. Turns out, I can't take my grant — or responsibility for the dig — with me. Looks like you'll be principal investigator on the grant now."

Jennifer slammed her tray down on the metal rack in front of them. Other students in line near her glanced at them and stepped away.

"You think that makes a difference? You think that makes me happy?"

"What? I don't get it."

"No, you don't. You really don't."

Jennifer left her tray where it was and ran out of the room, her footsteps echoing down the stairway.

"That was an odd reaction," Adam said quietly. "Interesting."

Isabel nodded, forgetting for a moment her anger at

Adam. "But not surprising."

She was about to say more, to point out Jennifer's obvious feelings for Sean, but she glanced at Adam and her anger returned. She bit her tongue. Adam Kaminski was the last person she wanted to talk to about love, particularly after so brutally exposing her own emotions the other day. She worked her mother's ring around and around her finger.

Sean picked up Jennifer's tray and carried it over to one of the tables. Eating the fruits of her labor, so to speak. What a bastard. Then again, who was she to judge? An image of the little girl pictured in the History Museum of Western Ireland exhibit came unbidden to mind. She pushed it away and turned to Adam. His eyes moved away as she looked at him, but he'd been looking at her hands.

"I need to track down Conn. You stay out of my way, right? Oh, for f—" Isabel cut herself off before she said anything worse and grabbed her phone. "Yes." She couldn't keep the anger out of her voice, but regretted it when she heard the voice on the other end.

CHAPTER THIRTY-FIVE

"DETECTIVE SUPERINTENDENT Sayers? This is Garda Jones." The voice on the phone was a young woman, nervous.

"Yes," Isabel said more calmly, trying to hide her irritation with the interruption. She needed to catch up with Conn, wherever he'd gone, and she didn't want to find herself chasing him all over the city.

"There's been an incident, Detective Superintendent. I was told to call you."

She glanced at Adam, who was watching her closely, and took two steps away from him. "What kind of incident?"

"Property damage. Over in Kilronan."

"Kilronan?" Isabel could picture the pretty little town at the main dock in Inis Mór. The tourist hub of the largest Aran island. "Why are you calling me?"

"A woman from the tourist board, Peig Browne. She said you'd want to know about this."

"Peig is there?"

"Not on the island, no. She's here, at the station. She came in looking for you, ma'am, but got me instead." Garda Jones' voice had been growing in confidence as she explained the situation to Isabel, and now she'd even reached a point of mock self-derision. Good for her.

"You're right to call me. Did Peig say anything more about why I'd be interested?"

"She thinks it's the same group, the group that's been protesting her offices."

"Wait, what kind of property damage are we taking about?"

"A boat, ma'am. One of those large, floating buses that brings the tourists out in droves, ma'am."

Isabel knew the boats. There weren't that many of them, despite the demand. She knew the owners of each of the companies that ran them. Whoever had just lost a boat had a tough season ahead of them, that was for sure.

"How'd they damage it? How bad is it?"

"It was burnt, ma'am. Set on fire. Overnight. Wasn't noticed until it was too late; it's burned beyond repair."

"Overnight? And it's just getting reported now?"

"No, ma'am, the local gardaí were on it early. It's just now that Ms. Browne came to us at Mill Street about it. And suggested you might be interested."

"Thank you, Garda Jones. You're right. I am interested."

Isabel slid her phone back into her purse and turned to see Adam staring at her. "How much of that did you overhear?"

"A boat was burned?"

Isabel nodded. "One of the boats that takes tourists out to the Aran Islands."

"Sure," Adam said. "I've seen the ads for those. Big draw around here, I imagine."

"Very big. And I need to get over there."

"You think this is the attack the eco group threatened? What did they call themselves, Warriors for Nature? But it's early."

She jogged up the stairs toward the light, Adam close on her heels. "This doesn't concern you."

"There's more to this you're not telling me." Adam's voice came from right behind her.

She stopped and found a perverse pleasure as he tripped slightly, pulling up short behind her. "This isn't just vandalism, this was a statement. An attack on the tourism industry as a whole." She continued up the stairs, pushing through a group of students as she moved quickly out onto the pavement in front of the building. "And I doubt very much this is the first time they've resorted to property damage."

"Wait, you think they're connected to the stolen necklace?" When Isabel ignored the question, Adam answered for himself. "So you think this is environmental protection gone crazy."

Isabel slowed for a moment. Stopped. She closed her eyes and pictured the largest of the islands, Inis Mór, quiet now but crowded with tourists in the busy summer season. She could see the narrow, winding roads, marked by low stone walls that ran throughout the island, defining not only roads but fields, paths, and homes. Even standing here, she could taste the island air, the scent of the sea, the sun on her face. From the rocky cliffs of Dun Aengus to the beaches of Kilmurvey to the strong but struggling town of Kilronan — there was a lot that needed protecting on Inis Mór. But not through violence. Never through violence.

"Moira was involved with something shady going on with the tourism council, I'm sure of it," she said aloud, opening her eyes.

"Maybe connected to the fraud with Conn's youth camp?"

"Maybe, maybe not. Peig's not talking about that. Conn's talking too much, about anything but the truth. Now I'm worried Conn might have a man on the inside..."

"Inside? You mean a garda?"

Isabel shook her head. "If this group is involved in some way, then I have to check it out. Look for any clues that could connect them to the theft. Or the murder." She shot Adam a murderous look. "Christ, I hope this isn't another waste of time."

ADAM WATCHED ISABEL race across the paved quad in front of the Arts/Science Building, her figure still visible as she cut behind one of the tall glass cubes that marked the location of the cafeteria below them. Maybe there was a connection between the eco-protestors and Moira Walsh. He could imagine the connection as well as Isabel could. If Moira was involved in shady dealings with Conn, who was using his influence with the tourism council to make a tidy profit — environment be damned — then, yeah, he could imagine one of those protestors confronting Moira.

Killing her, though? That was a different matter.

He toyed with the idea as he made his way back into the comfort of the cafeteria and grabbed a cup of coffee. Perhaps the killer hadn't intended to kill her. His emotions just got out of control. That happened.

Moira had received a note, a note that enticed her to leave the meeting, change her plans, and slip out to meet with her killer. What kind of invitation would an eco-protestor send her to get that kind of response?

It just didn't sit right with him. Plus, if this case was about eco-protestors and the environment, not about the ancient necklace or about Sean Rourke, then he was way off base.

He pulled out his smart phone, balanced the case on its side, and launched a video call. He loved free wifi.

Julia's face appeared on his screen, smiling at him. He felt his spirits rise. "Hey, Jules. How're things?"

"You calling to check in on me?" She laughed. "Pete said you were worried."

"Pete said that? He talks out his ass, don't listen to him."

"Hey." Pete's voice carried through to the Galway cafeteria, then his face appeared over Julia's shoulder. "What're you saying about me?"

"Oops." Adam grimaced. "I didn't think you'd hear. What, you taking a long lunch break?" He glanced at his watch. It would be an early lunch time in Philly. "I'm not calling to check in on you; I just wanted to talk."

"I hear you got caught up in a murder over there. Sylvia must love that."

He could hear the sarcasm in Julia's voice. She had a pretty good sense of Sylvia's estimation of his career.

"Actually, she asked me to be involved. The murder's hurting the success of her work over here, and she thought I could speed things up a bit, do a better job than the locals."

"Sylvia said that?" Julia asked, then gave him a sideways look. "How are things going between you two?"

"I don't know." He glanced down at his hands, resting loosely on his lap. "Something's off. I don't yet know for sure, but something's up. And don't say I told you so." He looked back at the screen. "I know you told me so."

"Adam, you know I love you. I just want you to keep your eyes open. Sometimes it's hard to face the truth."

"Look, that's not what I want to talk about, okay?"

"Okay…" Julia made a face toward someone off camera, presumably Pete. "So, you still doin' that mindfulness training?" Her face lit up as she asked, as if telling a great joke.

"I am, as a matter of fact."

Julia laughed out loud again, and he could even hear Pete laughing in the background.

"What the hell, guys. At least I'm trying, right?"

"Sure, sure." Pete's disembodied voice floated over.

"I guess," Julia said. "I mean, it's great you're trying to be more calm about things. More zen. It just seems like there are other ways you could do that — like cutting out the stress. You know, for starters."

"Sylvia thinks this is helping. And if it makes her happy, then I want to do it. And you know, I really do think it's helping."

"Are you being sarcastic?"

"No, it really does help." He closed his eyes, took a

deep breath in, then let it out. He opened his eyes. "See, I'm not annoyed with you anymore."

"Ha ha ha. All right, mister calm guy, tell me about Galway, then."

"It's beautiful here, Jules. You should come out sometime, see it for yourself." He described for her the beauty of the historic buildings, the bustle of the busy downtown, the young international visitors that seemed to be drawn to the city. He described the peacefulness and dignity of the university campus. And he described the way he'd found Moira's body, searching for the campus and finding death instead.

"I'm so sorry that happened to you," Julia said quietly. "What a shock. Even for a cop."

Adam nodded. "It's not right. Not for me, I mean — for Moira. I know, she wasn't perfect."

Julia laughed through her nose. "Please, who is?"

Adam smiled his agreement. "She was a strong woman, from what I've heard. Strong and smart." He ducked his head as he admitted, "And possibly dishonest."

"Dishonest how?"

"She made no secret about the fact that her interpretation of the numbers was up for sale."

Julia nodded, glanced off-camera again. "Hold on a minute." She stood and he could hear her talking away from the phone, but couldn't understand what she was saying. When she came back on the screen, she said, "So tell me about Isabel."

"Isabel? Is that you asking, or Pete?"

Julia made a face. "Why would Pete ask you about another woman, huh? I'm just curious, you haven't said much about her."

Adam shrugged. "Another strong woman, but with her own problems."

"Like what?"

He shook his head. "I don't want to talk about it. That's her business and I'm staying out of it. Suffice to say she's got issues, but she's a good detective. I have faith in her."

"I hope you're right. Is she off investigating right now?"

"Maybe. Or off chasing a false lead. But isn't that always the way?"

He heard a noise that was probably Pete, probably some type of agreement, knowing Pete. "What'd he say?" Adam asked.

"Nothing." Julia made a face toward Pete and turned back to Adam. "So what are you going to do about Sylvia?"

"I don't know. We need to talk, I guess. Clear things up. I'm probably imagining the problems. I bet she's just focused on her work."

"Uh-huh. 'Cause she's got such a good track record."

"Thanks, sis. That'll do for now." His voice was stern as he spoke, not wanting the memories of Sylvia's betrayal last fall to come back to his mind, not able to keep them away. "She keeps me grounded, Jules, realistic. She's good for me."

"What's wrong with being a dreamer? I love the way you can lose yourself in your work, or in a history book. Or even in your weird research into our family." She grinned as she spoke. "You're a good guy, Adam, don't let Sylvia take that away from you."

He took another breath. "I won't. But I still want her in my future. Hey, it really was good to see you. I miss you guys, both of you."

"You'll be home soon enough. What's your next step today?"

"I'm not sure." He glanced around the room, now emptying of students. He recognized Garret near the desserts, his bandaged hands making him hard to miss. "Maybe go visit the scene again. See if anything new strikes me. Talk to more of the suspects."

He kept his eyes on Garret as he said his goodbyes to Julia and Pete and dropped his phone into his pocket.

Garret struggled to balance a tray on one bandaged hand while shifting a plate of food onto it with the other. He somehow managed, carrying the tray to a table.

Adam walked over. "Need any help there?"

Garret looked at him with suspicion. "I was just going to go back for a tea."

"I got it."

Adam returned with two cups. The tea he placed in front of Garret, the coffee he held onto as he took a seat. "How're you managing?"

Garret shrugged. "It's not easy. But I get these off tomorrow, I hope."

"Bad burn, huh. How'd you do it?"

Garret kept his focus on the spoon he was ineffectually holding between his hands. He could manage to dig out only small pieces of steak pie at a time. A slow process. He didn't answer Adam's question. Didn't even look at him.

Adam took a sip of coffee, then said, "It's kinda suspicious you not wanting to say how you hurt yourself."

Garret finally looked at him. "It was nothing. Really."

"But keeping it secret makes it look like something. First you spy on me, now this."

"I told you, that wasn't me." Garret shrugged and returned his attention to his tiny morsels of food. "It's no big deal. I was just messing about with some friends. Look." He dropped his spoon. "I didn't mean to spy on you. I overheard you talking, then when you saw me, I got scared. Ran. And this?" He lifted both hands. "I shouldn't'a been in the lab, see? I don't want to talk about it because I don't want Sean to know what I was doing. That simple. I got a class in thirty minutes, and it'll take me that long to get through this. Thanks for the tea."

Adam dipped his head in recognition of the dismissal and left Garret to his tea and pie. For now. He was hiding something and Adam needed to find out what.

CHAPTER THIRTY-SIX

THE BREEZE PICKED UP, shallow waves running toward the rocky beach and slapping against the concrete pier that protected the dock at Kilronan. Isabel turned to face the wind, her eyes narrowed against it, her hair blowing back off her face.

Peig sheltered next to her, wrapping her sweater more firmly around herself, tucking her hair behind her ears in a futile gesture. "It's just terrible," she said. "I know he was insured, but even so."

Isabel thought about the owner of the boat. An honest man trying to make an honest living. A man who'd been making a quite good living, if she were fair. Until now. Until his livelihood had been attacked.

"He's got two other boats," she said aloud. "He'll make do with what he has. 'Til he's got a chance to replace this one."

The boat in question still sat next to the dock, nothing more than a burnt shell now.

"It's not right, though, is it? This group, these… Warriors for Nature. They shouldn't be able to get away with this."

"They won't," Isabel assured her friend. "This is vandalism, property damage true and sure. They'll pay for this."

The island of Inis Mór rose behind them, a paved road following the slight rise that led to the first main intersection on the island, a triangle of road and grass bordered by restaurants, bars, and stores that sold the famous Aran sweaters. The people who lived on this island relied on tourism, sure enough. They might hate it at times. Resent the visitors who swarmed over the islands in the warm months, cutting tracks across fields, posing for photos in front of private homes, leaving a trail of litter in their wake. But the industries that used to support the local population — farming, fishing, knitting, and basket making — no longer existed in a form sufficient to support them all.

"I love this island, and the others, as much as anyone," Peig said, turning her head to let her eyes run over the rise behind them. "That's part of why I do what I do, d'you see?"

"I know how important this is to you."

Isabel stared at the gutted boat and thought about a man with two burnt hands. The timing was off. But he could've been practicing, a trial run that went wrong.

"Could Garret be connected with the Warriors for Nature?" she asked Peig. "Have you ever seen him with that group, or anyone else you recognized?"

"Garret?" Peig sounded surprised. "I don't think so. But then, maybe..." She furrowed her brow as she tried to remember, tried to answer Isabel's question.

"It makes sense, doesn't it? Fits with everything we know about him."

"He certainly could've stolen the necklace," Peig agreed.

"But could he have killed Moira?"

Both women remained silent, unable to answer that question.

"He takes his work seriously," Peig finally said. "The archaeology, you know."

"Oh, yeah?" Isabel turned to face her friend.

"He takes it more seriously than the other one — Jennifer? I suspect Jennifer has a quite different motive for staying so closely involved in Sean Rourke's work."

Isabel grinned. "You picked up on that, too, huh? Kind of obvious."

"Oh, yes. She does enjoy it, don't get me wrong. She likes the archaeology, but it's more fun for her. Garret seems to care more about the ethical implications, talking about what it means for Ireland and Irish history."

Isabel couldn't help but show her surprise. "I had no idea you knew them so well, Peig."

Peig shrugged. "It's a small town, Galway is. Word gets around. I've been working closely with Sean, after all. He says things. I see things." She kept her eyes on the island as she spoke, and may not have noticed Isabel's skepticism.

How could Peig know all this? Simply from spending time with Sean on a tourism marketing campaign?

Isabel was about to voice her doubts when Peig shouted and pointed. "There!"

Isabel followed her gesture and saw a man leaving the bar behind the Celtic cross that marked the center of the triangle. "You recognize him?"

"Oh, yes, he's always about with that group. Protesting in front of the tourist center."

"Stay here."

Isabel jogged lightly up the slight incline, closing the gap between herself and her suspect, who rambled onward in a zigzag motion, his face down, gaze on the road below him, his dreadlocked hair falling into his eyes. As she got closer, she recognized him. He'd been arrested a few times in Galway. Nothing serious, nothing that put him in jail for more than a night or two.

"Hiya, Dara," she called out as she jogged up behind him and slowed to a walk.

He kept shambling forward, but turned his head to look at her, the expression in his eyes changing from apathy to confusion to fear.

"Aw, fuck."

Isabel was shocked by the speed with which he took

off. She watched him run for a second, amused at the energy he had to put into it, then she picked up her pace.

She let him run for a while. It was going to take more out of him than out of her, which would give her even more advantage once she caught up to him. He started straight up the hill out of town, but she could see him struggling against the incline. He made a sudden left, ducking around a hedge and cutting across a gravel path, between two old stone houses and out into a field beyond.

Once clear of the main road, he picked up his pace again, turning down paths Isabel wouldn't have noticed if she hadn't been chasing him, trying to take advantage of his knowledge of the land and built environment. He jumped over a low stone wall, dodged an innocent cow, and headed across an open field, a decrepit barn visible in the distance.

Isabel caught up to him just as he turned the corner of the old barn. She grabbed him by the shoulder and flipped him around, his back against the old stone, her right arm across his neck, her left hand flat on the warm stone next to his head.

"Why're you running, Dara?"

He only panted in return, his breath coming in great, rasping gulps. He didn't even struggle to break free, for which Isabel was glad. He might be high, but he was still stronger than her, and she wouldn't have wanted to use force to take him down.

"You burned that boat?" She put her face close to his as she asked. "You set it on fire?"

Dara shook his head.

Isabel took a step back, turned him around, and bent both his arms behind his back, pulling out the plastic cuffs she kept tucked into her belt. She marched him back the way they had come.

"It's not just vandalism this time, you know? If you know something about the death of Moira Walsh, you better talk now."

"Moira who?" Dara tried to turn, but Isabel tightened her grip on him. "What're you sayin'?"

"Did the Warriors for Nature think they could stop that dig? Prevent it from becoming the next big attraction in Galway?"

"You're crazy, for sure. I don't know what you're going on about." Dara spoke through gritted teeth. "If you got something on me, I'll listen. But I ain't involved in no dig. And I bloody well ain't involved in no death."

"Innocent, are you?" Isabel asked sweetly. "We'll see about that."

CHAPTER THIRTY-SEVEN

"I CAN'T. I'VE GOT nothing, no reason." Isabel tried, but failed, to keep the shock and disgust out of her voice.

"He ran from you, didn't he? He's clearly involved in something." McManus crossed his arms in front of him and leaned back in his leather chair as if discussing the weather instead of fixing up a potentially innocent man on a charge of murder. He looked at her expectantly.

"Sir. I don't know that he killed Moira Walsh. He was involved" — she held up a hand to forestall whatever idiocy he was going to come out with next — "in the arson, of that I'm sure. He was seen in the area and the evidence, once we get the analysis, will back that up."

"So what's the problem then?"

She threw up her hands and looked around his office, twice the size of hers, seeking some way to get this man to understand what she'd just told him: that there was no evidence linking Dara to Moira's murder, that he had an alibi for the time Moira was killed.

Framed photos dotted the walls, images of McManus paired with a variety of city and county leaders, both men smiling comfortably in each. A bookshelf displayed sporting trophies, a photograph of his family, an award from the city council. A photo of that award being handed to him by Conn O'Flaherty.

"He can't have been in two places at once. If he was

at the Banner's Dig having a few pints with friends, then he wasn't killing Moira." Isabel tried to sound patient. Tried to sound respectful.

McManus leaned over his desk, and the look he gave her made it clear she had not succeeded. "He has friends, Detective Superintendent. We already knew that. Friends who would commit arson with him." He jabbed his finger into the top of his desk as he spoke, driving home each point. "Friends who would lie for him. I'm not an eejit, got that?"

"No, sir, of course not." Isabel looked down at her hands. How had it come to this? She'd always had respect for McManus, even when he drove her crazy with his objections to how things were run in Dublin. He was the sort of chief whose door was always open.

She glanced now through the windows that broke up one wall of his office, windows that opened up onto the hall and the common workspace beyond. He never closed the blinds on that window. He claimed he always wanted to be visible. To be accessible to the officers who worked for him. He was that kind of leader.

So why was she so sure he was hiding something now?

"Look, sir. Why are you so sure Dara's involved in the murder? Murder's a long way from a little vandalism in the name of preserving the environment."

"A little vandalism?" McManus' voice rose as he did, walking around his desk toward her. "Tell that to Pauric Burke, whose boat was burned to a crisp. He's out more than a boat now, isn't he? He's out his livelihood. He has a family to care for, you know? And who knows how many people could have been hurt by that stupid act."

"Christ, I'm sorry." Isabel shut her eyes. "You're right. I apologize, that was a stupid thing to say."

McManus nodded. He stopped, put his hands in his pockets, and leaned back against his desk. Isabel glanced out the windows again and saw that their conversation had attracted some attention. Perhaps closing those blinds occasionally would be a good thing.

"It's been a long day, Detective Superintendent. For all of us." His voice had lowered.

She nodded. "I'll keep looking, see what I can find."

"Good," McManus grunted out the word. "Find a connection between this group, the Warriors for Nature, and the vandalism out at that archaeological dig. Must be a connection there."

Isabel nodded and left his office while he was still calm. He was right, of course. Dara was involved in some pretty bad things. He was a criminal. But it still bugged her. Why was McManus so intent on pinning the murder on him? Was he that sure Dara was a murderer, or was he trying to protect someone else?

LIGHTS FROM THE HOUSES that lined the Long Walk reflected off the water in shifting patterns, brightening the darkness already cut by the colorful glow from the city itself. Sitting here, on the front step of his B&B, Adam could see across the basin to the Claddagh, once an impoverished suburb of the city, now a popular tourist destination connecting the downtown to the Salthill beaches and resorts.

Sylvia wasn't home yet. He didn't really know when to expect her. Her meetings ended at six, but who knew where she would go from there. Hopefully she'd call.

The tide was in, the river coming in high under the bridge, filling the basin by the Claddagh Quay, lifting the small fishing boats that lined the curve of the waterway before it emptied out into Galway Bay.

A young couple passed him, walking arm in arm. Even in the chill of the March evening, the Long Walk still offered a romantic view, a little privacy. He watched them walk, envious of their calm, their peacefulness. Their trust.

He checked his watch, glanced up and down the

street. No sign of Sylvia. He took a breath, bit down on his lower lip, and waited.

He'd become involved in this investigation at Sylvia's request. It was her desire that he work with Isabel, find the real killer. To prevent any further damage to her ongoing work, she said. But did she really want him here?

Now that he was involved, he couldn't just drop it. He was beginning to get a handle on Moira, the elusive statistician who worked magic with numbers.

From everything he'd heard, she was rough around the edges, sharp with her words, and quick with her judgment. She didn't refrain from sharing her opinions, regardless of the impact they could have.

Sean was in love with her. He had some idea that she was good for his future. But how? He must have been applying for other jobs for several months; academic jobs weren't offered overnight. So if he already knew he was leaving Galway, how did he think Moira could help him? And Conn put him in the vicinity of the crime.

Conn wasn't in love with her. Conn wasn't in love with anybody but himself. But he did enjoy her company, that much was clear. He seemed a better match for her, two people who really only cared for themselves. Could this have been a fight over embezzled funds? An argument gone far, far wrong? Conn was a bully and Adam could imagine him getting a little too physical in his demands. And Conn had admitted being in the area at the time of the murder.

Nora didn't like Moira, didn't respect her or her ways. But was that enough to kill someone? It seemed unlikely. Almost as unlikely as little, round Nora Kane having the physical strength to strangle Moira Walsh.

The others at the university — Liam, Jennifer, Garret — hardly seemed to have been involved with Moira. Not enough to want her dead, at least. Peig Browne had more contact with her, particularly given her vement with Conn. He should do some more digging there, see what interaction Moira and Peig had had lately.

Another couple passed, moving in the opposite direction, back toward the water, following the walk around to the docks. Adam looked up and followed their progression. They passed a lone figure, standing just where the road curved out of view. Something about the still figure caught Adam's attention, though he wasn't sure what.

The solitary man moved, and Adam recognized Conn O'Flaherty. His heft, his shape, his bald head. Conn was staring out into the water. As Adam considered getting up and walking over to him, another figure approached. Adam didn't recognize him, though it did appear to be a man.

The two men stood close together. Whatever they said to each other didn't carry to Adam's location. From this distance they were one big dark mound. Then the mound shifted. Conn put a hand in his pocket and pulled it out. Did the other man just hand him something? Adam couldn't be sure.

It was a brief encounter, lasting no more than a few minutes. The other man left the way he had come, around the curve toward the docks. Conn waited a moment longer, then followed in the same direction, moving away from Adam rather than passing in front of him. He wouldn't know Adam had witnessed the exchange. Adam had to find out who that other man was and why Conn was meeting with shady characters in dark corners of Galway.

SHE CAME TO SEAN in his dreams again that night. The warrior Celtic queen, dark hair heavy around her face and shoulders, caressing him as she leaned over him.

He tried to stand, face her, but she pressed herself against him. Once again, he caught the peaty scent of the bogs clinging to her hair, her skin, her clothes.

He put a hand out to touch her and she faded into mist, only to reappear on his other side. He turned, trying to open his eyes, trying to speak, to ask her who she was and what she wanted.

Did she want to be left in peace? Had he unearthed a ghost?

Sean tossed and turned in his bed, then sat up straight, wide awake now. Dark shapes loomed from the corners of the room. He rubbed his eyes, took a few breaths, then looked again, now recognizing the familiar furnishings.

He lay back down on his bed, trying to retrieve the dream, trying to capture the sensation of her presence. She had been wearing the necklace, he remembered that. But she'd been angry. With him? With someone else?

Had he really found a significant site?

He laughed under his breath. He knew the truth. But at least he was getting away, moving to a new job. The university could have the damn grant and the dig that came with it. It wasn't his problem any more.

He rolled over to his side, punching the pillows, trying to shake the feeling of dread rising in him.

Maybe Jennifer really would find something. She was a talented archaeologist. Maybe he'd missed something and she would find it. He closed his eyes and the warrior queen was in front of him immediately.

She was definitely angry. Her eyes flashed and she raised a sword aloft, as if to bring it down on his head.

He gasped and sat up straight in bed. Alone again.

Maybe Jennifer would come over if he called her. Company would help. Help get him out of his own head. Away from the stress of the job.

Why was he stressed? He was leaving. He'd got out. He had a new job. It wasn't his problem anymore. He had no shame, no reason to feel guilty.

He thought of the quote Liam Dempsey had stuck to the bulletin board. "Better the trouble that follows death than the trouble that follows shame."

Would he better off if he had died? No, he had nothing to be ashamed of.

He lay back down in bed, but didn't sleep, his eyes wide open as the red flashing numbers on the clock slowly turned their way toward morning.

CHAPTER THIRTY-EIGHT

"I'VE SAID EVERYTHING. Over and over." Peig dropped her head dramatically onto her desk, her brown curls spilling out around her, then looked back up at Adam with a wicked gleam in her eye. "I've spoken more about Moira Walsh since she was killed than I ever thought I had to say about her when she was alive."

"I know it can be difficult," Adam said. "But you never know what will help point to whoever killed her. Sometimes the smallest detail..."

"Right, right, of course." Peig stared across the room, either searching her memory or trying to invent a memory.

Noises from tourists in the center seeped through the closed door. A child crying, complaining of being tired. A couple who must have been standing quite near the door discussing which restaurant to choose for that evening.

"Did Moira like working with Conn?" Adam finally asked. "Did she seem to get along with him?"

"Oh, yes." Peig's mouth worked its way into a straight line. "Those two were as alike as two peas in a pod. Both looking for the same thing, I suspect."

"And what was that?"

"Well, that's the kicker. I never could figure it out." Peig looked genuinely confused. "It wasn't money. That I could understand."

"How do you know she wasn't interested in money?"

"No, no, please don't misunderstand. She was very interested in money. But I don't believe that's what drove her. She'd get consulting jobs from a variety of sources. Some she'd take, some she wouldn't. And I couldn't figure out the logic of it." The confusion cleared from Peig's face as she threw her hands in the air. "But not really my concern, is it?"

"Do you think she had a special interest in the necklace Sean found? Or in his dig?"

Peig shrugged exaggeratedly. "I hadn't noticed that, no. Though I did get the impression she had a special interest in Sean, if you know what I mean."

Sean chose that moment to burst into the office, a rush of noises from the center following him in. He didn't bother to close the door behind him, just started blurting out garbled words.

"Torn up... All of it... It's a mess. A complete disaster."

As if exhausted by his own outburst, he collapsed into an empty chair.

Peig hurried to close the door, closing out the curious looks from visitors.

"What are you talking about? What's going on?" Adam asked.

Sean looked at Adam as if seeing him for the first time. "You. You brought all this on us. You must have. None of this happened until you came here."

"We're back to this again, are we?" Adam leaned back in his chair, straightening his jacket around him as he did so.

"Talk to me, Sean." Peig kneeled in front of him, gently guiding his face toward her with her hand. "Calm down and tell me what's wrong."

Sean nodded and gulped a few breaths of air. "It's the dig. Something... someone..."

"Yes?"

He shook his head, closed his eyes. He kept his eyes

closed as he answered, as if seeing the scene he was describing. "I got a call from the Garda this morning and went down there. It's all dug up, torn up. The tarps are gone. The trenches exposed, dug up like someone took a spade to them. It's ruined. A disaster."

Adam leaned forward. "First the necklace, now this. What's the connection to Moira Walsh?"

"What? Moira?" Sean glared at Adam. "There is no connection to Moira. This is about the dig." He shifted in his chair as he spoke to reach into a pocket. "They left this behind."

He moved his arm as if he was about to toss whatever was in his pocket onto Peig's desk, then thought better of it and leaned forward, gently placing the tissue-wrapped package on the desk's surface.

"Whoever did this left that at the dig."

Adam used a pencil to push away the tissues, to expose what Sean had found.

The gold was covered with dirt, tiny pebbles caught between the strands. Even the precious stones were smudged and darkened. But the beauty of the necklace nevertheless jumped out from its white tissue wrapping.

"That's the necklace," Adam said, thinking it through as he spoke. "Whoever vandalized the dig also stole the necklace."

"But then why give it back?" Peig asked. "That doesn't make any sense."

Adam looked at her. "Could they have been returning it to where it belonged?"

"You're thinking of my eco group, aren't you?"

"They said they'd do whatever it took to keep the tourists out. Maybe they want the dig closed up, the necklace returned to history."

Peig shook her head. "That doesn't make sense. If they're Irish, they want us to learn more about Irish history, not less."

Sean replied in a soft voice, "They may not like what I have to teach them."

CHAPTER THIRTY-NINE

"ARE YOU CRAZY? We need to go now." Jennifer's voice held an edge of disbelief that bordered on fury.

Sean sighed heavily and raised his eyes from the stainless steel tray in front of him. "You need to wait. Both of you." He looked back and forth between Jennifer and Garret to make his point. "Don't touch anything, don't even go out there until I tell you to, got it?"

"And when will that be?" Garret asked, more calmly than Jennifer was probably capable of at that point.

"I'll let you know."

Isabel watched the exchange from the doorway, trying not to cough as the smell of chemicals hit her. None of them had heard her approach the lab in the back of the museum. She figured she'd use the opportunity to learn something. But after Jennifer's outburst, she seemed to want to bite back the rest of her words.

Jennifer took a few deep, loud breaths, worked her face into an angry knot, then stalked up and down the room. On her way back to the bench where Sean worked, she noticed Isabel.

"What are you doing here?"

"I heard the necklace was retrieved. I wanted to see for myself." Isabel leaned over the bench where Sean worked, studiously ignoring her. "What're you doing?"

"He's cleaning it," Garret answered when Sean didn't.

"You can do that here? Is it damaged?" Isabel asked.

Sean finally dropped the small brush he'd been applying to the artifact and looked up at Isabel. "Of course I can do it here. This is what we do. Is there something in particular you need, Detective Superintendent?"

Isabel raised her eyebrows. "I didn't think I'd be in the way. A valuable stolen item has been found. But we still need to figure out who took it."

Sean shrugged. "Amazingly, it's no worse for wear."

Isabel leaned closer. "Looks dirty."

"And that's all it is." Sean stood, twisting his hands together. "It was surprisingly well cared for by whoever took it. It's just got some dirt on it."

"Fingerprints?"

Sean shook his head. "Your team was in here already, that's the first thing they looked for — under my very careful watch," he added, his voice stern. "If you want to look at anything else on it, you'll have to wait until it's back in its case and look through the security glass."

"New and improved glass," Jennifer added, nodding. "But I still don't understand—"

"Drop it." Sean practically bit the words off. "You don't go back there until I tell you."

"Is there something you're worried about at the dig site?" Isabel asked. "We've got gardaí protecting it now. No one else can get to it."

"See?" Sean raised his hands. "It's being protected. We need to finish our work here. Finish our plans for the summer as we originally intended."

"We can't wait till the summer, Sean." Even Garret was letting his frustration show through. "You said the site had been exposed. We can't leave it like that."

"I did re-cover the trenches, of course. And yes, we will need to speed up our timeline a bit, you're correct. But that does not mean we go running off half-cocked like a bunch of knee-jerk imbeciles."

"So you'll stay to work on our original plan, then?

This summer?" If Jennifer was trying to keep the hope out of her voice, she failed.

"No," Sean answered through gritted teeth. "I am not. This dig is no longer my concern. I'm leaving as soon as the semester ends. If not sooner."

"Excuse me." A light cough from the doorway caused them all to spin around. "Sorry to interrupt."

"Michal?" Isabel stepped toward her brother. "What are you doing here?"

"I came to see this exhibit you've been talking about. Look at the great necklace. Is that so surprising?"

"But it's not back in its exhibit yet. In fact, we only just got it back."

"Back? From where?"

"Oh, Michal, you're hopeless. You don't read the news at all, do you? The necklace was stolen."

"But it's back now, safe and sound," Sean interjected, giving Isabel an odd look. "It will be on display again soon enough. Probably later this week."

"Michal" —Isabel put her arm around her brother, turning him back through the door and away from the others in the room — "Why did you come?"

He shrugged again. "Like I said, I wanted to see the exhibit." He looked at her. "Are you okay then?"

She shook her head. "I'm fine. You know I am. But I'm glad you're here."

"I heard you had a difficult time at the museum. I'm sorry," he added quickly as she felt her face burn, "but it's a small place, people recognized you."

"I suppose they would, wouldn't they?" She saw again the image of the girl in the photograph, the image that had finally broken through her defenses. The image that had driven her to see her own daughter. She smiled and played with her ring. Adam Kaminski even now was digging into his past, trying to find the truth. Why had she spent so many years running away from hers?

Aloud, she said, "I'm sorry you came all this way to see an exhibit that isn't available. Will you at least stay for dinner? I'd like to talk to you about something."

"Ah, sorry. I'm meeting some colleagues. That was the other reason I came, you see, I've arranged to do a bit of research in the library here."

"Of course you have. That's grand. I'm glad to hear it." Isabel made sure her expression reflected the satisfaction of her words. "I'll see you around then, right?"

She left the room before he could read the disappointment on her face.

CHAPTER FORTY

THE OLD MAN WAITED at the bar, the inevitable pint of Guinness in front of him. He looked like he'd been there for hours, but it couldn't have been more than thirty minutes, since he'd only decided that day to come to Galway. At least, that's what he'd said on the phone when he called Adam that morning.

The message was short and to the point. Konrad Rupiewicz had found references to Adam's great-grandfather in his father's papers. He was coming to Galway and Adam would want to meet with him. Would want to see these for himself.

"Konrad. Good to see you again," Adam said as he slid onto the barstool next to him. He gestured to the bartender, then ordered a whiskey. It was far too early. And he was far beyond caring. Sylvia hadn't come home last night. He needed a drink.

"You won't be thinking that once you see what I've brought you."

Konrad pulled a rubber-banded mess of papers out of his pocket. A thick, leather-bound diary stuffed with odds and ends of papers, tickets, handwritten notes.

"What's this?"

"That's Da's diary. And notes."

Adam took the bundle carefully, slowly removing the rubber band while holding the whole mess together. Even the binding of the diary seemed weak, ready to burst at the seams.

"The part you want is there, with the red ribbon."

Adam turned to a page marked with a thin, torn piece of red fabric. A ribbon as old as the book itself. He opened the book carefully, focusing on the narrow, almost illegible scrawl before him. He ran his eyes up and down both pages, trying to make sense of the few Polish words he recognized, and then his great-grandfather's name jumped out at him.

He squinted at the pale ink, worn down over the years. "Does this refer to a debt?"

Konrad nodded. "A debt to the town, from what I can tell."

"I don't understand." Adam shook his head as he gave up trying to decipher more of the text.

"It's a sort of shorthand, I suppose. Not everything is spelled out."

"No—" Adam looked at Konrad. "I mean I don't understand what he's saying. That my great-grandfather skipped out of town to avoid paying a debt?"

Konrad shrugged, turned back to his pint. "There are documents, tickets." He ran a gnarled finger through the notes tucked into the back of the diary and Adam followed the trail of his gray finger. When Konrad paused over one item, Adam slid it out and turned it over.

"It's a train ticket stub. What does it have to do with my great-grandfather?"

"Can't you read that?"

The printing on the ticket was even more worn than the notes in the diary. Only every third letter or so was visible, and he had to guess at the words based on the few clues he had.

"You think this says Marek Kaminski. But I don't see that."

He passed the ticket stub back to Konrad, who shrugged again and tucked it back into the diary. "It's from Poznan. Isn't that where your great-grandfather was from?"

"That doesn't prove anything." Adam felt his anger rising and tried to call on one of the lessons from his mindfulness training. He couldn't. All he could see were random notes, random documents that had nothing to do with his great-grandfather, but for some reason Konrad was interpreting them in the worst possible way. "Why are you showing me this? What do you think this means?"

"My father, he was not a nice man," Konrad muttered. "These notes, they were not good to read. I wish I had never found it." He downed the rest of his beer, slamming the pint glass back on the bar.

"What else did you see about my great-grandfather?"

"My father seemed to like him. Perhaps they had much in common." He looked at Adam. "Let this go. This is ancient history. This is not about you."

"What else does it say in that diary?" Adam pressed.

Konrad looked back at the bar. "As I said, my father was not a nice man. And he was a friend to your great-grandfather. They were in the party together."

"The Nazi party? I don't believe that."

"Believe what you will. It's in his notes."

"Let me take this. I want to spend more time reading it, deciphering it. To see what it really means."

"No." Konrad shook his head. "I came here because I thought this was a piece of history. There is a man here, at the university, who studies this history. But now… now that I have read it…" He shook his head again. "No. This must be destroyed. This is not a good part of history."

"What?" Adam asked, incredulous. "You can't destroy this. It's too important."

"Detective Kaminski, according to my father's notes, your great-grandfather was a Nazi, a coward, and a cheat. Is that what you want the history books to say?"

Adam turned to stare at his whiskey, sitting untouched on the bar in front of him. His hand shook as he reached for it, downed it in one gulp.

"That's not the truth. I know it's not."

Konrad raised his hands in a question, then nodded when the barman gave him a quizzical look. "I am surprised, myself. This is not what I remembered at all. I am sorry that I misled you."

"It doesn't make sense. Why would your memory of what your father said be so different from what's written here?"

The two men sat in silence, Adam considering the question, trying to make sense of the discrepancies between what Konrad had remembered from his childhood and the notes in this book.

"Perhaps my father told me the past the way he wanted it to be," Konrad finally said as a second Guinness appeared before him. "Perhaps he wanted me to believe that. To know him as he was at the end of his life. Not as he was during that time… during the war." Konrad let his head hang over his beer. "It was a very bad time. You know that."

"What else is in that diary?" Adam asked again.

"I don't want to tell you." Konrad took a long drink. "My father was not a nice man," he repeated.

"So what will you do?"

"I'm going to burn it. This needs to end. This bitter, evil history needs to end."

"That's a terrible loss to history. To the truth."

"Is this the truth?" He shrugged. "I don't know what is true or not." He took a deep breath, leaned more heavily on the bar. "I feel older now than I did yesterday. I don't believe I'll see eighty. This must end with me."

"But perhaps this person at the university, he could do more research. Cross-reference the notes in this diary with other evidence—"

Konrad hadn't heard him or perhaps he didn't care. He simply started talking, ignoring Adam's ideas. "I was so sure, you know. About what my father had said to me. Until I read this."

"Memory can be tricky. I know."

"That's true. Perhaps even my father's memory. Maybe he really did remember things differently."

"Or maybe he just wanted to."

A CHATTERING GROUP of young women came toward him from the river, following the path toward the university campus. Adam headed the opposite direction, the campus to his back, passing the old lime kiln on his right.

He had a moment alone, then another pair of young people came towards him, a solitary figure not far behind them.

This path was far from deserted, at least not in the middle of the day. Why would someone choose this location to commit any crime, let alone murder? Even if the original intention was mugging, as Isabel seemed to think, it still didn't offer much privacy.

On the other hand, the killer succeeded. There were no witnesses. Or at least, none willing to come forward. If Adam was trying to identify suspects who could intimidate potential witnesses, Conn O'Flaherty was the first person to come to mind. He'd oh-so-helpfully told Isabel about seeing Sean Rourke near the cathedral that night. But not only did that put Sean in the vicinity of the crime, it also put Conn there.

"Detective Kaminski."

He'd been standing on the edge of the path, looking out at the river and the Salmon Weir Bridge, when David called out to him. Adam had no interest in talking to this colleague of Sylvia's. He'd seen the way David looked at her.

He simply nodded and waved, hoping David would keep going. No such luck.

"Detective Kaminski. Adam. I was wondering if I'd run into you."

"Were you looking for me?"

"Um, no, not exactly. But thinking about talking to you."

Adam took a deep breath, accepted the fact that he was going to have to chat with this guy, no matter how annoying he was, and turned away from the river to face him.

"How are your plans coming?"

David shrugged, wagged his head from side to side. "Not great, really. I think Sylvia told you. Moira's murder put a bit of a chill on the excitement for the event. Now the added potential threat from the eco-protestors. People are backing out."

Adam tried to look interested. It wasn't easy. "You can still hit them up for donations, though, right? Even if they don't come?"

"Sure, sure. Yeah. It's just better odds if you get them in person. With a little bit to drink. Tend to get better figures, if you know what I mean."

"I understand. Sylvia asked me to help, and I'm doing what I can. Trying to learn more about the victim, the people who knew her." He tried to give David an encouraging look. "So if there's anything you know, I'd love to hear it."

"About the murder?" David took a step back, both hands held out in front of him. "Oh, no, not about that."

"Then what?" Adam couldn't keep the impatience out of his voice, and David reacted with irritation.

"I'm sorry if talking to me is such a burden. I felt I needed to see you. To tell you the truth. Man to man."

Adam felt his hackles rise. He knew his face was turning red. "Tell me the truth about what?"

"Sylvia. Your fiancée?"

"I know who she is," Adam said through gritted teeth.

"Do you? I think you don't. And you should."

Adam took a step toward the other man, his fists clenched. "Did you come find me to insult Sylvia? To insult me?"

"I'm not here to insult anyone. Call it what you will. I'm not comfortable with what's going on, and if Sylvia won't tell you, then I will."

It took a moment for Adam to speak. His rage blurred the edges of his vision. All he could see was the man in front of him as the river, the gravel path, the other pedestrians all faded from view. He was way beyond mindfulness.

"What's going on, David?"

"It's just... I saw you looking at Sylvia and me. And... well, you seem like a decent guy." He lifted his chin, as if proud of himself. "Before you came out here, Sylvia and I. Well, we... You know."

It seemed possible that David had been going to add to that statement. Perhaps some graphic description of exactly what he and Sylvia had been doing.

Adam didn't give him a chance to get the words out. David went down with one punch.

Adam had put all his anger into it, sure, but David was a serious wuss if one hit really knocked him to the ground.

He moaned and rolled over.

"Don't get up," Adam ordered, and David lay back down again. "Don't let me see you again. You see me coming, you run. Got it?"

Adam left the man lying in the mud by the path, a group of students gawping at him.

"GOOD, GLAD TO see we're on the same page again," Adam said, not really surprised to see Isabel approaching Conn's offices from the other direction. "Conn's guilty as hell and you need to arrest him."

"Whoa, hold up." Something in Adam's expression must have worried her. "I'm just here to talk to him, to ask him where he was that night. To get some straight answers about the lottery funds."

"You know where he was. He saw Sean standing outside the cathedral just before the murder. That means *he* was outside the cathedral just before the murder."

"I know." Isabel nodded. "A few minutes' walk from the scene. But that doesn't make him guilty."

"You found his motive. He was skimming money from the lottery fund. Moira must have found out."

"And what, threatened to turn him in? That doesn't sound like Moira."

"No? Then maybe she was blackmailing him. That sounds a little more up her alley."

Isabel frowned. "Could be. He's pretending they had some kind of relationship, and meanwhile it was a completely different kind of relationship."

Adam nodded encouragingly, eyebrows raised. "So, motive, opportunity…"

"And means. He's certainly big and strong enough to have strangled her."

Adam grabbed the glass door and pulled it open, but Isabel put her hand on his arm. "I need to talk to him. Officially. And that can't include you."

"You don't know what I saw last night."

"And what was that?"

Adam shook his head. "I'll tell you when I tell him."

"Don't be daft," Isabel almost shouted, then glanced around and dropped her voice. "I'm not going into a suspect interview with only half the information."

Adam dropped the door and it swung slowly back into place, only to be pushed open again from the inside. A woman in a drab suit left the building. Adam and Isabel both stepped to the side to let her pass them on the narrow sidewalk and she nodded her appreciation.

"Are you going to wait here?" Isabel asked, her eyes narrowing.

Adam took a deep breath and shook his head. "I saw Conn meeting someone. Out on the Long Walk."

"Who?"

"I didn't recognize him."

"What did they say?"

"I couldn't hear them."

"So why does it matter?" Isabel almost laughed out the question.

"It was odd, that's why. He meets a guy in a dark corner late at night. How does that make sense? He's up to something."

"I know he's up to something," Isabel said, raising her voice again as she spoke. "I know about the lottery money. I'm sure there's more I don't know. But just because he has a late night meeting doesn't necessarily have anything to do with Moira's murder."

"Seriously? You were willing to link a robbery of an artifact to the murder, but not this? Are you kidding me?" Adam flung his arms up in despair and turned his back on Isabel. And saw Conn standing across the street.

Conn crossed the narrow cobblestoned street in two long strides. "Detective Superintendent, Mr. Kaminski."

They both nodded, wary.

Conn continued, "Are you standing on a public sidewalk, where anyone can hear you, talking about me? Talking about embezzlement, about murder?"

"Conn, where were you the night Moira was killed?" Isabel asked.

"I don't have to answer that question, Detective Superintendent, but I will. I was with Nia O'Keenan. We met outside the cathedral and were together all night." He glared at them both. "All night."

"And she'll verify this?"

"Too bloody right, she will."

"Sure, of course she will." Adam stepped closer to Conn. "And who were you meeting last night, out on the Long Walk?"

The color rose in Conn's face, starting around his neck and working its way up to his forehead, then out to his ears. His voice, on the other hand, dropped. "Who the hell do you think you are? How dare you question me?"

"I'm the man who's going to prove that you killed Moira Walsh."

"You? You couldn't prove you're the son of your own sweet mammy."

Conn grinned as he insulted him and Adam's anger rose out of control. He took another step toward Conn, his arm raised, his fist balled.

Conn was no David. He blocked Adam's punch with a thick forearm, his right fist landing on Adam's kidney like a battering ram. He shoved himself against Adam as Adam jerked back, pushing him hard against the building.

He turned back to Isabel, jabbing a finger into her chest. "You really balled this one up, Detective Superintendent. Bringing this arsehole with you."

Isabel didn't flinch. "I don't control him, Conn. I came to talk to you."

"Well, you just did." He looked from one of them to the other, his voice still low. Dangerous. "You just made a terrible enemy. Both of you. You" — he jabbed his finger at Isabel again — "can count yourself out of a job. And you—" he pointed at Adam, but then dropped his arm. "You and your fancy girlfriend will be on the next flight out of here if I have anything to do with it."

He jerked the door open and stalked into the building, leaving Adam and Isabel standing on the sidewalk.

CHAPTER FORTY-ONE

THE GROUNDS AROUND the academic buildings were empty of students, as was the quad within. Adam slumped onto a bench along one wall, trying to breathe in that air of satisfaction he'd felt last time he'd been here. Trying to recapture the peace this environment brought him.

No peace came. He tightened his hands into fists, felt his fingers digging into his palms, and tried to breathe.

He saw the familiar rotund figure leaving the building, passing through the quad toward him. He spoke and she stopped her progress.

"You hated Moira Walsh."

"So you heard that, did you?" Nora said.

Adam nodded. "I heard a few things."

Nora stared off across the quad, as if watching students bustling past, though the space was empty, then sat next to him. "It's true, I did."

"Why?"

She gave Adam a small, sad smile. "Same old story. Oldest story in the book."

"It was about a man?"

She nodded. "It was another faculty member. Long since gone now. Oh, it was nothing serious, nothing untoward, I assure you."

Adam couldn't help himself; he grinned. "I believe you."

She ducked her head in recognition. "We went to dinner once, talked a few times. I really liked him. I thought we might have a future together. Then Moira arrived on the scene."

"And what happened?"

"You didn't know Moira. Not really. Her flashy clothes, her impish smile, so petite, so pretty. So willing to do anything."

"He fell for her?"

"She was out of his league. Why did she even flirt with him? But she did. And he fell for it. They had an affair. Very brief. It didn't take Moira long to break his heart. He left the university, got a job elsewhere." Nora toyed with the hem of her skirt. "We didn't stay in touch."

She paused there, leaving Adam to fill in the blanks. To think about what that must have done to Nora's feelings, to her self-esteem. To wonder why she didn't try to stay in touch with him. And to respect her a little bit more for not doing so.

"I didn't kill her," Nora said.

"Where were you?"

"I was at the reception with everyone else, then left early. I came here to finish up some paperwork. Alone."

"No one saw you?"

"No, I don't have an alibi. I didn't know I'd need one." She shook her head, then perked up. "Oh, I did see Jennifer."

"Did she see you?"

Nora shrugged. "Perhaps not. She looked like she was clearing out some paperwork of her own. Struggling with the office equipment, silly girl."

"You didn't offer to help."

She shook her head. "I didn't kill Moira, Detective. I hated her. She was demeaning, demanding, rude. But I didn't kill her. She was still up to her old tricks, though."

"What do you mean?"

"Oh, you know. Flirting, and not just with one man.

She always had at least two men on the side. She even received a love note at the reception."

"How do you know?"

"Well, I don't really, do I? But she did receive a note. I saw that."

Sylvia came through the same door that had released Nora a moment ago. As if sensing the change in Adam, Nora stood silently, walking away without another word. Adam tried to release the fists his hands had become, but found he couldn't. He left his hands in his pockets as he stood.

CHAPTER FORTY-TWO

THEY DIDN'T WALK FAR. They stopped in the drive leading to the frail white pharmacology buildings, so different in appearance to the rest of the elegant campus. Holdovers, they looked to Adam, of another time. Another spirit.

His mind did always move to the past, no question. He glanced at Sylvia but had to look away. He'd thought she held his future.

She kept her head down, her eyes on the path ahead of them. No doubt she was as confused as he was. He understood that. It didn't help.

She broke the silence. "Thank you for meeting me."

He nodded, trying to gain control of his emotions before answering. Trying to be mindful.

She waited, giving him the time he needed.

"We have to end this," he finally said.

She bit her lip but nodded. "I understand." She looked up at him. He saw her out of the corner of his eye, but intentionally kept his face away, refusing to meet her gaze. "I am sorry, Adam."

"Me too." It was all he could say. He waited for his anger to surge, but it caught him more by surprise when it didn't. He felt sad. Betrayed. Hurt.

"Thank you for trying to help with this murder," Sylvia said. "I know you wanted to help me."

"It's all I wanted." He laughed, a dry, hacking sound.

"I thought this trip would be a fun diversion. A chance to spend time together."

"Adam." She put a hand on his arm.

He jerked his arm away, the spot where she had touched him burning. He took a step back.

Sylvia took a deep breath, looked at the ground. "Our event is tomorrow."

He heard her words, but didn't register the meaning. Didn't think about the fundraising event she'd been here to work on. Didn't even think about what he'd learned about his great-grandfather. He didn't care. He really didn't care.

He felt tears hot in his eyes and turned his face away so Sylvia wouldn't see them. If she started crying, he didn't know what he'd do.

But when she spoke again, her voice was normal. Strong even. "Do you think you will ever catch the murderer?"

Adam had to take a moment before he could answer. He swallowed hard. "I truly have no idea. We have a few leads. A few clues. But nothing certain. Not enough proof of anything."

Sylvia shivered and Adam resisted the urge to put his arm around her. "It is a terrible thought, that someone might kill Moira and get away with it."

"It is." He thought about the desires that had brought him here, to Galway. The desire to learn more about his great-grandfather. That hadn't gone well. The desire to be near Sylvia. That had gone even worse. At least if he could've helped Isabel figure out who'd killed Moira, he could have left with some semblance of pride. As it was, he had nothing.

"Is there anything else I can do? Anything else I can tell you, to explain?"

He shook his head. "I'm not sure, Sylvia." He turned to face her. "I love you. I still do. But I need to go. You need to figure out what you want."

"I know that, Adam. I am so sorry. I will find another

place to stay."

He leaned forward, kissed her on the cheek, and walked away.

CHAPTER FORTY-THREE

"YOU KNEW. You always knew."

Sean threw his pen down with a loud sigh and turned his most condescending glare on Jennifer, who had stomped into the room and slid into one of the armchairs by the window. She flicked a finger at the dead branch of one of his plants as she accused him.

"What are you talking about?" he asked.

"The dig."

He felt his face go red and tried to control his emotions. "I told you not to go out there."

"And now I know why." She gave him a half grin.

"When were you there?"

"Just now. I know what I saw."

He folded his arms and leaned back in his chair, the creaking making him feel professorial. Superior.

"And what do you think you know?"

Jennifer raised her eyebrows and one shoulder. "You're no fool, Sean. You know exactly what you're doing."

He stared at her for a moment longer, then shook his head and turned his attention back to the paper form in front of him. "I have a lot I need to do, to make the transition to my new job, to transfer the responsibility of the dig to the university. So, if you don't mind."

He moved his pen as if he were writing, though he couldn't keep it from shaking slightly in his hand.

Jennifer didn't move. She just sat there, watching him.

"How the hell did you think you were going to get away with this?"

Another dramatic sigh. Again, he dropped his pen and looked at her. "Get away with what?"

She leaned forward in her seat, the dead branch now lying on the floor near her feet. "There was no great find."

"You must be joking. I ran every test in the book on that necklace. It's authentic."

"Oh, sure, the necklace is." She shrugged. "But that's it. It's not the tip of the iceberg, like you claimed. It's a one-off."

Sean bit down, blinked a few times. When he spoke, it was through a clenched jaw. "There's really no way to know that until we go back in. Dig some more. You know that."

"Kind of. We're not digging blind."

"So what's your point? What do you want from me?"

She scootched her chair closer to his desk, still leaning forward. He could smell her flowery perfume, overwhelming in this little space. Much like she was, her large frame threatening the little chair she sat in.

"I can keep a secret."

He looked at her. Nodded. "Did you go out there alone?"

She shook her head, a frown creasing her forehead. "I already spoke to Garret about it. But I can get him to stay quiet."

He laughed at this. "And how can you do that?" He held up a hand as she started to answer. "Never mind. It doesn't matter. I'm leaving anyway."

Her eyes darkened. "Don't go. I can help you."

"It's no use, Jennifer, there's no point. I'm leaving."

"You'll lose your job once they find this out."

"Maybe. Maybe not. So I was wrong about the dig. I still found that necklace; my expectations just won't pan out."

"You doctored the photos."

"Oh, really?" He leaned over his desk, their faces now only inches apart. "How dare you accuse me of that?"

She hesitated. She leaned back slightly, rubbed her hands together. "I saw the photos. You must have changed them."

"You can't prove that."

Now she leaned completely back in her chair, hands on the armrests. "Are you denying it? You really think you can get away with this?"

He shrugged and smiled.

"You're even crazier than I am," she swore under her breath as she slipped out of the office.

CHAPTER FORTY-FOUR

"TAKE A SEAT, PEIG." Isabel eyed Adam coldly as she welcomed Peig to her office. "The desk clerk said you insisted Detective Kaminski join you."

"That's right." Peig's brown curls bobbed against her neck and shoulders as she nodded. "I know it's probably not what you want."

"I don't understand. I asked you down here to talk about the vandalism at Sean's dig. To see if we can find a connection with any of the people who have been protesting your work." Isabel only hoped she could come up with some connection, anything to offer in her defense once Conn made his complaints to McManus.

"And you don't really think I'm involved in some way?"

Isabel smiled at her friend. "You know I don't, Peig."

Peig nodded decisively. "Then that's why I needed Adam here."

"Wait." Adam finally jumped into the conversation. "I'm not following."

"Everyone in town knows Isabel and I are friends."

"I am perfectly able to put my personal feelings aside to work on a case. I think everyone knows that as well," Isabel said.

"I suppose. But I wouldn't want there to be any doubt. With Adam here, a disinterested third party with an expressed interest in the case..." Peig let her voice trail off, as if not sure how to finish the sentence.

Isabel smiled at her again. "Peig, you're way off base here, but I appreciate what you're worried about. We could've had any of the gardaí in here with us."

"Since I'm here, I'd still like to stay." Adam sat in one of the wooden chairs and crossed his legs, his right foot on his left knee.

Isabel glared at him again but retook her seat behind her desk. "So let's talk about vandals. Peig, I'll need as full a list as you can give me of the people involved in the protest to your tourism efforts. Starting with the group Warriors for Nature."

"They're just kids, university students." Peig voiced her doubts. "It seems unlikely any of them would have been able to pull off something as difficult as the museum theft, doesn't it, or the vandalism at Sean's dig?"

"I'm not ruling anything out," Isabel answered. "They may seem like bit players, but they may well have bigger connections."

The door to Isabel's office burst open. "I'm sorry, ma'am, I did try to stop her, but short of arresting her..." The uniformed garda at the door held Jennifer tightly by the arm, preventing her from getting any further into the office.

"That's all right, Garda Simmons. Let her in." She turned to Jennifer, who remained standing by the door, rubbing her arm. "What can I do for you?"

Jennifer's eyes were wide, strands of blond hair flying free of the rubber band that held the bulk of it in place. She spread her hands out to her sides as she spoke. "It's a fraud. It's all a fraud."

ISABEL STOOD IN the doorway watching the uniformed officer guide Peig and Adam to a small interview room, then turned back to Jennifer, who paced restlessly around the office. Isabel couldn't help but think of a similar scene only a few days earlier with Sean in this office.

"Please, Jennifer, have a seat."

Jennifer shook her head in small, jerky movements and kept pacing.

"What did you mean when you said it was a fraud? What's a fraud?"

Jennifer looked at Isabel as if she didn't recognize her for a moment, then turned her back and addressed her words to the window with its view of the mill wheel in the river.

"The dig. The dig is a fraud."

"What?" Isabel felt her heartbeat rise, and she stood to lean over her desk toward Jennifer. "Do you have any proof?"

Jennifer shrugged, still staring out the window. "I don't need proof, do I? He won't find anything more. That's proof enough."

"Sean won't find anything because he's leaving. He's taking another position, outside Ireland. Did you know that?" Isabel asked gently. Could this all be a stunt to get him to stay?

Jennifer was nodding. "I know. He told me." She turned back to Isabel and her face was pale. "He's a liar and a fraud. Completely incompetent."

"You can't go around making accusations like that without proof." Isabel sat back in her seat. "Is the necklace a fake?"

"That? No. That's the only thing about this that's real."

"So if the necklace is real... And that's the only artifact he's claimed to have found so far...?" Isabel left her question hanging, but Jennifer just stared at her. "Then where's the fraud?" she finally asked.

Jennifer sat. "There's nothing else there."

"He hasn't done the rest of the dig yet," Isabel pointed out.

"You're as blind as he is, aren't you?" At least the

color was coming back to Jennifer's face. "He faked the photos. The evidence of a potential encampment? That's what the grant is based on, and they're fake."

Isabel leaned back in her seat and considered what Jennifer was saying. Was this a crime?

"Why are you telling me this, Jennifer? Do you think it's connected to Moira's murder? Or to the theft of the necklace?"

Jennifer's face screwed up into an angry knot. "He may have stolen it. I wouldn't put it past him."

"I thought you liked him," Isabel said gently. "A lot."

The look Jennifer shot at Isabel was full of venom. Isabel sat back, surprised.

"He's a liar and a fraud," Jennifer repeated.

"Can you prove this?"

"I can show you the photos. Now that I know what I'm really looking at. Now that I went back to the dig and saw for myself."

"Perhaps I need to talk to Professor Rourke again." Isabel stood. "Jennifer, thank you for bringing this to my attention. I'll take it from here. I'd encourage you not to get involved any more than you already are. Have you told Sean of your suspicions?"

Jennifer nodded, her eyes on her own lap.

"Then perhaps you could take the day off, spend it in town. No need to go right back to the university, is there?"

Jennifer took a moment before standing.

"Is there anything else?" Isabel asked.

Jennifer just shook her head one more time, then stood and left the office in a few quick strides.

PEIG JUMPED UP as soon as Isabel entered the room, her expression one of concern. And confusion. Isabel felt for her. Maybe it was a good thing Kaminski was with them after all.

"Take a seat, Peig." She gestured to the metal chairs

around the table that took up most of the room. As Peig and Adam sat, Isabel took a chair across the table from her. A far cry from the cozy conversation they'd been having in Isabel's office.

"What is it? What's happened?" Peig's pretty face scrunched up, as if she were about to break into tears.

"Things have changed a bit, Peig. I need you to tell me the truth."

"The truth?" Peig's voice rose to a squeak. "What do you think I've been telling you?" She looked back and forth frantically between Isabel and Adam.

Adam stepped into the conversation. "What's going on? What did Jennifer mean was a fraud?"

Isabel ignored Adam, directing her question at Peig. "How much do you know about Sean's dig?"

Peig frowned, shrugged. "As much as anyone, I suppose. He found a place on the coast that may have been the site of a Roman encampment." She looked at Adam as she answered. "And I know that's a big deal."

"Do you think it's real?" Isabel asked. "The encampment, I mean. Do you believe he really found it?"

"Well, he said he did, didn't he? So I suppose he did." Peig was looking more and more confused, but at least she'd pulled back from the threatened tears. "Why?"

The confusion that had clouded Adam's face cleared. "It isn't, is it?"

Isabel tried to forget it was Peig sitting across from her. Tried not to think about their chats over coffee. The times they'd met for drinks after work. She had so few true friends, women she could respect and trust. She knew that if she let herself, she'd give Peig a pass to preserve this budding friendship.

She took a deep breath. "You're doing really well with this dig, aren't you?"

"How do you mean?"

"It's turning out to be a good thing for you, professionally," Adam said. "You've been using the dig,

Sean's discoveries, to create a strong marketing campaign."

Peig shifted in her chair to lean away from Adam. "Yes. I took the available information and turned it into something positive for the city. What's the problem?"

From anyone else, the question might have sounded defensive, but Peig was so open, so honest, coming from her it sounded like she really wanted to understand. And to help.

"Did you know it was a fake?" Isabel asked.

"What d'you mean, a fake? I don't understand."

"The dig," Isabel explained. "I have reason to believe Sean didn't find any remains of a Roman encampment after all."

"What?" Peig looked truly surprised. Isabel let her breath out. "Are you telling me he faked it? That necklace's not real?"

"The necklace is the real thing," Isabel said. "But it was a one-off. Just the necklace and some other trinkets. That's all that was real. The rest..." Isabel let her voice trail off, curious to see how Peig would finish the thought.

Peig nodded as she listened, but then shook her head. "The rest what? What rest?"

Isabel smiled. "The evidence of the encampment. He may have faked that."

Peig was still looking a little bit lost, as if she'd stepped into the wrong room somehow.

Adam said, "The reason we all thought there was more to find there, that there was a Roman encampment, is because Sean said so. But if he doctored the evidence somehow, made it look that way..." He gave Isabel a questioning look, but she didn't respond.

"Okay..." Peig sounded wary now.

"There is no more there." Adam answered his own question, putting it all together. "Even if they dig up the rest of that field, they won't find anything else."

"But the necklace is real?"

Adam and Isabel both nodded. "They got outside verification on that," Adam said. "There's no question."

Peig furrowed her brow, looked down at her hands. Finally she looked back up at her two interrogators. "I didn't know. I'm not sure I really understand. But what does this have to do with me?"

"You were counting on that dig," Isabel kept her voice low. "Once news gets out that it's a fake, your marketing campaign will be rubbish."

Peig pursed her lips as she considered this. "I can still use it." She shook her head. "As long as the necklace is real."

"Where were you when Moira was killed, Peig?"

"Me?" The squeak had returned to her voice. "I was home. Alone."

"Did anyone see you?" Adam asked.

Peig shook her head. "Why would you ask me where I was? Why would I want to hurt Moira? She got it. She knew what I was trying to do."

"I have to ask, Peig. I hope you understand. The truth of this dig will affect you, even if you say it won't. Maybe Moira told you the truth and you killed her to keep her from telling anyone else."

Peig actually laughed at this. "Me? Kill Moira?" She held her hands out in front of her, examining them. "I just want to make beautiful things. You know that, Isabel. What you're saying, about fake evidence? I don't know anything about that."

"So you'll move forward with your plans to promote the dig, promote the find?" Adam asked.

Peig nodded. "That necklace is beautiful. And historic. It's a dream come true."

Isabel finally turned her attention to Adam. "Did Jennifer's news surprise you?"

"That Sean was faking his results?" Adam asked. "I don't know, I guess I'm not all that surprised. He never was completely open about his work."

"That's not what I meant."

Adam considered her question for a minute or more, his eyes on Isabel. Finally he nodded. "Did he drop her? Break it off somehow? Is sharing the truth about his fraud her way of getting back at him?"

"And did she really not realize the truth before?"

"Good point. Perhaps keeping his secret was her way of showing how she felt about him. But I'll tell you what," Adam added. "It makes me wonder who else knew about this."

CHAPTER FORTY-FIVE

THEY FOUND SEAN back in his lab, bent over the cursed necklace wearing an expression of intense focus. He used a minuscule brush on the surface of the gems, barely touching them. Adam couldn't tell what difference, if any, he was making to the stones, but Sean must have seen some changes, for at one point he blinked and tssked to himself, pulling his hand away.

It had taken some effort to convince Isabel to let him join her. His arguments of the benefits of teamwork, of what he could contribute to the investigation fell on deaf ears. It was only as Isabel was escorting Adam out of the building that her resolve lessened. Adam suspected it had something to do with Conn O'Flaherty at the front desk, asking for Chief Superintendent McManus. With faint mumbles about not knowing who she could trust, she'd finally acquiesced.

"Professor Rourke." Isabel spoke first.

Sean straightened and looked at them. He nodded, placed the brush on the table next to the steel tray that held the necklace, and took a step away from the artifact. "Detective Superintendent. Now what?"

"We need to talk to you. About your student Jennifer Hughes."

Sean smiled lopsidedly. "Yes, I suppose you do. She's been to see you?"

"Can we have a seat?" Adam asked, indicating a group

of tall stools clustered around a table across the room from the necklace.

Sean nodded and led the way, perching on the stool closest to the wall and leaning back, his hands folded on his lap. "Whatever she's saying, you shouldn't listen to her. She's very angry right now."

"Tell us about your relationship with her," Isabel said.

"My relationship with her? I don't see how that's any of your business."

"Maybe not," Adam said. "We just thought you might have an idea as to why she was making up lies about you. Accusing you of some pretty bad things."

Sean's lips twisted into an uneven smile. "Yes. I see your point."

"So?" Isabel asked again.

"Okay, we had a relationship, you're right. Started a few years ago. Before she was my student." Sean raised a finger as if to highlight that last point. "This was all above board, you understand. Nothing unethical. We met at a conference, we... well, we had some fun."

"And since she's been your student here?"

"Completely ethical, I assure you. Teacher, student, that's all. Well, except..." Sean bit his lip.

"Except?"

"I may have slipped. Around the holidays. Holiday parties can be very trying; sometimes we forget ourselves. But she is a grown woman, you know that. She makes her own choices."

Adam shook his head. "You may have slipped. Slipped accidentally into bed with her, is that what you're saying?"

Sean grinned and shrugged. "It happens."

Adam felt his face growing red. This was hitting a little too close to home. "It shouldn't. She says you doctored the photographs of your dig. To make it look like you found more than you really did."

Sean's face dropped. Hardened. "She has no way to prove that."

"We do." Isabel's expression was equally firm. "You'd be surprised how easy it is to retrace the digital history of a picture."

"What are you talking about?"

"It's fairly basic, Sean. You shouldn't be surprised. We have experts at the station right now looking at those photographs. They'll know within the hour if they've been changed."

Sean's steely expression faltered, one eyelid fluttered. "You can't prove it was me."

"Who else would do that?" Adam asked. He was doing a pretty good job of controlling his anger, but as he looked at Sean, a man who could slip and accidentally sleep with a student, he could only see David. David and Sylvia. "You're a real creep, you know that? You take advantage of your students. You fake your own research."

"I had no choice." Sean's voice had taken on a whining tone Adam hadn't heard before. "There was nothing else there. Just that necklace. I was so sure. I kept researching, kept looking for more. But there was nothing. How could that necklace be there alone?"

"Surely that must have been a significant enough find on its own?" Isabel had risen from her stool and now stood facing Sean, who had slumped back even more against the wall. "You didn't need to pretend there was more. And how did you think this was going to end?"

"I don't know. It happened accidentally."

"A lot of things seem to happen accidentally with you," Adam said.

"You have to understand." Sean's words came out as if he were begging for their help.

"So explain it to us," Isabel said.

Sean shivered as he answered. "I've wanted to be an archaeologist for as long as I can remember. I started out great — the golden boy, when I first joined the graduate program. But…"

"It didn't turn out the way you expected?" Isabel

asked.

Sean shrugged. "I got a few job offers, but only one-year renewable positions, nothing tenure track."

"And you were expecting something better?"

He blinked as if confused by the question. "Of course. I deserved better. I was one of the best archaeologists in the country. I just needed to get back on track, something that would stir up my career, throw a spotlight on my creativity… my genius."

Isabel's brow lowered and Adam was pretty sure she shared his sentiment. "But not your humility, huh, Sean?" he said.

"Whatever. When the opportunity here came up, I took it. It was just a one-year renewable fellowship, but it gave me exactly what I needed."

"And what was that?" Isabel asked with growing skepticism.

"The ability to stay here, near the field site, so I could continue my work throughout the year. And I was right." He straightened on his stool, squared his shoulders. "I made my greatest find." He leaned back again. "The find that ruined my career before it even started."

CHAPTER FORTY-SIX

SEAN SAT SLUMPED on his stool, Adam and Isabel leaning toward him. He seemed to have run out of strength. His hands shook in his lap; his eyes blinked rapidly. Adam didn't care.

"Tell us about this dig, Sean," Adam said. "What did you find?"

"It was a treasure trove," he explained. "And it wasn't just the quantity — which was surprising enough — it was the context. We'd found a collection of Roman origin — coins, weapons, pitchers, you name it — along with Irish artifacts. In the same context, together. This was unheard of in Ireland."

"The Romans never invaded Ireland." Isabel nodded as she spoke.

"Or so the prevailing theory goes," Sean agreed. "They were chased away by naked, screaming, crazed natives, some say. Others point out that at the time the Romans were taking over England, they were fighting numerous other battles on the continent and their attention was divided. Whatever the reason, there was no archaeological or historical evidence of a major Roman incursion onto Ireland. Until now."

He stood from the stool, stuffed his hands in his pants pockets, and wandered back across the room to the table that still held the necklace. Adam opened his mouth to ask another question about who else worked with him on the dig when Sean spoke again, as if finishing his earlier thought.

"And the juxtaposition of the Irish and Roman artifacts was particularly interesting. Could the invading Roman army have been working with a local king or chief? A traitor to his own people, perhaps?"

"You found the necklace," Adam prompted.

"And the necklace… ahh, the necklace. Perhaps not a king at all. Perhaps a queen. You can't imagine… stories of Queen Maeve and Boudica filled my dreams." He closed his eyes, as if calling back the images from his dream. "Night after night, I would dream of the ferocious Irish warrior queen who may have worn that necklace. Beautiful. Daring. Brave. Sensual. I could almost smell her, she became so real to me."

Meanwhile, he and his students diligently recorded their find, he explained. It was a small area in which they found the artifacts, which clearly meant that whoever had been using them was living in close proximity. They belonged together, they weren't items from separate encampments. Dating proved they were from the same time period. Irish and Roman living together.

As they recorded their finds and analyzed them, they continued their investigation, because of course there must be more. What they'd found was tremendous, but only assuming it was part of a larger encampment. Or even a fort. It wasn't simply a bag of loot that a marauding Irishman had brought back from some incursion into Roman-occupied England.

"There have been other finds like that. Roman artifacts, brought to Ireland by raiding armies, thieves even," Isabel interrupted him.

"Sure, there was plenty of that. A stray Roman coin found among a collection of Irish artifacts. Trophies grabbed by warriors who saw the wealth over on the other island and practiced stealth invasions." Sean shook his head, his eyes squeezed shut. "No, this was so much bigger than that. There was so much here. I was sure it wasn't an isolated trove; it had to be part of a larger encampment."

"And was it?" Adam asked. "Is it true?"

Sean ignored his questions. "My dreams of the Irish warrior queen grew more frantic as the summer progressed and we found nothing else. Nothing. No further artifacts. No indications of a larger encampment. No human remains. Only that first trove of treasures. As if a bag of loot had been dumped and abandoned."

"Perhaps that's exactly what happened," Isabel said.

"I couldn't accept that," Sean said. "I hadn't found a bag of random loot. It had meaning. It changed Irish history. I could write the book about the failed Roman invasion, an invasion encouraged by a vengeful Irish warrior queen who seduced — who? A Roman general, perhaps, or other military leader. She seduced him and convinced him he could succeed in his invasion of this wild, unruly, and wet island."

"But despite your expectations, the season ended with no new discoveries?"

"August drew to a close. September loomed." He rested both hands on the table now, leaning his full weight on it. It shifted slightly, but held him up. "I knew my season was coming to an end. While the find was interesting, as an isolated group of artifacts it lent nothing new to the story of Irish history. And then… finally… I found it. Discoloration, along the side of a trench."

"Wait, you did find it?" Isabel leaned toward him.

He nodded. "It was subtle. Too subtle. I could so easily have missed it. Or I could so easily have invented it, a figment of my desire. I wanted to find it so badly, could I really have imagined seeing it?"

"Are you asking us, or telling us?" Adam asked.

Sean turned his head to look back over his shoulder at Adam. There were tears in his eyes. Tears of shame for what he had done? Or anger that he'd been caught?

"The discoloration marked the line of a wall," Sean

continued. "A stone wall. Straight, long, smooth. Roman. This was no Irish cottage or even castle. This wall proved that the Romans had been here. They'd built a wall around their encampment. Or perhaps it was the beginning of a fort. Or temple even. Who knew? This was just the beginning."

"And who else was with you, when you found this?" Isabel asked.

"Garret was out that day, sick or something. Jennifer was the other leading archaeologist there. I called her over. Asked her to look at what I'd found. Her reaction was less than thrilling."

"She couldn't see what you saw. What you'd imagined."

"It was so obvious to me. But I was the expert, she just the student. I'd been doing this for longer than she had. And these discolorations aren't always obvious. They're hard to see. You have to know what you're looking for."

"So what happened next?"

"We documented the new find. With notes, maps, drawings, and photographs. Jennifer still seemed skeptical, but she trusted my judgment. Thank God for that."

"And that marked the end of the season for you."

Sean nodded, his attention back on the table in front of him. "But my God, what a season. What a find. I spent the next month writing it up. Applying for grants. Applying for jobs. This was the find that would get me that tenure-track job. Each morning I ran to my lab, eager to continue the analysis of what we'd found, to continue my interpretation into this little-known aspect of Irish history."

"What changed?"

"I'm trying to tell you. It was an accident. An honest mistake. I started really focusing on the photographs. It didn't happen suddenly. It wasn't like that."

He realized, he explained, that when he looked at the

photographs, he couldn't see the line of discoloration he'd identified on the site. The site was closed, covered and secured for the winter. He couldn't go back. The photographs were all he had to work from for the next few months. And he couldn't see the line. Had he imagined it? Was Jennifer right?

The fraud started accidentally. He was playing with one photograph and thought he'd jog his memory by simply adding some color to the image. A line of red-colored stone where he knew he'd seen it before. It was so simple to do. Just a light-colored smudge along the image. And it worked! The line became clear, this is what he'd seen on the site.

He pulled out the other photographs. In each, the line wasn't there. At least until he added it. He grew frantic, realizing that the line wasn't visible in any of the photographs. Hundreds of them. One by one, he went through each one with a magnifying glass, looking for that sign, that slight discoloration that would exonerate him, prove he wasn't crazy. But it wasn't there. The stratigraphy was clear, sure enough, but none of it indicated a stone wall. He was well and truly screwed.

Once he realized what he was looking at, really understood, he became more intent in his manipulation of the images. He went through each and every image, even those that only showed the trench tangentially. In each image, he found the place where the line should exist and he added it. Just a smudge sometimes, nothing drastic. Just a slight indication, enough to convince anyone else who looked at it that he wasn't crazy. That he had seen the line of a wall.

"But it wasn't there." Adam's question broke into Sean's story.

Sean had been talking with his eyes closed, as if trying to recapture the heady emotions of that time, when he truly believed he'd made a great discovery. He straightened and opened his eyes. "I knew it wouldn't last. As soon as anyone else went out to look, they'd see it wasn't there. I wasn't thinking about that. Hell, I wasn't thinking at all. I just wanted that line to be there so badly I'd do anything. Even something as stupid as fake it."

"And it worked, people believed you."

"Of course they did. My career took a wild leap forward after that. I had a series of articles published. Not on the wall, not yet. The articles were all good, solid analyses of the artifacts we'd really found. Some speculation, perhaps, about what they could mean. But it was all phrased as speculation. I claimed nothing to be fact that I couldn't fully defend." He glared at Adam and Isabel as if daring them to prove him wrong. "I stand by my work in those articles."

"But at the same time, word was spreading about the wall. About the potential implications. Surely you realized that was why your work was getting the attention it was?"

"I knew." He laughed. "Applications started pouring in from students and young archaeologists around the world who wanted to work on the dig. I put them off. I knew the problem. I just didn't want to face it. And the dreams of the warrior queen continued. The Celtic queen who had worn that necklace. She beckoned to me."

"So when the job offer from the States came in, you jumped at it."

"Of course. It was getting harder and harder to build momentum from the find without digging myself in any deeper. I thought maybe if someone else took over the dig, they'd accept the mistake of the wall as just that, a mistake. Or perhaps a product of the weather or the light at that time. Or something else. I don't know. I just needed to get as far away from this dig as possible, as soon as possible."

"And no one questioned you? No one wondered why you were walking away from the archaeological discovery of a lifetime?"

Sean wiped a hand across his face, then leaned again on the surface in front of him. "I wasn't walking away, you see. Not really. Everyone assumed I'd take the position but return to Galway to continue the dig each summer. Being based in a U.S. institution wouldn't preclude that."

"But you had no intention of returning."

"Of course not."

"When did Moira find out?" Isabel asked. "About the fraud."

"A couple of months ago. I told her. It was stupid. We slept together. I thought… well, I thought I could trust her."

"Why did you tell her?"

Sean shrugged and let out a breathy laugh. "She seemed to know about these things."

"Fraud?" Adam asked.

Sean nodded. "Exactly. I thought she'd be able to give me some advice, to get out of the hole I'd dug." He laughed at his own pun, then glanced at Adam and Isabel and stopped laughing. "I didn't kill her, I swear. I needed her. I needed her help. I didn't know what I was going to do. Hell, if this job hadn't come through…"

"You'd've been screwed." Adam finished the sentence for him.

"Damn straight. I didn't kill her. I needed her."

CHAPTER FORTY-SEVEN

"HOW DARE HE?" Isabel paced in a tight circle, her arms wrapped around herself.

"Sean? I can't say I'm that surprised. He always came across as a smug, self-centered bastard, didn't he?"

Adam was only relieved Isabel had waited until he'd pulled the door shut behind them before venting her fury. Her inexplicable fury. If she did end up arresting Sean, his lawyers would have a field day if they thought Isabel had some personal grudge against him.

"What are you so upset about?" he asked.

Isabel stopped pacing only long enough to glare at him, then continued her tight movement as she answered. "He's a fraud. A fraud and a liar."

"So are a lot of people we deal with in our business. Do you always take it this personally?"

Isabel shook her head and stopped moving again. "I thought… I thought he might be on to something. Something new. About Ireland, our history, who we are. I thought…"

Adam stepped closer to her, ducking his head to look in her eyes. Was she really thinking about Irish identity? Or about her own past? "A lot of people will be disappointed by this, I'm sure. A lot more will be relieved. But it's just one dig. One relatively unknown archaeologist. It won't change anything, not really." He smiled at her, but she didn't return the smile.

"He had no right to mess with our history like that. To pretend."

"It would've come out eventually anyway. Once he went back to work over the summer and didn't find anything. I can't imagine what he was thinking."

Isabel's words came out fast, her voice low and tight, her words betraying a stronger accent than Adam had noticed before. "He was thinking he was more important than us. That his accomplishment, his name in headlines, was all that mattered. He was thinking that we don't matter. The people of Ireland, the people whose history he was trying to rewrite."

"You gotta calm down. Take a breath. Go for a walk. You're letting him get to you, and you're better than this."

Isabel started to say something, then clamped her mouth shut, sucking her cheeks in. She took a breath, then another.

"If Sean did kill Moira," Adam continued, "we need to prove it. Right now, all we know is that he faked a few photographs, lied on a grant application. That's hardly proof of murder."

"He killed her, that liar. It's exactly what he would do."

"Why would he kill her? He's the one who told her about it. He thought she'd help him."

"Maybe he realized too late she had no intention of helping him. Maybe she blackmailed him. Maybe she just said she was going to tell people the truth."

"Now that doesn't sound like the Moira I've been learning about," Adam said gently, trying to keep his voice light. "Blackmail, maybe, but we have no evidence of that."

"She got a note. We've heard this from a few sources. What was in that note?"

"That's what we need to find out," Adam said. "What was in it and who sent it to her." He looked carefully at Isabel. "Are you okay now?"

She nodded, but her arms were still tightly wrapped around her body.

"Take a few breaths," he said. "I've found that helps."

She grinned, unwrapped her arms and shook them out. "You're right, of course. I'm sorry I overreacted. I'm not sure why, that just made me so angry."

"This is a tough case. It hits home."

"Not for me. I'm no historian."

"No? You could've fooled me."

Isabel shook her head and produced another small smile. "But I know a historian I need to talk to right now."

"MICHAL?"

"Up here." Michal responded to Isabel's call from the top rung of a worn, wooden ladder. The ladder leaned against a high bookshelf, and Michal was propped precariously as he looked through the books on the top few shelves.

"What are you doing? That doesn't look safe."

"No? No, I suppose it's probably not. But it's only a six foot drop; I don't think I'll kill myself." Michal grinned as he climbed carefully back down the ladder. "Is the exhibit back in place?"

"Not yet, no. In fact..." Isabel wasn't reluctant to tell Michal about the fraud, though she knew how much it would distress him. On the contrary, she realized, she was looking forward to it.

"In fact what?"

"I don't know if it will go back on display."

"Oh, dear, was it damaged that badly then?"

Isabel shook her head, looked up and down the long aisle of the university library. Only a few students were visible; perhaps others were tucked away in the stacks or behind the tall reading desks. "No, it's fine. But the dig itself is not."

"Yes, you told me about the damage."

Isabel shook her head again. "Not that. Turns out it's a fake. Like you said."

"Now, Sibéal, I never said any such thing." He put a hand on her arm as he spoke, his voice lowering. "Why do you say that?"

For the first time that she could remember, she felt no annoyance at his use of her Irish name. If anything, it brought a hint of peace. Of belonging. "Okay, you didn't say it was a fake, but you didn't believe it would prove to be real."

"Which is completely different. Now, how do you know it's not really a Roman encampment?"

Sibéal laughed softly. "The archaeologist himself admitted it. He found no evidence, he faked it."

"Wait, he really did commit fraud?"

Sibéal nodded. "He did. He doctored the photographs so it would look like evidence of something more."

Michal leaned against the shelf behind him and a few books shifted, the last on the end making a dramatic bang as it fell to the side. He looked around sheepishly as he stood straight. "That's hard to believe. There's no reason for anyone to do such a thing. No way it could possibly work out."

Sibéal shrugged. "I know. He knew. But he did it anyway."

Michal turned to carry the two books he'd selected to the main reading room and Sibéal walked next to him. "I can't tell you how distressing this is," he said. "To think that someone — and an American at that — thought he could fake Irish history."

Sibéal saw his knuckles whiten as Michal tightened his grip on the books he held.

"I do understand," she said. "I had the same reaction. Detective Kaminski didn't know why I was getting so upset." She looked up at her brother. "But you do."

He stopped and faced her, a sad smile on his face. "I knew you'd come around eventually."

She lifted one shoulder, ran a hand along the old

wooden bookshelf to her right. "It's who we are, isn't it? This is our land. Our history. It defines us."

"It does." He rested his free hand on her shoulder, the closest they'd come to a hug in many years. "What brought on this change of your heart, Sibéal?"

She shook her head. "I don't know. But…"

He waited for her to complete her thought, not pushing her, simply smiling down at her.

"I want to meet her," she finished.

He nodded. "Of course you do."

She laughed, a tear slipping in with the laughter. "I don't even know her name."

"You will, Sibéal. You'll know her name. You'll know her. And she will know where she came from."

ADAM LEANED ON the gray stone rail of the Wolfe Tone Bridge, watching the water flow below him on its way through the basin and then out the bay. It was surging again today. Good for the fishermen, he supposed. He could hear the bustle and music of the Latin Quarter to his left, the traffic and voices of the Claddagh to his right. He shut out the sounds and tried to let his mind work through everything Sean had told them.

The dig was a fraud. There was no great Roman encampment to be found. Moira had known this. Who else had known? And who would kill for it?

He shut his eyes, breathing in the cold, clean air. The smell of fresh baked bread coming from a bakery to his right was so strong he could almost taste the bread, the reedy smell of the water providing a subtle backdrop. The scent of lavender on the air… No!

He straightened and turned in a sharp movement. And almost knocked Sylvia down as he bumped into her.

"Adam."

"What are you doing here?"

"I'm just on my way to get some coffee. I didn't expect to see you here."

"No, me neither."

He shoved his hands in his pockets and walked past her, then paused. He tucked his chin low, took a deep breath. He could work around his emotions. He was a cop. He was good at this sort of thing. He turned back to Sylvia and said, "Tell me again about the note Moira received."

She blinked, surprised at the question. "There is not much to tell. Someone came up and handed her the note. She read it. She put it in her pocket. She left."

"Did she look upset when she read it?"

Sylvia thought for a moment. "No. No she did not. She didn't seem upset at all. In fact, I believe she smiled."

"That would explain why Nora assumed it was a love note," Adam thought out loud. "And that would make sense."

"Maybe." Sylvia hesitated, then continued, "But I don't think so. No, it wasn't that kind of smile."

"What do you mean?"

"Well, you know when someone smiles because they're happy. Or excited. But this… this was an unhappy smile." She shivered again. "Frankly, it was a nasty smile. I remember now, it made me wonder. It made me think that perhaps Moira wasn't as nice as she pretended to be."

That put a different spin on it. Perhaps Moira had arranged the meeting, and someone was simply confirming it. Perhaps this added weight to Isabel's theory of blackmail. "Who brought her the note?" he asked.

"One of the students. That archaeologist."

"Jennifer?" Adam asked, surprised.

"No, not her. The young man who works with her."

"Garret." Adam hadn't given much credence to Isabel's theories about Garret. "Garret brings her a note that makes her grin, then she leaves to meet someone and is killed. I wonder…"

"Adam." Sylvia put a hand out toward him, then pulled it back. "Can we talk?"

He saw her in front of him. As beautiful as ever, her blond hair floating around her head as it was jostled by the light breeze, her pale blue eyes full of concern, fear, hope. But something inside of him had snapped. Something was broken.

"Not now," he said as he walked away.

CHAPTER FORTY-EIGHT

"IF THERE WAS a fraud involved, I guarantee Moira knew about it." Conn laughed out loud. "That was my Moira, no question."

Isabel heard Conn's voice echoing out of Chief Superintendent McManus' office. Christ. The last two people she wanted to see.

She picked up her pace, hoping to pass by the open office door without attracting attention. She failed.

"Detective Superintendent, come in here, will you?"

She stopped in the doorway, not happy to see Conn engaged in a tête-à-tête with McManus. She tried to read his expression, but couldn't tell if Conn had made his complaint about her yet. Surely he had; he wasn't the type to let moss grow under his feet.

"If Moira knew about the fraud, Sean could have killed her to keep her quiet," McManus said.

"It's a definite possibility," Isabel said. "Of course, she only knew about it because Sean told her. He had no reason to kill her for it, unless he really thought she wouldn't keep his secret."

"Moira wouldn't have ratted him out." Conn shook his big head firmly. "No way, that is definitely not Moira. Not who she was." His eyes dropped to the table as he spoke, and Isabel felt a little bad for him. He did miss her, in his own way.

"Maybe Sean didn't trust her?" she asked.

Conn shook his head again. "Moira was direct, one of the most direct people I knew. She would never have told anyone, and Sean would've known that. No, if he killed her — and I'm not saying he didn't, mind you — but if he did, it was for some other reason."

"It may have been blackmail." Adam spoke from behind Isabel, and she stepped away from him, farther into McManus' office.

"What are you doing here?" she asked, but her words were drowned out by Conn's question.

"How d'you mean?"

"Sylvia remembered something else about the note, the note that called her out of the event that evening. About the way she reacted to it. I came to tell you." Adam glanced at the two men in the office, as if unsure about his audience, then spoke to Isabel. "You should know that Moira seemed somehow happy about it. Satisfied."

"Like she was looking forward to the meeting? It was something she wanted?"

Adam nodded. "Something like that. Which could support your theory about blackmail."

"It does." Isabel considered. "Look, we have to assume the dig is connected to Moira's murder. It keeps coming up — first the murder, then the theft of the necklace, then the vandalism, then we learn the anticipated discovery is a fake. That can't all be coincidence."

"Agreed." Adam said.

"And only two people knew about the fraud: Sean and Moira."

"Unless Jennifer knew, too," Adam added.

Isabel made a face and shook her head. "I don't think so. You saw how upset she was about it. No, Sean's our killer, I'm sure of it."

"She was upset, sure, but that doesn't mean she didn't already know. Or that Moira didn't already tell her."

McManus cut off Isabel's reply. "You clearly haven't

made a case yet, Detective Superintendent, against anyone. Perhaps you should get back to work? Or do I need to call Dublin to get someone else on this case?"

"HOW DARE YOU imply I'm not doing my job in front of my superior?" Isabel spoke the words through clenched teeth as soon as her office door closed behind Adam.

"Hey, I held back. Don't pin this on me if you're up a creek without a paddle."

"Up a what? Never mind, I don't care. Your comments back there didn't make me look good."

"It's not my comments you're upset about, it's this case. We're missing something, I know we are."

"That, I agree with." Isabel smiled, and Adam let out his breath.

"Finally, something we agree on. So, what are we missing?"

Isabel paced back and forth across her office. Not a large space, it didn't take long. "We need to get a different perspective on this. Maybe revisit the scene?"

Adam shook his head. "We do need a different perspective, but not from a different place, from a different person." He pointed at the phone on her desk. "Can you make long-distance calls on that?"

Isabel gestured for Adam to take her seat behind the desk. He punched out Pete's number and set the phone on speaker. Isabel remained standing until Pete's voice crowded into the room, then took a seat in front of her own desk.

"Sure, if you think I can help," Pete answered when Adam had explained why they were calling.

"We need to sort through the facts, and right now Isabel and I aren't seeing them exactly eye to eye."

"Sorry you're stuck with him, Isabel, you sound like you're a good detective."

She smiled at that and Adam saw her shoulders lower

a fraction. Good. She needed to relax, to let her mind work.

"So where do we start?" Adam asked, leaning toward the phone. "The victim? Motives?"

"Of course you want to start with the people, the psychology. That's your strength, partner, not mine. You called me, so let's talk about what I would be focusing on if I were on the case, right?"

Adam grinned and shut his eyes. "Evidence. Paperwork. Reports."

Isabel raised her eyebrows. "A detective who knows how to do his job. How refreshing."

Adam opened his eyes but didn't take the bait. "All right, then, Detective Superintendent, what's our evidence?"

Isabel frowned as she considered the question. "I reviewed all the witness statements, people who were in the science building that evening."

"Nothing jumped out at you?"

"Too much, really." She waved a hand. "It was a busy evening. So many people were out and about. Conn, Sean, Nora, even Peig. Someone saw each of them at some point."

"Not enough to tie it to the right time though?" Pete asked.

Isabel shook her head. "We have the report from the scene analysis." She gave a quick run-through of the evidence found at the scene. "No smoking gun, as they say, in that list. The report from the medical exam is only preliminary. There could be important evidence there." She tapped her ring on the wooden arm of her chair and pursed her lips.

"Everything has new meaning when you know what you're looking at," Pete said.

Isabel nodded. "Right. The coroner's report confirmed strangulation as cause of death. Possible DNA evidence, but too soon to have identified it yet."

"But if we make an arrest, we can do a comparison."

Isabel nodded at Adam even though the comment had come from Pete. "We can. It was odd, though, about her ears."

"What about her ears?" Adam asked, confused.

"They weren't torn."

"You lost me, Isabel. Come again," Pete's voice said.

"Her earring." Adam sat up straight. "It was lying on the ground near her body when I found her."

"It could've simply fallen out." Isabel toyed with her own gold studs. "It happens quite easily."

"Especially if she was fighting for her life," Pete agreed.

"But then where's the other earring?" Adam asked. "You said only one earring was found at the scene. We assumed it was hers. What if it wasn't?"

Isabel frowned, considering. "Interesting. Let's see, what else? The theft from the museum and the vandalism at the dig. I tracked down a potential connection with an eco-preservation group with violent tendencies, but there's no evidence at all linking them. And the ring leaders all have solid alibis for both. Though I have a strong feeling about Garret."

"He's up to something, no doubt. You think he's part of that eco group, involved in the vandalism?"

"Makes sense, doesn't it? But I've got nothing to connect him to the murder. At least not yet."

"So what connections do you have?" Pete's voice encouraged her to continue.

Isabel frowned again. "I've got a paper trail connecting one of our suspects to an embezzlement scheme, but no evidence connecting the victim. Suspicions, but no evidence."

"Suspicions aren't good enough. Not for me, anyway. Now for Kaminski, maybe…"

"Very funny," Adam finally chimed in. "I think we all know the evidence is short on the ground here. I want to focus on the people. On the motives."

"You can't charge someone just because they have a

motive, partner. If we did that, hell, half of Philly would be in jail."

Isabel grinned again and Adam started regretting having her and Pete on this call together. "All right, enough. Focus."

"We know she received a note just before she died," Isabel said. "But we don't have that note."

"That would be evidence, if you had it," Pete said. "Anybody know what it said?"

Adam and Isabel both shook their heads. "We think it was an invitation. To a meeting or something," Adam said. "She changed her plans right after getting it."

"Nope, that's a big leap, partner, can't go there with you. Without the actual note, you can't assume anything."

"Jeez." Adam pushed himself up from the desk with force. "Let me speculate, will you?" He walked over to the window, his back to Isabel.

"We don't have that note. If the techs had found it at the scene, they would have let me know immediately. They wouldn't wait to include that in their final report…" Isabel's words fell away.

"They found an envelope," Adam reminded her. "The killer probably took the note away with him. He knew it could tie him to the murder. If it was an invitation—"

"But you don't know, do you?" Pete cut Adam off. "What if it was a note agreeing to something completely unrelated? Don't assume."

Adam felt his anger rise. He turned to glare at the phone, then shifted his gaze to Isabel. When he saw the surprise on her face, he shut his eyes. Took a breath. "Right, don't assume. So, we need to find that note."

"We have to assume it's been destroyed," Isabel said, then held up an apologetic hand. "I know we shouldn't assume, but that's a safe bet."

Adam opened his eyes. "No. I saw something. What was it?" He ran his mind back over the past few days, trying to put his finger on the thing that was bugging him. Isabel watched silently and Pete knew enough not to interfere. He finally snapped his fingers. "Jennifer had a note. In the file of pictures she showed me."

"You saw it?" Isabel asked.

"No, not really. But it was a note card. Just like the kind Sylvia" — he clenched his teeth for a second — "Nora described seeing."

"It could have been anything that you saw. There's no reason to think it was the same note."

"But it might have been." Adam thought about a note card stuffed in with papers to be shredded, a dangling earring catching the light, a woman in love. "I think it might have been."

"I'm with Isabel on this one, partner. If the killer had the note — and that's a big if — he would've destroyed it by now."

Adam closed his eyes, remembering Nora's fixation on her office equipment. "Damn. The shredder. Jennifer and Nora were both going on about the shredder."

"No." Isabel sat forward in her chair. "Fire. Easiest way to get rid of paper is to burn it, right?"

"You're thinking of Garret's injury?" Pete asked.

Isabel opened her mouth to respond when voices carried through the closed door. McManus and O'Flaherty. Laughing.

Isabel sealed her lips tight.

"Look, maybe it's been destroyed, maybe not," Adam said. "Right now, it's the best lead we have. At least it's something we can do."

CHAPTER FORTY-NINE

"IF YOU TELL ME what you're looking for, perhaps I could help."

Adam saw the smirk on Jennifer's face but ignored it. What did Jennifer have to worry about? Even if she did kill Moira, she'd had more than enough time to destroy any evidence. Besides, he had no legal right to be in her room, searching her things.

When they'd parted ways at the station, Isabel had headed upstairs to do the paperwork necessary for a search warrant for the house that Jennifer and Garret shared. Adam didn't want to wait. He only hoped Isabel would show up with that warrant before Jennifer changed her mind about letting him search.

"I told you, Detective, I have nothing to hide. Here, you want to look through my clothes?" She crossed the room and held open a closet door. "Or maybe my lingerie?" She grinned wickedly.

He pulled open another drawer. Rifled through the books on the shelves. Dug through duffle bags tucked under her bed. It was a small room, not a lot of places to hide anything. If she even had anything to hide.

A wide window took up most of one wall, a bow window with a cushioned seat. Thin drapes were pulled back from the window, tied to the side with neat ribbons, letting in the afternoon sun. A frilly bedspread matched the curtains, a peach area rug adding even more color to the room. The flowery scent of Jennifer's perfume lingered in the air. It was a feminine room, which surprised Adam. He hadn't really seen Jennifer that way. What else had he missed?

"Garret's room is just the other side of the hall." Jennifer gestured with her hands. "He's not in right now, but I can help you dig through his things, too."

He didn't respond and she laughed. She pulled open the small top drawer of her long dresser and pulled out something black and lacy that she dangled from one finger. "This what you're looking for, Detective?" She laughed again.

Adam felt his face turn red. Jennifer must have misinterpreted his anger at himself for embarrassment and decided her little game was working, because she sashayed around the room, waving the black lace.

Adam followed her with his eyes as she moved, watching her. Where would she hide something she didn't want found? What did he know about Jennifer?

She passed back and forth in front of the dark wood dresser, casting a pale shadow against the wall and dresser. A flicker of light caught his eye.

He didn't look at it, kept his eyes glued to Jennifer. He took a step sideways, as if moving out of her way, turning as he did so. There it was again. As she moved, the changing light caught on something lying on the dresser. Something long and shiny, almost, but not quite, covered by a lace doily.

She must have seen something in his expression because she stopped moving. Her hand still in the air, dangling whatever piece of underwear she'd picked up, she looked at him, then solemnly followed his gaze.

It took her a second. She didn't see what he saw. Not at first. He knew she'd seen it when she put a hand to her ear.

Their eyes locked. She shook her head silently.

"I have that warrant." Isabel came into the room. "Now we can start searching." She gave Adam a meaningful look.

He pointed toward the long, glittering earring lying on the dresser. "I suggest you start there."

JENNIFER COLLAPSED ONTO her bed, her head hanging. Isabel wondered if she'd break down, start to cry perhaps. When Jennifer looked up at her, all thoughts of tears vanished. She was furious.

"You had no right to go through my room."

"I have a warrant," Isabel said. "I had every right."

"He didn't." She cast her venomous gaze on Adam.

"Is this your earring, Jennifer?" Isabel held up the clear plastic bag in which the earring was now safely stored.

Jennifer shrugged.

"We'll test it for DNA, Jennifer. We'll know soon enough if you've worn this earring."

Jennifer still said nothing, so Isabel continued, "And I have its partner down at the station, found next to Moira's body."

One side of Jennifer's mouth turned up into a smile. "So it's my earring. I use that path all the time. You can't prove I was there that night."

"We can also match the DNA found on Moira's scarf," Isabel said softly.

"Did you write the note Moira received?" Adam asked.

Jennifer jerked her head away from Adam at the change in topic. "What note?"

"Why did Moira want to meet with you?" Adam kept pushing. "Did she want to tell you something?"

Jennifer's eyes narrowed, her lips pursed. "She had things she wanted to say to me, yeah. Doesn't mean I killed her."

Adam leaned back against the wall, his arms crossed in front of him. "Did you talk to her?"

Jennifer shrugged, glanced back and forth between

Isabel and Adam. "What if I did?"

"You weren't expecting what she had to say." Adam kept his voice low, calm. Isabel kept quiet, let him take the lead. His methods were unusual, but they seemed to work.

"She lied. She said awful, terrible things about Sean." Jennifer was getting angry again and Adam didn't seem to mind. If anything, he was goading her.

"What makes you think they weren't true?" he asked.

She laughed out loud at this. "Well, in the end, they were true, weren't they? But I didn't know that. How could I? That bitch."

"You saying it wasn't your fault?" Adam almost laughed as he asked the question.

Jennifer looked down at her hands clasping and unclasping in her lap. Her voice was low, but strong. "This is all on Sean."

"Tell us what happened," Isabel said.

Jennifer sniffed. Took a deeper breath. Looked up at Isabel and Adam. Her face cleared, a decision made. "She came down that path, all perky in her fancy clothes. I wanted to strangle her just for flirting with Sean. He didn't care about her. He cared about me."

Isabel could picture Moira Walsh as Jennifer described her, striding down that path, antagonizing Jennifer with every step.

"Then she started telling me he was a fake. A liar. A cheat." Even as she spoke, Jennifer's hands clenched into tight fists, the muscles on her legs tightened.

Isabel considered Jennifer's strength. Isabel wasn't sure she could take Jennifer in a fight, and she was well trained. What chance did little Moira Walsh have? "You didn't want to hear what she had to say."

"I wanted her to stop saying it. I wanted her to just shut up. But she kept going on. About how she could help. About how I should be happy about it because she was keeping my boyfriend safe. She said she was taking care of him."

Moira probably thought she was giving Jennifer good news. Telling her not to worry, in what Isabel was coming to recognize as Moira's normal, condescending way. Telling Jennifer that she, Moira Walsh, would take care of everything. Not realizing that Jennifer had no idea about the fraud. Not realizing that Jennifer didn't believe it. That Jennifer would do anything to make it not true. That Jennifer was very, very angry.

"You love Sean."

"Of course I love him. But it's not just him, it's everything he is, what he stands for. It's my dream, it's always been my dream. He was my future. He was living the dream. Ever since we met at the Global Archaeology Conference, ever since he took me back to his hotel room… I've been in love with him. I came here, to Galway, to be with him. And he loved me, too."

"I don't understand. What dream?"

"All I ever wanted was to be an archaeologist." She glanced again first at Isabel, then shifted her gaze to Adam. She must have found what she wanted in his eyes, because she continued, "To travel to beautiful places, learn about the world, write about what I found to share this knowledge with others. To spread understanding, to make the world more peaceful."

She dropped her gaze to her lap, her fingers moving up and down her legs. "Sean was living that dream. He had it all. That's what I was in love with. Him and who he was, what he was. I wanted that. I wanted him." Her voice dropped to a whisper. "I was afraid I'd lose it all."

"I understand." Adam kept his own voice to a whisper. "When Moira told you the truth, she wasn't just breaking your heart about Sean, she was threatening your dream, your future."

"Moira said he'd lied, he'd faked the photos. I knew I hadn't seen that stratum. I knew it. It wasn't there at all. But Moira said he didn't care, he faked it for kicks. And he asked her to help him cover it up because he was in love with her. With her, not with me." Jennifer shook her head. "I couldn't let her say things like that. Not to me. Not to anyone."

CHAPTER FIFTY

THE BOOKSTORE WAS pleasantly full. Customers browsed along the shelves that filled most of the small store. A couple of young families occupied a seating area in a back corner. Adam turned his attention away from the picture window that fronted onto the street to the woman in front of him. "Will you be okay on your own from here?"

"I will. And thank you, Adam." Isabel smiled. "I wouldn't have come this far if you hadn't pushed me, forced me to..."

"I know," Adam said quickly, before Isabel felt obliged to finish her sentence. This hadn't been easy for her, that much was obvious. He was glad he could have been of some small assistance.

Isabel laughed and pointed at a sign propped up in the window display. "Find your dreams in Galway," she read aloud. The words were printed in green fairy letters over an image of the necklace Sean had found.

"Peig's not wasting any time, is she?" He laughed with her.

"She's very creative, she is. I'll give her that." Isabel smiled up at Adam and he felt good. Good for the first time in days, possibly the last time in a lot of days. "Thank you," she repeated.

He nodded, not sure if she was thanking him for helping her or for helping Peig. "She explained to me that her campaign was always about dreams, anyway. It doesn't matter if they don't find anything else at that dig."

"I know, dreams of Irish queens. Irish fairies." Isabel shook her head, but her expression didn't carry the disapproval she used to show when talking about Irish myths and legends.

"How about you and your work? You going to be able to get back into the routine, after…" Adam bit back the harsher words he was going to say. "After your doubts about your coworkers."

Isabel laughed again, this time softly and without mirth. "Are you asking me if I still think McManus might be crooked?" She tilted her head, looked down at the ground. "Who knows. Maybe he is, maybe he isn't. Maybe he's just using Conn. We'll have to wait and see. But I will be careful with him."

"By the book?" Adam asked.

"By the book. And speaking of books, I can officially confirm that our friend Garret is one of the Warriors for Nature. We found his face in a group of surveillance photos. We'll have to keep an eye on him, too. Jennifer confessed to vandalizing the dig and stealing the necklace, but I'm fairly certain Garret was involved in torching that boat."

"It would explain why he was worried about me sticking my nose in, sniffing around. You'll certainly be busy, then, won't you? I'm almost sorry to leave; sounds like things will be interesting around here."

She dug through her shoulder bag and pulled out a thin file. "Look, I need to give you this. I should've given it to you earlier."

He took it, glanced at the first page. "My psych report. I was wondering when you'd own up to having it."

"How'd you know?" she asked with surprise.

He shrugged. "Nora didn't have it, didn't mention it. I knew you were the only person she'd trust with it."

Isabel's lips narrowed into a frown. "Well, I just wanted you to know, I never had reason to contact your superiors. Since you never were part of the case." She raised an eyebrow. "Officially, that is."

"Thanks." Adam kept his eyes down on the report, not wanting to engage her in a discussion of what the evaluation contained.

"Why did you even have this sent over?"

"I wanted to see it for myself." He raised his eyes to her without lifting his head and said pointedly, "before anyone else saw it."

"Ah, sorry about that. I did read it. You have to understand, I didn't know what it was. I'm really sorry."

He let out a breath. Raised his head to look around, then back at her. "I know, I understand."

She put a gentle hand on his arm. He glanced at it and she lifted its weight for a moment, as if to move it, but let it lie. "It looks like you're on the mend, Adam. From a terrible experience, I understand. But it will get better."

"Better?" He laughed bitterly. "I accused the wrong man. I lost my fiancée. I've found evidence that my great-grandfather may have been a Nazi."

"But at least Mr. Rupiewicz turned that diary over to the university instead of burning it as he threatened. That's good, isn't it? Someone else can look at it, perhaps find a different truth in it."

Adam shrugged. "It doesn't look good for me right now."

"It will get better," she repeated stubbornly.

"Yeah, how do you know?"

"I read your pysch eval, remember?" She moved her hand to punch him gently in the arm, then lowered her arm. "I'm slagging you. Look, I just know."

She looked into the bookstore where the little brown-haired girl sat with her parents, her attention riveted on the picture book she held on her lap. The little girl Isabel could finally get to know. A stuffed bear was squeezed into the child's seat with her, its arms stuck straight up in the air, as if in full surrender. Isabel pulled the ring off her finger and held it in her closed fist. "I just know."

THE PROMENADE STRETCHED before Adam and Sylvia, the paved path following the water as far as the eye could see, curving out of view with the edge of the bay ahead of them. They weren't alone on the path. Well-bundled children trotted along after their parents, briskly moving walkers marched past, out for their daily exercise. Adam shoved his hands deeper in his pockets, not used to walking along next to Sylvia without holding her hand or putting his arm around her waist.

Her conference yesterday had been a big success, from what he could tell. No more violence from the Warriors for Nature. He didn't know if they had ever really intended to disrupt it. Hell, he wasn't sure if they intended to burn that tourist boat, or if it had been a symbolic message gone horribly awry.

A group of young men stood on a yellow metal platform jutting out into the bay. They took turns jumping into the chilly water from the height, getting a thrill, he supposed. A very dangerous thrill. He'd been down here when the tide was out. He knew how close those men were to the rocks that hid just below the surface. He turned away, then looked back again when he recognized one of the jumpers.

Garret stood on the platform, smiling, laughing with his friends, waiting his turn to leap off into the unknown. The bandages were gone from his hands. He looked happy. Relaxed. Adam hoped that feeling would last for him.

The sky caught fire as the colors of sunset — pinks, oranges, yellows, reds — took over. The giant orange sun peeked out from behind the buildings along the street, casting shadows that slowly crept toward them.

"I thought the sun was supposed to set over Galway Bay. Isn't that what the song says?"

Sylvia shrugged. "Things are not always as they're supposed to be."

The promenade curved away ahead of them. He could only assume they were on the wrong stretch of the bay to appreciate the sunset. Why was he always in the wrong place at the wrong time?

"Adam," Sylvia started, but he cut her off.

"There's nothing left to say, Sylvia. I don't know what you want. If you even know what you want. But I can't trust you."

She nodded, biting her lip as tears appeared in her pale blue eyes.

They stopped walking. He looked away, out at the water, deep dark green in the twilight.

"I'm sorry I hurt you. I never meant to," she whispered, as if speaking to herself.

He sniffed, nodded. "But you have hurt me. A lot. I don't..." He clamped his jaw shut, shut his eyes for a moment. He couldn't trust himself to speak.

"The honeymoon. We've already paid for it. You should take it. Go away, take a vacation." She smiled sadly at him. "You deserve it."

He laughed through his nose. She could afford to give up the tickets, and she knew he couldn't. Not on a policeman's salary. "I thought we had a future together. I was counting on that. Looking forward to it." He took another breath. "You took that away from me. And for what? A fling with a colleague? Why would you do that?"

She looked up at him. "Do you really want an answer? Because there is no answer. No good excuse. I... I don't know why I did what I did. I know that I regret it." She followed his gaze out over the water.

For a moment, just a flash, he understood that someone could be so upset, so angry, as to hurt another person. He felt his hands tighten into a fist. Then release. He wasn't angry. Not really. He took a deep breath and let it out.

He leaned forward, kissed her on the cheek, and turned around to head back to town. He didn't care if she followed or kept walking forward. He heard a shout, and from the corner of his eye, he saw Garret leap off the platform into the water below.

Author's Note

I hope you enjoyed reading *What She Fears* as much as I enjoyed creating it. Writing a book is never a solo effort. I am grateful for all the support I received from my early readers, mentors and friends who took the time to read, comment and critique, particularly the fabulous professionals at TanMar Editorial and Bookfly Design.

I'd like to thank the late Gerald Horgan, who took time out of his life to show my husband and me around Dingle, to teach us a bit of the culture and the way of life. I also want to thank the Sisters in Crime and all the Guppies for sharing their wisdom, their experience and, when necessary, their commiserations. I extend my appreciation to the An Garda an Síochána for responding to my inquiries. Most of all, I want to thank Chuck, for his unwavering belief in my writing.

In each of my books, I try to share the experience of traveling to a different place. I add touches of reality to give the setting depth and complexity. To make it more real. But rest assured this story is not real.

NUI Galway is real, but the faculty departments mentioned in the book are not, nor are the faculty themselves. To the best of my knowledge, none of the students or faculty at NUI Galway have committed or are contemplating murder!

Many of the venues described in this book are real, though not the Tourism Center, the Banner's Dig or even the B&B at which Adam sits on the front step to stare out at the Claddagh (which is, of course, real).

There are so many books I could recommend you read, if you're interested in Galway or in Irish history, but I will limit myself to three (if you'd like more suggestions, just email me!). Fist, *McCarthy's Bar: A Journey of Discovery in Ireland*, by Pete McCarthy. You won't find a more entertaining (laugh out loud!) true story about traveling through Ireland. And if you read that, you might also want to go online and get yourself a copy of Dara Ó Maoildhia's book, *Legends in the Landscape: Pocket Guide to Árainn*. For some traditional Irish mythology, I recommend finding a good translation of the Irish epic Táin Bó Cuailnge. I enjoyed *The Táin*, translated by Thomas Kinsella.

To keep up on news about the Adam Kaminski books, including the fifth book in the series (coming Summer 2017), please visit my website to sign up for my newsletter or follow me on Twitter or Facebook.

www.janegorman.com